THE BARON

was a legend. He was surrounded by an
aura of glamour and romance – the
most brilliant, dare-devil cracksman in
the annals of crime!

THE BARON AND THE BEGGAR,

one of the Baron series, is by John
Creasey writing as Anthony Morton,
of which there are now over forty titles
and many have been published by
Corgi Books.

Born in 1908, John Creasey died in
June 1973. Overall, his books have sold
nearly a hundred million copies and
have been translated into 28 languages.

As well as travelling extensively, he had
a particular interest in politics and was
the founder of *All Party Alliance*,
which advocates a new system of
gov   He
fro   He
fou
by-

D1419764

Also by John Creasey

and published by CORGI BOOKS

John Creasey
writing as
Anthony Morton

The
Baron and the Beggar

CORGI BOOKS
A DIVISION OF TRANSWORLD PUBLISHERS LTD

THE BARON AND THE BEGGAR

A CORGI BOOK 0 552 09513 3

First publication in Great Britain

PRINTING HISTORY

Corgi edition published 1974

Copyright © 1950 by John Creasey

This book is set in 10pt Plantin

Corgi Books are published by Transworld
Publishers Ltd.,
Cavendish House, 57–59 Uxbridge Road,
Ealing, London W.5.
Made and printed in Great Britain by
Cox and Wyman Ltd, London, Reading and Fakenham

The
Baron and the Beggar

CHAPTER ONE

THE BEGGAR AND THE JEWEL

IN the narrow window of Quinn's, that exclusive antique shop in Hart Row, W.1, a single diamond lay upon rich black velvet. This background was sombre, but the diamond gave the window life and brilliance. A dozen jewel-merchants in London's West End could have displayed diamonds of larger size and even of greater purity. Yet this gem without a setting was unique.

There was nothing to inform curious passers-by about its origin and history; nor was there a price ticket; only the diamond in its pristine beauty. It was an open invitation, as a surly patrol sergeant put it to a police constable, to every smash-and-grab raider in London.

Hart Row led off New Bond Street, and the few shops there were centuries old. The woodwork of Quinn's had recently been oiled. Fresh gilt lettering on the facia board was in Old English style, which suited the shop's appearance of great antiquity.

Outside Quinn's stood a beggar.

Near by, the constable who had been warned by his sergeant of the temptation in the window, stood and watched the beggar.

Inside the shop, an old man and a young one worked among the miscellany of jewels, *objets d'art*, silver, glass and porcelain. Quinn's did not specialize only in jewels; it was the Mecca of those who sought rare curios of East and West. Everything was steeped in history, none greater than the diamond.

The beggar stood looking at the diamond for a long time.

He was neither old nor young. His greying hair was long and untidy, and draped about the frayed collar of his patched and torn sports coat. His baggy flannel trousers were also patched, and frayed at the bottoms. He wore a pink shirt without collar or tie. In one hand he held a battered cardboard tray on which stood a few bootlaces and boxes of matches. He looked thin and hungry, yet in his blue eyes was an expression both wistful and longing; they were like the eyes of a man in love.

He had been there for some minutes when the constable pursed his lips and approached with heavy, regular tread. The beggar did not appear to see or hear him, and started when the constable's deep voice rumbled:

'Seen enough?'

The beggar turned to look at the massive figure in blue uniform; after a long pause, he shook his head.

'No,' he said.

'Well, *I* say you have,' announced the constable. 'You'd better move along.'

'I'm doing no harm here.' The beggar's quiet, protesting voice was not unpleasing.

'I didn't say you was doing any harm, I said it was time you got a move on. You won't sell many bootlaces along here,' added the constable, with heavy humour. 'Move along, now.'

The beggar's eyes lost something of their wistful look. He straightened his shoulders and took a firmer hold on his tray.

'You have no right to move me on,' he said firmly. 'I am not interfering with anyone. I don't intend to commit a crime – and I haven't anything on me with which to break the window, if that's in your mind. In any case, I am going—' he paused, glanced up at the gilt lettering, and added firmly, 'to see Mr. Quinn.'

'Oh, *are* you.'

'I am.'

'Oh, no, you're not.'

'I tell you—'

'Because Old Quinn's been dead these eighteen months. And young Quinn nearly a year.'

'Oh,' said the beggar, and pondered. 'Who is the new owner?'

'How should I know?'

'You knew the original owner.'

'Never you mind,' said the constable, tired of arguing. 'It's time you moved along. Don't give me no trouble, now.'

'I'm not giving you any trouble,' said the beggar. 'Please move aside.'

8

The policeman was so startled by the request that he actually obeyed. The beggar nodded his thanks calmly, and went into the shop. He moved so quickly that by the time the constable peered into the gloomy interior of the shop, the elder of the two men working there had begun to come forward.

The constable pushed the door open an inch – and was too astounded by what followed to interrupt at once.

'Good afternoon, sir,' said the assistant, as courteously as to a millionaire. 'Can I help you?'

'Good afternoon,' replied the beggar. 'I am interested in the diamond displayed in the window.'

'It is a wonderful jewel, sir, is it not?'

'It is superb.'

'I fully agree with you,' said the assistant, a pale-faced man with white hair. He stood a head taller than the beggar, and appeared to be as deferential as he sounded. 'I do not think I have ever seen a finer – no, indeed. The faint rose tint . . .'

'It's South American, I suppose,' interrupted the beggar.

'That is so. Early South American.'

'Early? One of the *original* stones.' The beggar's voice was reverent.

'Yes. One of those found when the Aztec treasure houses were looted during the Spaniards' first visit. We know its history for the last hundred and fifty years, but little before that.'

'That's a pity, a great pity.'

'It is indeed,' agreed the white-haired man. 'I sometimes stand and look at it and try to imagine what happened before European eyes fell upon it. It has been cut since then, of course.'

'Yes, yes – beautifully cut.'

The constable could stand the strain no longer. He pushed the door open wide and entered, heavily. The assistant looked round, murmured what might have been an apology to the beggar, and spoke clearly.

'Good afternoon, officer.'

'I'm sorry to bother you, sir,' rumbled the constable, 'but I was just wondering if this man is worrying you.'

'*Worrying* me?'

'Yes, sir. *He* didn't come to buy.'

The white-haired man smiled gently.

9

'Many people come without wanting to buy, officer.'

'They do?'

'A great many, yes.'

The constable looked at each man in turn. His expression hardened, and his tone became authoritative.

'Is he begging?'

'Begging?'

'You heard me.'

'I assure you that you need have no cause for complaint,' said the white-haired man, his voice sharper. 'I appreciate your carefulness, and will tell Mr. Mannering of it when he arrives.'

'I see.' The constable hesitated, glared at the beggar, touched his helmet by force of habit, and said: 'You'd better be careful yourself.'

'Thank you. Good day, officer.'

'Good day,' echoed the beggar, with great satisfaction.

The constable let the door slam, disappeared, took out his notebook and wrote furiously; his description of the beggar was adequate. He went to the nearest police box and called his Divisional Station, reporting on recent events of the neighbourhood in great detail. Duty done, he returned to keep an eye on Quinn's.

Inside the shop there was a long silence after the constable had gone. Then the beggar sighed.

'May I ask another question?'

'By all means.'

'What is the price of the diamond?'

'I am afraid that you have asked me something which I cannot tell you,' said the old man. 'Mr Mannering has not yet set a price upon it. If I judge Mr. Mannering's attitude correctly, he will sell only to a chosen client, and the price – well, the price will depend on the means of the client.'

'I see.'

'I should perhaps add that I do not think the price will be under one thousand pounds.' The assistant seemed sorry to have to say so.

'Oh,' said the beggar. 'It is possible to learn its history?'

'I wish I had time to go into detail. As it is, I can do no more than tell you a little. The modern history is fascinating. The Duchess Zara—'

From the dark bowels of the shop appeared the other assistant, a young man with enormous eyes, a large forehead, and a chin which disappeared into his high stiff collar, with its grey bow tie. He was dressed in black. He did not speak, just attracted attention by standing there.

'Perhaps I should start at the beginning,' the older man said. 'The diamond was brought to Spain by the Conquistadores, and was for many years recognized as one of the priceless gems of the Spanish royal collection. Towards the end of the eighteenth century it was given to a courtesan then in the King's favour. By then it had acquired a strange legend: that it rightly belonged to the reigning Queen, and any other who possessed it would die of violence. It was stolen from the King's favourite. She was left dead.'

'Dead?'

'With a knife in her breast, exactly where the jewel had rested.'

'Ah, I see.'

'It was the main gem of a necklace of Zara, fifth Duchess of Adalgo. She was the wife of a Pretender to the Spanish Throne. She was murdered for political reasons. Her children were exiled. They managed to take the family jewels with them, but were compelled to sell them, piece by piece. Some were eventually returned to Spain, not to the Adalgo family but to the Royal House. This particular diamond was among them, but was later stolen. Soon afterwards, the King lost his throne. It was returned to him while he was in exile, and sold, like many other royal jewels. It had several owners, but,' the assistant shrugged, 'never remained in the same hands for long. Women who wore it died – some by violence, some mysteriously. Eventually Mr. Mannering was offered it and, paying no attention to the chatter of the gullible and superstitious, he bought it.'

'I see,' said the beggar, and added. 'Superstition?'

'It is a blood-diamond, or more properly a rose-tinted diamond. Its history has made it a jewel of ill omen. It is said that violent death will overtake all but its rightful owner – the true Queen of Spain. Today, there is no Queen, but much poverty and persecution. There has been much intrigue outside the country, of course, to restore the throne. You may have heard of Pedro Lopez, who came to England years ago to plead for British recognition of the Duke of Adalgo's claim to the Spanish Kingdom.'

'I've an idea I remember that,' said the beggar.

'One day, perhaps, the diamond will grace the present Duchess of Adalgo. After that, who knows?' The elder man paused, and turned at last to the younger. 'What is it, Simon?'

'I am sorry to interrupt, sir, but tea is ready.'

'Tea? Is it so late? I was expecting Mr. Mannering before now. Tea, yes. Will you have a cup of tea with me, sir?'

'You're very kind,' said the beggar.

'Not at all. I am fascinated by that gem – as you are. Come with me, please.'

The beggar followed, still holding his battered tray. In a small office, which could not be seen from the shop door, the tea things stood on a carved oak desk; bread and butter and cakes. There were two cups.

'Your assistant,' began the beggar, drawing back.

'He will have his later, that is the custom.'

On one wall was an oil painting of a dark-haired, handsome man, whose smiling face dominated the office. The beggar studied it as he ate.

'That is Mr. Mannering,' said the assistant. 'It is an excellent portrait, painted by his wife. They are a gifted pair, delightful people.'

'Lorna Mannering? The – the great artist who has painted so many famous people?'

'Yes. I think the word great is justified, yes. More tea?'

'Thank you.' The beggar had cleared the food, the assistant eaten little.

'A cigarette?'

'No, thank you. I have lost the craving for tobacco, at considerable pains to myself.'

'You were wise.'

'Yes.' The beggar hesitated, glanced at the portrait, and went on slowly: 'There is one other question I would like to ask.'

'Yes?'

'Will you please tell me why you have treated me like this?'

'I assure you I would have behaved exactly the same way with whoever had come in. I would have talked less with many, those lacking your obvious interest in jewels and in that gem particularly.'

12

'The constable was partly right, you know.'

'You came hoping to sell, but the diamond hypnotized you,' murmured the old man. 'I have Mr. Mannering's permission to use my own judgment about callers. Had he been here, he would have done exactly the same. He is as absorbed in precious stones and those who love them, as his wife is in her painting. And of course, he is known wherever gems are known.'

The beggar gave a curious smile.

'You would be surprised to hear where I first heard of him.'

'Indeed?'

'Yes. I was in prison. I had been sentenced for – jewel robbery. It was for jewellery that was like tinsel compared with that diamond.'

'In*deed*,' breathed the old man, and pondered. 'How strange that Mr. Mannering should be known in prison! I – but here is Mr. Mannering.' The front door opened, firm footsteps sounded in the shop. 'I know he will be very glad to meet you.'

CHAPTER TWO

THE ARTIST AND THE MODEL

LORNA MANNERING thoroughly disliked herself. It was only by exerting painful self-restraint had she avoided being rude to the model who had just left this Chelsea studio, and clearly the girl had realized it. Earlier, she had been unbearable with John; the fact that she had controlled herself with the girl and not her husband angered her. She had delayed him, although knowing that he wanted to be at Quinn's by half past three He had left late, worried by her mood, which had been on her for several days. Nothing either of them did improved it.

Why was that?

Almost entirely, Lorna believed, it was because she could not find *the* model.

At times, painting the famous and the fashionable, palled. She could hardly tell one face from another. All seemed to have the same bone formation, the same blankness, hardness or forced geniality of expression, and there was no life in them. It was nonsense, but whenever she began to feel like that, she stopped accepting commissions and looked for a model on which she could really spend herself.

The girl that afternoon had been the fifth; a plain-faced creature with the figure of a Juno, who caught the eye quickly only to disappoint; well, the girl had been disappointed, too.

Lorna looked dispassionately at the sketch she had made of her, and the first bright patches of colour on the canvas. Dreadful! It showed as much imagination as a pavement artist. Less. This came of thinking she was good. Some fools even called her brilliant! Idiots.

If she could get the right model . . .

She didn't want the bizarre – or even particularly arresting features; just a human being who loved, feared, grieved, lived. She would not get it from a professional model if she tried for a month, and when she got it, she would probably do a pretty picture everyone would say was *lovely*.

'Oh, damn! I can't breathe up here!' She tore off her green smock, left the attic studio without another glance at the easel, and climbed down a rickety staircase to the apartment proper. She slipped on the last step.

'That's a thought,' she said. 'I could break my neck.'

At least it made her laugh at herself.

The bedroom mirror soon banished laughter. She tried to smile in it, but a frown showed through; she looked a shrew. Her heavy eyebrows seemed to meet in the middle; simian! It was like her to 'be different' to keep her eyebrows bushy; with her dark hair falling in natural and now untidy waves to her shoulders, they made her pale face pallid; distinctive, some said; she had even agreed with them.

How would *she* like to live with a face like this opposite her at the table?

She snatched up a pair of tweezers . . .

'At least I'm no longer a hairy ape,' she said five minutes later, and laughed at herself again. Laughter cleared her frown, hinted at her beauty. She combed and brushed her hair furiously, did it up – and everything went right, even her hat set well. She unbuttoned her frock and stepped out of it. Then she caught sight of herself in slip, brassière, and green hat with a long, sweeping feather, and felt better still.

Was the mood on its way out?

She dressed in a bottle-green two-piece, this season's best Hartnell model.

'I'll grab the first ugly man I see and drag him here,' she told her reflection. 'I'll paint a *person* if it's the last thing I do.'

She hurried into the hall.

Before opening the door, she caught sight of a portrait of John. It was the second one she'd painted of him, and had hung last year in the Royal Academy. She seldom went out without casting a quick glance at it. It pleased her, because she had caught not only his looks but the man himself.

It was a strong, arresting face. There was the half-smile which was so often played at his lips and in his hazel eyes. It hinted that he was laughing at a secret joke; humour was always lurking in him; he looked upon everyday things in a different way from most people. He seemed to be smiling at her now; yes, he could see a bright side to these moods of hers, moods which would have driven most men to a pitch of desperation and smashed the marriage.

'Sorry, sweet,' she said, and turned to the front door.

Someone rang the bell.

She had been too absorbed to hear the footsteps outside. Now, she saw a shadow against the frosted glass panel of the door. Her frown came back. It was tea-time; a friend might have dropped in for a leisurely gossip which would drive her silly. She actually thought of tip-toeing away, but conquered the impulse and opened the door.

A stranger stood there, tall and dark-clad.

'Good afternoon, madam.'

'Good afternoon.'

'Is Mr. Mannering in?'

'No, I'm sorry.'

'Oh.' The man had a plum-pudding face, ordinary except for rather sad eyes; unpaintable. 'I want to see him urgently. Do you know when he will be back?'

'Some time this evening,' said Lorna.

'Not earlier?'

'You might find him at Quinn's, if you hurry. Do you know the shop?'

'Yes, but I have no time to go there, now. Are you Mrs. Mannering?'

'Yes.'

'I wonder if I can leave this with you?' asked the stranger, holding out a small packet, wrapped in brown paper. 'Mr. Mannering knows about it. Perhaps you will tell him I will call for an answer this evening.'

Lorna took the packet.

'Yes, I'll tell him.'

'Thank you very much,' said the stranger. He smiled; it was a pity that he had such a round pudding of a face, it made his anxiety seem comic. 'You'll excuse me if I say that it ought to be put somewhere safe, won't you?'

'I'll look after it,' she promised.

'Thank you *very* much.' He touched his forehead, turned and made off.

Lorna closed the door and went into Mannering's study. This was a small room, with a Queen Anne writing-table and a few old etchings on the panelled walls, two book-cases, one for modern works, one for classics, and a brown carpet. In one corner was a Cromwellian oak settle with a box-seat.

The seat was locked and no key would open it; it was lined with steel, and electrically controlled. She pressed a switch concealed in the carved back of the piece, then was able to lift the seat easily. Inside was a steel box. She pressed another switch, concealed inside the seat, and took a small key from her bag and unlocked the box. A second box was inside it, with a combination lock; this was the safe itself. She knew the combination by heart, and twisted and turned with the tumblers clicking, until it opened. Inside here were a few small packages and one or two jewel cases. She put the packet in, closed the safe, and locked it. Soon, there was just an old oak settle against the wall.

Opening the safe seemed to have opened a partition in her mind. The caller with his shy, awkward manner was one of several whom John had arranged to see here lately. Judy, the cook-general, had twice given her brown paper packets, left as this one had been.

Judy was out—

Never mind Judy!

Who were the callers? Why didn't John see them at the shop? The packages contained jewels, of course; yet he had never referred to them or the callers.

Why not?

Had her moodiness discouraged him?

Was there really mystery?

She laughed, but not easily. John thrived on mystery; always had, always would. Mystery, trouble, crime – they were part of his life, the only part she hated.

Hated? The truth was, it frightened her. She had been frightened, over the years, because he would never leave a mystery alone. He had to solve it, no matter where it took him. Some were trivial, some . . .

Why had she had to fall in love with a man who had always lived dangerously? His passion for jewels was responsible. She'd persuaded him to buy Quinn's, hoping the shop would absorb the passion, but it hadn't. Nothing would, nothing could. Probably he had not mentioned the callers because she'd flare up at him, driven on by her fears — that this would lead to a danger he couldn't escape.

Nonsense?

She'd see him — now. Talk to him, make him talk; he'd probably be able to banish her fears.

She laughed.

He might still be at Quinn's.

She hurried out, slamming the front door.

Twenty minutes later, her taxi pulled up at the end of Hart Row. A heavy van was waiting to come out, and as Quinn's was not far from the corner, she paid the driver and walked towards the shop. As she drew near, a man came out; not a man likely to come from Quinn's. He carried a cardboard tray with some matches and bootlaces, and wore an old coat, old flannel trousers and a pink shirt. He was hatless — his greying hair long and straggly. He came towards her slowly, with a dreamy expression on his face. Only once did he turn away from her; to glance at the window and its single diamond.

They were nearly level when he looked round again.

Lorna missed a step

This *was* the model! The dreamy eyes held a glow, like the eyes of a girl in love. The fact itself was interesting — weak yet with a hint of stubbornness; no, not exactly weak; arresting, in a strange way. The mouth was good, so was the chin. The cheekbones were a little high, the halo of hair gave him the look of an Old Testament prophet. If she searched London high and low, she wouldn't find a better subject.

He moved towards the road, to let her pass, and looked at her, surprised to find her staring at him so intently. He smiled, and fingered a box of matches.

'Good afternoon, ma'am. I'm afraid I haven't got much of a selection, but—'

'Selection?' She stared. 'Oh, those. No, thanks. Are you busy?'

The question was absurd; she was absurd; but he looked at her with a sparkle of humour which reminded her of John.

'I am not overworked,' he said.

'Could you sit for me for a few days?'

'I don't understand you,' replied the tramp. 'Sit for you?'

'As a model. I am a painter. I'd like—'

He gasped.

'Are you Mrs. *Mannering*?'

'Yes.' It didn't matter how he'd guessed, he was a gift from the gods. 'Will you—'

'I have just seen Mr. Mannering,' said the beggar.

The door of Quinn's opened, and Mannering came out. No one else was in Hart Row, so the contrast between the two men was heightened. The beggar, slow moving, gentle voiced, dressed in little more than rags, short, unkempt; Mannering, brisk, tall, lean and lithe, dressed by the artists of Savile Row, with all the assurance of wealth and well-being in his manner He looked exactly as he did in the portrait at home.

They were both perfect models.

Mannering's smile widened.

'Hallo, my sweet. You two don't know each other, do you?'

'I haven't that pleasure,' Larraby said.

'Mr. Larraby – my wife.' Mannering's eyes said: 'Now what imp of the devil's in your mind, darling?'

Larraby murmured: 'How are you, Mrs. Mannering?'

'I'm feeling wonderful! I've been looking for you for weeks – *can* you sit for me, Mr. Larraby?'

Mannering said: 'What's this?'

'It's less a case of whether I can but whether I may, Mrs. Mannering. Isn't it, sir?' Larraby looked at Mannering wistfully but amused and not really hopeful.

Mannering was studying Lorna's plucked eyebrows.

'I don't see why not,' he said, after a long pause.

'Darling,' said Lorna, 'Mr. Larraby will sit for me, you know, not for you.'

'Oh, yes.' Mannering chuckled. 'I still don't see why not. But not today, my sweet, no matter how your fingers are itching, we've several things to do. Tomorrow morning, if you like.'

'That'll do. The light's no good now.'

'11b Green Street, Chelsea,' Lorna said to Larraby. 'It's a turning between King's Road and the river – the Embankment.'

'I am well acquainted with the Embankment, Mrs Mannering,' said Larraby dryly, 'and I'll be there any time you like.'

'Nine o'clock? You will come?'

'Nothing would keep me away,' said Larraby. 'And I may even live to repay you both. Good day.'

He turned, and walked off.

'Repay?' Lorna looked blank.

Mannering laughed. 'Did I ever tell you that you're beautiful, my sweet, while a policeman looked on?'

The constable was in the doorway of the next shop to Quinn's.

No. Have I ever—' Lorna broke off, looking at the diamond for the first time.

'Nice little thing, isn't it?' Mannering asked.

'Darling, *are* you crazy? To put a thing like that in the window is—'

'I know. Asking for trouble. Don't forget that window's so strong you'd need dynamite or a pneumatic drill to break it. Talking of Larraby—'

'We weren't.'

'We are. Before you start to dab him on canvas there are things you should know. I'll be in for dinner. Seven-ish.'

He kissed her.

But when he'd left, she wondered why he had hedged from the subject of the diamond in the window.

CHAPTER THREE

THE POLICEMAN AND THE REPORT

SUPERINTENDENT WILLIAM BRISTOW, of New Scotland Yard, sat in his large airy office and read the reports on his desk. The desk, like Bristow, was very neat and tidy. So was the room. So was the other desk, in the corner by the window, which was normally occupied by the Inspector who looked after Bristow's routine work when the Superintendent was not in the office. A wall-clock ticked on a hushed note. Footsteps sounded clearly on the stone floor of the passage outside the office. Sounds of traffic came from Whitehall, the Embankment and the river, but none of these things disturbed Bristow.

He came upon a manila-coloured slip, a report from 'A' Division. The writing was laboured, clearly the work of a constable who had no love of writing reports. It had the bold clearness of a schoolboy's hand, and the phraseology was a cross between that of a schoolboy and a policeman in court. Bristow ignored many repetitions; they were there because years of training had taught the constable that when making a statement before a magistrate, he had to be sure that he could not be misunderstood by a child of ten.

The report was headed: 'Quinn's, Hart Row.'

Bristow read it closely. It was now a little after six o'clock, and P.C. Baynes, author of the report, had come off duty at four-thirty. He hadn't lost much time. 'A' Division, knowing that Scotland Yard had recently requested information about anything unusual that happened at Quinn's, had sent it to the Yard by special messenger.

Bristow read about the beggar and his tray, about his interest in the diamond, about the policeman's pursuit of his duty and the reaction of the old assistant at Quinn's. There was more. The policeman knew that the beggar had been inside the shop for over an hour. Mr. Mannering had followed him from the shop, and a well-dressed woman had stopped the beggar; Mannering had joined them and, the constable prosily deduced, Mannering knew the well-dressed woman. The constable had heard them make the appointment for nine o'clock the next morning.

Bristow lit a cigarette from the butt of another.

'Now what's Mannering up to?' he asked aloud.

He finished the other reports, scribbled instructions on some of them, and then picked up P.C. Baynes's masterpiece. As he was reading it again there was a tap at the door.

Bristow looked up. 'Come in.'

The door opened to admit a tall, gangling man, who seemed all hands and feet. He was dressed in a new blue suit. His sparse grey hair, which, judging from a few blond streaks, had once been yellow, was carefully brushed and oiled but wouldn't lie down. His face shone. His eyes glowed.

'Hallo, Tring,' greeted Bristow. 'What's on your mind?'

'Good evening, Mr. Bristow,' said Sergeant Tring, formally. He approached the desk slowly. Obviously he was excited, and trying to repress it. His hands were clenched and his face looked ready to break into a broad grin. This was remarkable, for by nature Tring was a gloomy man and proverbially the unluckiest sergeant on the Force.

'You wouldn't know, sir, would you?' replied Tring, and rested his beefy hands on the desk. 'I want – I want to thank you very much indeed. Mr. Bristow.'

'Thank me? For what?'

'Come off it,' said Tring, relaxing. The grin turned his face into a mass of wrinkles. 'You know about it if anyone does. I've got it!'

Bristow looked blank.

'You know what I'm talking about,' insisted Tring. 'Strewth, I never thought I'd get it. I wouldn't have, if it wasn't for you. Twenty-seven years – *twenty-seven ruddy years* – I been a sergeant, and now Detective Inspector Tring, Mr. Bristow! Come to report.'

'Well I'm damned!' exclaimed Bristow. 'Well done, Tanker! He put out a hand and shook Tring's warmly. 'I *am* glad. I knew that the A.C. was trying to get it through, but didn't know that he'd managed it. Sit down – have a cigarette.' Bristow pushed a box of cigarettes across the table, and opened a cupboard in his desk, producing a bottle of whisky and two glasses. 'This is an occasion, we're going to celebrate.'

'This is a real treat, this is,' said Tanker Tring, dreamily. 'I used to think, once a sergeant always a sergeant. I said to the missus only yesterday morning, "Daisy," I said, "I've 'ad it. I'm due to retire at the end of this year, and you'll have to manage on a sergeant's pension." That's what I said – only yesterday. She won't half be pleased.' He took a generous glass of whisky. 'Ta. Mr. Bristow.'

'You'll want to get off to tell her,' Bristow said.

'She's at the flicks,' said Tring. 'Thursday evening she always goes to the flicks. I go to the club.' He pronounced the word 'club' as if it had an aura of sanctity. 'Am I waiting to see the looks on their faces when I tell 'em there. Inspector Tring – it don't sound right, somehow, does it?'

'You ought to have had promotion years ago.'

'Oh, I dunno,' said Tring, with a devastating flash of honesty. 'I dunno so much. I've never 'ad no luck, Mr. Bristow, and I'm not clever, like you are. I'm sound, though, and I stick on – a grip like a bulldog, I've got, and that's no exaggeration. I dunno that I ought to 'ave had it years ago; the thing is, I've got it now.' He finished his drink. 'Cor lumme, I could jump over the moon!'

'On one shot of Scotch? Have another?'

'No ta, Mr. Bristow, I'd better not.' Tring was still beaming. 'I've got a lot to put away tonight. I was talking to my club only a few weeks ago about my bad luck. It's a kind of joke, me and my luck. They don't mean any harm by it, but they think it's funny I never have none. Some silly fool said I'd never get promotion an' I said I'd buy every member of the club a pint if I had to retire on a sergeant's pension, and one of them said: "We'll take you, Tanker," he said, "and if you ever get promotion," he said, "every member in the club on the first Thursday afterwards will buy you a pint *and* you'll have to drink it," he said. So I took him on. I never expected I'd have to do it, that's the truth. Think I can 'ave a day off tomorrow?'

Bristow chuckled. 'Why not? You've a lot of leave due to you.'

'It ain't the leave I want. I'll need a rest after tonight,' said

Tring. 'Well, I really am grateful, Mr. Bristow. I wouldn't never have got it if it hadn't been for you, I know that. Anything turned up?'

'You don't want to worry about work tonight,' said Bristow. 'You get off, Inspector.'

Tring's smile nearly split his face in two.

'I shan't half feel funny when they call me that. Not that it won't make some of the sergeants look down their noses, and I'll make one or two of the cheeky baskets sit up before I've finished. Cor, I—'

He broke off.

He had glanced down at the desk, and the report from 'A' Division had caught his eye.

'Don't that say Quinn's?'

'Reading upside down, are you? It's a routine report about a beggar who went there today.'

'Routine,' echoed Tanker. 'Just routine, is it? Well, you've got it on top of all the others, that don't look much like routine to me. You aren't keeping anything back from me, are you?'

'I am not,' said Bristow, firmly.

'Because if there's anything doin' about Quinn's, I'm in it,' said Tanker. 'They can buy my beer next Thursday. Mannering's not up to anything again, is he?'

'I don't think so.'

Tring sat back in his chair.

'That means you think he might be. Don't put anything across me, Mr. Bristow. You know—' he paused, and licked his lips. 'You know I've got a conscience, don't you?'

'It's the biggest at the Yard.'

'And I've been doing a lot of thinking about Mannering this last few weeks,' confided Tring. 'I like Mannering as a man, no one ever heard me say I don't; but right's right, that's what I've always said. He's a rich man, he's living in the lap of luxury, as you might say, and his conscience don't prick *him*.'

'I wouldn't be too sure,' said Bristow.

'But I am sure, Mr. Bristow,' insisted Tring. 'Living in the lap of luxury, that's what he's doing, on the proceeds of his crimes.'

'I don't think that's true,' Bristow argued.

'It ain't far out. I know you've got a soft spot for him, and so

24

have I, in a way, but right's right, and it don't matter if he has given a lot o' money away to charities, he can afford it, can't he? And he *was* a thief. The cleverest jewel-thief we ever came up against. There's no getting away from that. When I sit back and think about the old days, when he was the Baron and always putting his finger to his nose at us, I go all hot and cold.'

'Forget it.'

'That's not so easy,' said Tring. 'Every now and again, I get an urge.'

'An urge?'

'I reflect that it isn't right that Mannering should be living in the lap of luxury, like he is, and other poor beggars who never had half the nerve he's got, nor pinched half the stuff, do their stretch. It's all very well to say he cut out the funny stuff years ago. Maybe he did.' Tring paused, and then added heavily: 'And maybe he didn't.'

'Now, Tanker—'

'And maybe he didn't,' repeated Tanker Tring, ominously. 'I used to think he had, but since he bought Quinn's I've wondered. That shop's a wonderful cover for a fence, Mr. Bristow. And he has some funny customers there. D'you know who I saw go in there only last week?'

'No. Who?'

'Flick Leverson.'

'Flick's been out of the game for years, to my knowledge. Mannering's been out for eight years. Don't get worked up about Mannering. I've often wondered why he took to burglary,' Bristow added, in an effort to distract Tring's attention. 'I think he was badly hit during the slump, had a knock from a woman, and—'

'It's my opinion that once a thief you're always a thief,' announced Tring. 'Once a thief, you've always got it in the back of your mind. You may resist temptation for years and then something turns up and you fall for it. It's an attitude of mind,' Tring went on, elaborating with great care. 'I don't know that it's even his fault, Mr. Bristow, it's a moral matter, that's what it is. Psychological.'

'Mannering wouldn't play the fool now.'

'You've often thought he was playing the fool, and he's pulled the wool over your eyes,' said Tring, darkly. 'I've never been really sure. Do you know what? I've got about six months to run at the Yard, and if I could get something on the Baron in that six months I'd retire happy.'

'We've never had a spot of proof against him. Any counsel would tell us that we can't prove he was ever the Baron.'

'Oh, can't we,' growled Tring. 'I know what I know, and you know it, too. *Is* he up to something fresh?'

Bristow shrugged and passed over the report. Tring read it, grunted two or three times, then handed it back as if it were precious.

'There's not much in that, I agree,' he said, 'but that's one of the things I'm always telling you, he's got a lot of queer friends. Why should Mannering and his wife want to see a hobo at nine o'clock tomorrow? How do you know he is a beggar? How—'

The telephone rang.

Tring sat back, Bristow picked up the receiver.

'Yes, I'll speak to him,' he said, and covered the mouthpiece with his hand. 'It's Parker, of "A" Division.'

'Anything brewing there?'

'I don't think so ... Hallo, Parker ... Yes, I'm all right, thanks. There's plenty to do, you know ... Eh ...? yes, I've had Baynes's report ... What's that?'

He listened intently, staring at Tring, while Tring tapped the P.C.'s report significantly and looked almost smug.

'There isn't any doubt, I suppose,' Bristow said at last. 'No ... Fine, thanks. I'll look into it. Goodbye.'

He replaced the receiver, and lit a cigarette; his small moustache was stained bright yellow with nicotine. He eyed Tring through a cloud of smoke, and the new Inspector continued to tap the report and to look as if he wanted to say: 'I told you so.'

'Well?' asked Tring, at last. 'Something is up, isn't it?'

'It's a queer business,' said Bristow, 'but I can't believe there's anything in it. The man at Quinn's this afternoon has been identified. The sergeant placed him.'

'Who is he?'

'Josh Larraby.'

'Larraby! The man who stole that stuff from the Mace Gallery? I thought he was inside.'

'He's been out for three months, on his ticket of leave.'

'Cor, strewth!' exclaimed Tring. 'And Mannering's pally with *him*. There you are, what did I tell you? I don't think I'll take a day off tomorrow, after all, Mr. Bristow, thanks all the same.'

CHAPTER FOUR

THE BARON AND HIS WIFE

MANNERING hurried up the stairs to the Green Street flat, just before seven o'clock. Lorna opened the door before he took out his keys. He beamed.

'Wonderful! Anyone would think you were glad to see me.'

'I am. Getting soft in the head, aren't I?'

'You said it. A plucked beauty.' He kissed her between the brows, where there was a faint pink puffiness. 'Food?'

'Plenty.'

'Work?'

'I've done some sketches of Larraby.'

'Why aren't they round the walls?'

They sat at the table, where dinner was served.

'You can go upstairs after dinner and see them,' said Lorna. 'I couldn't have picked a better subject if I'd tried for a year.'

'As a model, maybe.'

'I know he's a tramp, but—'

'Oh, he's not such a tramp,' said Mannering. 'He's known better days. Trust you to pick our Josh to come here.'

'What *is* the mystery about?'

'His past. He was a jewel-merchant in a small way, and gradually increased his business, and then one day fell for some stuff which he pinched. He had a big failing as a dealer – he loved gems for their own sake.'

Lorna sat, very still and silent, frowning.

'There was a small collection at the Mace Gallery, five years ago. It was a private show, carelessly arranged, and there was a diamond Josh coveted. He took it and was caught. He's still on his ticket of leave.'

Lorna said heavily: 'What a fool I am. We can't have him here.' All her brightness had gone.

'Light fingers being dangerous in the flat? He may genuinely have reformed. Such things happen! I'm inclined to think that he fell to temptation and wished he hadn't, even before he was caught. I took to him.'

'You would.'

'You wouldn't!'

Lorna forced a laugh. 'I didn't know his past. What was he doing in the shop?'

'Apparently he was passing the window and saw the Adalgo diamond. He wasn't the first to stand and stare. A policeman wanted to move him on, but the proud Josh wasn't having any. He swept the said policeman imperiously on one side and entered the shop. Carmichael had heard most of what went on, thanks to the new speaker system which works perfectly, and greeted him as he would anyone else.'

'As instructed,' said Lorna, dryly.

'Yes. I'm glad he did. I think Larraby might have had a sharp knock if he'd met with the usual rebuff. You see how sentimental I'm getting! Carmichael thought that Larraby was genuinely interested in the stone – its history and so on.'

'Not to mention its value.'

'He did ask its value, yes. Oh, I know it might not be all it appeared to be on the surface, our beggar may be a sinister villain, but I doubt it. I had a chat with him myself.'

'Did he tell you about his past? Or did you recognize him?'

I didn't know him from Adam,' said Mannering. 'He volunteered the information first to Carmichael then to me. We discussed *jools*, my love. The man has a fever for them.'

Lorna didn't speak.

'But he's been so stung by his fever that I fancy he'll keep his own temperature down,' said Mannering. 'After all, if a man really goes for sparklers and sees the Adalgo in a shop window, you can't expect him to ignore it.'

'No. You wouldn't suspect him of being a spy, sent to find out if it's genuine and to weigh up the chances of breaking in, would you?'

'With my innocence? No!'

'Seriously—'

'The jewel fascinated him, that's all. He has a one track

mind. That's what you saw in him, what you want to put on canvas. It had struck me, but I daren't wish a jail-bird on you.'

'Ought I to let him come?'

'I don't see why not. Judy will be in all the time. If you'd feel happier, I'll send young Simon round to keep an eye on things while he's sitting.'

'I'll paint him,' Lorna decided. 'Two or three days should be enough. I can finish it after he's gone.'

'And he'll be glad of the sitting fee, I fancy,' said Mannering. 'He's not a man who takes charity easily, in spite of his boxes of matches. Part of what you saw in his face was pride.'

'I suppose so. But—'

Mannering laughed. 'I know, I know! Would a man who was really proud come to Quinn's with a tray in his hands and "beggar" written all over him? Would he push past a policeman to enter the shop, just for the sake of inquiring about a jewel which he couldn't hope to buy if he lived to be a hundred? I still think it was a chance visit, and the Adalgo fascinated him.'

After a long pause, Lorna said:

'I wish you'd sell that diamond.'

'Gem *fatale*?'

'All right, laugh at me, but—'

'If it's burglary you're worried about, you can rest happy. Quinn's has all the latest burglar-proof contraptions. Carmichael's vastly intrigued by the listening-in system. It isn't bad, either, although I thought of it myself.'

'I don't see how it helps to scare off thieves.'

'Take an example. Carmichael saw Larraby outside, and heard the policeman speak to him. Both voices sounded at the back of the shop. The microphone picks up whispers. Supposing a pair of toughs came along to smash and grab. Supposing, as is likely, they gave each other last minute instructions. Carmichael would be able to call the police before the job had started. It has commercial possibilities, too. People come and stare, and talk outside. Carmichael knows in advance whether they're likely to buy. Not bad?'

'Oh, you're full of bright ideas.'

They finished the sweet.

'John.'

'Hmm-hmm?'

'I've been foul to you, lately.'

'Forgotten.'

'I know you don't let it rankle, but—'

'I don't even remember it.'

'It isn't the only thing you forget to talk about.'

Mannering said: 'Oh? What's the other?'

'Mystery callers, mystery packets – there's another in the settle.'

'So that's it,' Mannering said slowly.

'Not why I've been unspeakable, but—'

'We'll talk over coffee,' Mannering said.

He led the way into the drawing-room, the largest room in the apartment. It was a treasure-house of lovely furniture, with grey and blue decor, richness of colour and of age. Small Dutch panels, exquisitely painted, hung on the walls, each with its separate light.

Outside, it was dark: the curtains weren't drawn. They stood side by side, looking towards the Thames, its broad, flat bosom reflecting lights from the two bridges in sight, and from the Embankment. Heavy clouds were blowing up; the window shook in a sudden gust.

Mannering drew the curtains.

'Well?' asked Lorna, and sat down.

Mannering perched on the arm of her chair.

'A further adventure in the life of a certain diamond,' he said.

'The Adalgo,' Lorna said heavily.

'There is one, and only one, Adalgo. It's now in the safe at the shop. But there are a number of replicas, or similar gems. They've popped up all over the world. Some are real stones, very like the Adalgo at a casual glance. Some are paste, and perfect copies. After I bought the Adalgo, and put it in the window for the first time, three separate men came to see me and told me that *he* had the Adalgo.'

'Oh,' said Lorna.

'I broke the news to them. They didn't like it, and asked me to examine their gems. Two were genuine diamonds, with slightly different measurements. The other was a paste thing, worth about thirty shillings.' Mannering laughed. 'I spread word among the trade that I was interested in similar gems.

There may be only one Adalgo, but if I could get a collection, each diamond about the same size and quality, there would be something worth having.'

'For your own collection?'

'That's how it started. I didn't know what I'd let loose. Many mysterious merchants telephoned the shop, they didn't want to see me there, so I told them to bring their stuff here. Each, of course, thought he had the Adalgo. You had one this afternoon.'

'Why didn't you tell me?'

Mannering said gently: 'Fuel to the fire? By then, it was an outsize mystery. I could understand finding two or three replicas and even two real stones pretty much alike, but altogether, a dozen have turned up. Odd, isn't it?'

'Odd! It sounds crazy!'

'It's worse. Hold tight!' He rested a hand on her shoulders. 'The police have been paying some attention to Quinn's. Tanker Tring was in the street the other week, when Flick came along to see me. Our bad luck! Tring always thinks the worst. He can't really believe that Flick Leverson and the bold bad Baron have really retired.'

Lorna jumped up.

'Steady,' Mannering said.

'How *can* he believe you've stopped being the Baron? Flick visits you. Whenever you get half a chance, you fling yourself into crime. You're a friend of thieves and fences, even when you investigate a case you thumb your nose to the police – look at *this* one. It shouts crime. Have you told Bristow?'

'Why should—'

'You've kept it to yourself because you've some silly notion that you'll find excitement in it. You laugh at me because I've never liked the thing, but who's really superstitious? Don't interrupt! *You* are. It's a diamond with a history, a blood-diamond, that's why you bought it. *Isn't it?*' She almost shouted.

Mannering snapped his fingers.

'I've an idea!'

'Never mind your ideas. Isn't that why you bought it?'

'Not in a thousand years. I'll tell you why. Every woman who's worn it has died a violent death. So—' he went to her and poked a finger between the full swell of her breasts, '—my tortuous mind worked fast. If *you* were the beauty, one day I'd be free from—'

He took her in his arms, and kissed her fiercely. She caught her breath, then slowly yielded her body against his.

He drew his head back.

'Now you know what a villain you married.'

'I wish I hated you.'

'I wish you did. I'd have to woo my fiery beauty over again. It wouldn't be so easy.'

'Easy!'

'That's what I said. I held all the cards, then. Wasn't I the Baron and in the height of his career? Wasn't there a risk that I'd never give it up? Would you have married a sedate, middle-aged antique dealer who flares up now and again as a dude detective?'

'No!'

'There you are, you see.' He kissed her again, more gently. 'I couldn't resist this mystery any more than I can you, my darling. You know it. But if—'

'If it's dangerous, you'll tell Bristow. That is, when it's so dangerous you're half dead. Did you buy the Adalgo because you wanted excitement?'

'I bought a lovely jewel, and I didn't think of it as a gem of ill omen. Just as a jewel. This other business may peter out.'

The ringing of the front door bell broke across his words.

CHAPTER FIVE

A VISITOR AND A REQUEST

LORNA pulled herself free.

'That'll be Pudding-face.'

'Who?'

'The man who brought the packet this afternoon.'

'And started all this.'

'So it's only just started!'

'Let's say it's warming up.' Mannering stood and looked at her. Her cheeks were flushed. She'd made up carefully before dinner and was at her best; it was a lovely best. She wore a black dinner gown, with a high neck; one creamy shoulder was uncovered, one long, slender arm was bare.

'Hate me?' he asked.

'Yes!'

'Good! Open the door to Pudding-face while I see what he's brought, will you? Keep him amused. Ask him if he's really a thief or a murderer, anything will do.'

'I could ask him how much he'd want to murder you.'

'That'll be fine.'

The bell rang again.

Lorna said in a choky voice: 'Darling, be careful.'

He nodded and hurried into the study. As he opened the settle and went through the various processes to get at the safe, he listened. Lorna hadn't yet opened the door, and the bell rang for the third time. Lorna wanted to compose herself before meeting a stranger.

Mannering took out the packet, and heard Lorna open the door. When she spoke, the surprise in her voice made him look up sharply.

'Good evening.'

A woman answered, not Pudding-face.

'Good evening. Is this Mr. Mannering's apartment?'

'Yes.'

'Please, I must see him,' the woman said.

She sounded young and alarmed; Mannering could hear her breathing, as if she had hurried up the stairs. He opened the packet. Inside was a small jewel case, without a lock. Inside the case, a single diamond glowed up at him from a velvet lining; few would have been able to tell the difference between this and the one on display at Quinn's.

He slipped it into his pocket, then went to the door. Lorna was taking the caller into the drawing-room. Her profile hadn't much wrong with it. She was very young and had fair hair, wavy, attractive. She wore a perfect fitting dark suit, and walked well.

They entered the room, and Mannering heard her say:

'I must see him quickly. I hope it's not a bad time, but—'

'I think he's free. Who shall I tell him?'

'He doesn't know me. I'm Marjorie Addel – *Miss* Addel.'

'Do sit down,' said Lorna.

The girl wouldn't sit down. Mannering knew agitation when he saw it, so did Lorna.

Lorna came hurrying out of the drawing-room, saw him, but spoke as if he could have heard nothing, pitching her voice rather high.

'John, a Miss Marjorie Addel says she is anxious to see you. Can you spare her a few minutes?'

'Eh?' Mannering stepped close to Lorna's side, speaking quietly, to sound as if he were in another room. 'Who did you say?'

He stood by the partly open door of the drawing-room, peering at the girl through the crack between door and wall. Agitated? She was anguished. Her hands were raised to her breast, she stared at the door as if ready to rush at him when he appeared. He saw that her eyes were a clear, cornflower blue; beautiful eyes; she was really beautiful.

'Coming,' he said more loudly, stamped his foot several times, then pushed the door open.

She rushed towards him.

'Mr. Mannering!'

He smiled. 'Hallo. Do we know each other?'

'No, no, we haven't met, I've called on behalf of a friend.' She could hardly get the words out.

35

'A friend of yours?'

'Yes, I – he came to see you this afternoon. He left a packet with you. I must have that packet, he – he can't come here to collect it himself. He's changed his mind about it being for sale and asked me if I would come to collect it.'

He didn't answer.

'You must let me have it!' the girl cried. 'You must!'

'I'm afraid it isn't quite so simple as that,' said Mannering, recovering slowly.

Lorna followed him into the room and closed the door. She looked dazed by the tempestuous Miss Addel.

'It must be!' cried the girl. 'What do you want to know? Don't you believe that I've come from him?'

He considered.

'Well, you certainly know that he brought it.'

'Of course he did. We're friends.'

He did not know Pudding-face well; he did know him for a man who did not move in the same circles as this girl, whose clothes came from Mayfair, whose youthful intentness could not rob her of an air of good breeding; of quality. She hadn't even named the man.

'Just a friend?'

'Yes! Yes, of course. He told me he'd brought it to you, who else *could* have done? He – he's had to go away and can't get here himself. He was going to offer it to you for sale but he's changed his mind. I have come from him, honestly.'

'Perhaps he gave you a note,' Lorna suggested faintly.

The girl glanced round at her.

'What? I – oh, no, there wasn't time. He had to *hurry* away. Mr. Mannering, please believe me. I'll give you a receipt for it. I – I'll pay a security, if you like, and leave you my name and address. I've brought some money with me.'

Lorna glanced at Mannering in blank astonishment. He watched the girl fascinated. She had opened her bag, and began to take out a bundle of five-pound notes; several hundred pounds were there. She thrust the untidy wad into his hands, and went on:

'Here are three hundred pounds. I wouldn't give you *that* unless I meant what I said, would I?'

'I suppose not.' Could anyone be so naïve as this?

'You will give me the diamond?'

36

Mannering frowned, and did not have to try very hard to sound undecided. 'It's most irregular, you know.' Lorna stifled a snigger. 'Where do you live, Miss Addel?'

'Here's my card.' She thrust a white card into his hand, to join the money, and watched him intently as he read:

Miss Marjorie Addel,

Gowns,

21, Lander Street,

W.1.

'I have a shop in Lander Street,' she said superfluously. 'Mr. Mannering, I must have that diamond. My friend told me it – it was a serious matter, he must have it back. There's the money and you can check my identity, if you like, but please let me have it.'

'Where do you intend to take it?'

'To – to my friend.'

'I see,' said Mannering. Lorna glanced at him over the girl's head. 'Let me have a few minutes to think about it, will you?'

'*Please* hurry!'

'I won't be long,' promised Mannering.

'I'll get Miss Addel a drink,' Lorna said brightly.

'No, thank you, I – oh, well, thanks.'

Mannering went out, closing the door. Lorna would keep the girl occupied for ten minutes, while he dealt with as odd a situation as he'd ever met. There was an attractive honesty about the girl's appearance . . .

Honesty?

Mannering grinned to himself as he switched on a special light above the writing-table in the study. He took out the diamond, and studied it closely. The girl, Lorna, everything but this jewel, faded from his mind.

The diamond was real.

Its brilliant, darting lights were dazzling; the colours were beautiful; and there was a faint rose tint at one side; very like the Adalgo. He took out a glass and screwed it into his eye, to make quite sure.

This was a beauty.

He went to the settle, unlocked it, and took out another jewel case. Inside was a diamond which looked like the first, but had

37

no real sparkle; it was paste. He put it in the original jewel case, and placed the real stone in the safe. When he'd locked up again, he went into the hall.

Marjorie Addel was saying: 'Can't you *please* ask him to hurry?'

Lorna promptly said: 'I'll try,' and opened the door. Mannering stood waiting near the study. She came across quickly.

'What are you going to do?'

'Give her a fake, and follow her.'

'I was afraid of that.'

'Nice girl, isn't she?'

'She's frightened out of her wits.'

'That's why I want to see where she goes.'

Mannering went into the drawing-room. The girl jumped up from an easy chair and knocked an empty glass from the arm. She did not seem to notice that as she stared at him with desperate eyes. He drew the jewel case out of his pocket and opened it. In the comparatively poor light the paste gem sparkled as if it were real.

'That's – that's it!' the girl cried.

'I shouldn't really do this,' said Mannering ponderously, 'but you're leaving a security, and – well, I'll take a chance.'

'I – I do appreciate it, I really do,' said Marjorie Addel.

She still hadn't named her 'friend.'

Mannering made a great fuss of preparing a receipt for her to sign. Lorna found a pen. The girl looked down at the jewel case, clutched tightly in her hand, and seemed as if she had been given the world. Naïveté could hardly be carried further. She believed that she had a diamond worth a fortune, and that he'd given it to her, on a flimsy excuse, for a tenth of its value.

Her hand was unsteady as she signed the receipt.

'There!' She was radiant. 'He'll be so glad. Thank you very much, Mr. Mannering.'

'Not at all.' Lorna, behind the girl, raised her hands in mock despair.

'I must go now.'

Mannering showed the girl out, and watched her hurry down the stairs. She tripped, halfway and grabbed the hand-rail. The only light came from the flat.

Lorna was just behind him, as Mannering closed the door loudly.

'*Is* she real?'

'Of course she isn't, none of this has happened. Put the light out,' he said.

Lorna touched the switch. Mannering opened the door again and stepped on to the dark landing. The girl had reached the front hall.

'John! Have you anything—' Lorna's whisper was hoarse.

'To defend myself with? Forget it!' Mannering didn't laugh, but she could imagine his smile as he went down the stairs, sure-footed, ignoring the darkness. He made no sound.

Lorna closed the door quietly and hurried to the drawing-room. She moved the curtain aside. A street lamp showed a small two-seater parked a little way in front of Mannering's *Talbot*. The girl took the wheel, and drove off.

A minute later, Mannering followed.

Lorna didn't move, when the car's rear-light disappeared, but let the curtain fall a little. Her face was pale and tense. There was no sound anywhere.

Suddenly, a man moved from the doorway of a house opposite. He walked beneath a street lamp, and she saw his tall, clumsy figure and familiar features; she knew him as Sergeant Tanker Tring, of the Yard.

Tring walked heavily towards the end of the road and entered a telephone kiosk.

Lorna said involuntarily: 'Darling, be careful!'

The words echoed about the room, mocking her helplessness. She knew Tring's tenacity; knew that he had never given up hope of catching the Baron. Day in, day out she was haunted by the fear that one day, perhaps soon, John would make some trivial slip with which the police would brand him for all the past.

He was no longer the Baron, but nothing else in him had changed. He'd want to know why that girl had come, who had sent and frightened her, why there were so many diamonds like the Adalgo. Wherever the trail took him, he would go.

She turned away from the window, lit a cigarette, and poured out a drink. Then she picked up an illustrated book, which Mannering had brought home a few days ago. Jewels and their wearers filled its pages. She found what she wanted; a portrait of a dark-haired beauty: Zara, fifth Duches of Adalgo, the first owner of the diamond; and in an inset was a drawing of the diamond.

Lorna closed the book and went up to the studio.

The sketches of Larraby were on the easel.

As she studied them, she imagined a sinister twist in his expression. Imagination? Now that she knew about his past, how could she believe that he had come into Quinn's by chance? Once a thief, always a thief—

She caught her breath.

That wasn't true; mustn't be true.

She made herself work on one of the sketches. Every line and stroke of her pencil seemed to increase the touch of the sinister. She dropped her pencil, tore the sketch across and across, and flung the pieces aside. Then she took a new sheet of paper, picked up the pencil, and began to draw blindly. A likeness of the pudding-faced man appeared on the sheet, then one of Marjorie Addel.

The girl was a picture postcard beauty.

No, that wasn't true. She had – quality. It forced its way thro' into the sketch. Lorna caught her expression of delight when she'd been given 'the' diamond. Youthful, naïve – and relieved beyond words.

Lorna said: 'I wonder what he'll learn about her,' and made a colour sketch of the girl. It absorbed her. She was putting the finishing touches to it when she heard a creaking sound behind her. She turned.

'John—'

It wasn't John, but a stranger, with a gun in his hand.

The man stood behind her, near the door to the studio. She had left the hatch at the top of the rickety staircase open, and he'd stepped on a loose board.

He was squat and broad-shouldered, with a handkerchief over the lower half of his face, and an old trilby hat pulled low over his forehead, the brim shading his eyes. His right, gloved hand pointed the gun towards her. He stood quite still, a figure of silent menace.

Lorna did not speak; her mouth went dry.

'Come here, sister,' the man said. His voice was low-pitched and hard; with an accent.

She did not move.

'I told you to come here,' the man repeated and advanced a step. 'I don't want trouble.' He moved the gun.

Swift, wild thoughts flashed through Lorna's mind – of Tring, outside; surely he was still there, he must have seen the man come in. If she flung her palette it would spoil his aim. A brush would do – any missile. If she screamed, people in the neighbouring flats would hear her; people in the street would raise an alarm.

'If you open your mouth, I'll shoot you in the stomach. You wouldn't like the feel of that.'

He meant it.

Would sounds travel far from the attic?

'Get a move on,' the man said.

She had to obey. Every step was mental agony. She could not see the man's eyes clearly, but they seemed dark and brilliant. If she could strike at his arm—

As she drew nearer, he stood aside, out of reach.

'Turn round and go down, backwards.'

She glanced down through the open hatch. Another man stood in the hall below. She hadn't a chance. If she weren't careful, she would fall. She fumbled for the top step, then went down slowly. The man below moved forward and caught her arm as she reached the bottom. He also wore gloves. Without a word, he pulled her towards the drawing-room door, and the other came down; both moved with uncanny silence. When they were all together in the big room, she waited for the next order.

Would it never come?

They just stood staring at her. They were trying to frighten her. Trying! They were hoping to break her nerve, and were already near success.

The squat man spoke abruptly.

'We don't want trouble. We have come for the Adalgo. Understand?'

She didn't speak. That accursed diamond—

'We're going to get it. Don't make any mistake about that. Because you're going to tell us where it is.'

'I don't know!'

'That's a lie!'

'It's at Quinn's!'

'Make up your mind.'

'My — my husband doesn't tell me where—'

'Forget it. Which room?' asked the squat man.

The other moved forward swiftly and seized her arm again. His fingers were cold, like steel bands. He twisted her arm; it didn't hurt much, but carried the threat of torture.

'Which room?' he demanded again.

'I tell you I don't know whether it's here.'

'You know, all right.' The man waved his left hand to the other. 'Fix her. Be quick about it.'

Her arm was bent back so that she couldn't move without pain. The man pulled a scarf from his pocket, and twisted it round about her face, covering her mouth. The other moved and held her arms as the scarf was tied behind her head, drawn tightly across her lips, pressing them against her teeth, blocking her nostrils, making it hard to breathe. Then they pinioned her arms with cord, and moved away. She swayed drunkenly. The men watched her, their glittering eyes very bright. She lost her balance, tried to save herself, but fell. Either of them could have saved her, but neither moved.

They let her lie there, watching her struggle for breath. The scarf shifted from her nostrils. The second man came and knelt down, gripped her hair and dragged her towards the drawing-room. It was agony, but she could not shout, she daren't struggle, for fear of losing her breath again. Her scalp burned, seemed to tear.

In the room the men picked her up, one taking her shoulders and the other her feet, and slung her on to the settee. They looked at her steadily, until the squat man stepped forward and unfastened the scarf. His movements were rough, he meant to hurt. The corners of her mouth were already red and sore, and her mouth was dry, her head seemed red hot.

The squat man sat her up against one end of the settee.

'Learn some sense. We don't want to hurt you, but we're going to get that bit of ice. Don't make any mistake.'

She closed her eyes; the man slapped her face, and said:

'Look at me. Which room?'

If John knew what was happening, he'd expect her to tell them; would want her to. Could she hold out?

'I'll give you two minutes,' said the squat man, and the menace in his voice was foul.

She was so frightened that her heart thumped sickeningly.

Tring had seen nothing of these men; rescue was a silly, vain hope.

The second man drew out a pocket knife with a long blade. He made it flash, but didn't speak.

She couldn't hold out.

'In – his study.'

'Where's the study?'

The other man came forward, and helped her up; the knife touched her hand. This time he was more gentle, and he unfastened the cord. The squat man stooped at the cocktail cabinet, poured out soda-water and handed her the glass. She was able to stand without support.

'We won't hurt you, if you do what we want,' the man said. 'We'll cut you up if you lie.'

She led the way into the small study. The knife glinted. She hadn't the strength of mind to try to fool them again. She hated herself, but couldn't fight any more When she neared the settle, she swayed.

'Steady, sister!' A powerful hand gripped her. She felt dizzy and there was a mist in front of her eyes.

She pressed the first switch, and opened the seat.

'Say, that's neat,' exclaimed the second man. 'Electric control?'

'I – I need – a key.'

'Where is it?'

'In my handbag.'

'Go and get it,' the squat man said.

The other brought the bag in and emptied the contents on a table, lipstick and money fell to the floor. He picked up several keys and held them out to her on the palm of his hand.

If she flung the key away—

His eyes bored into her.

'No tricks.'

She chose the right key.

The second man pushed his hat back. She saw his light grey eyes, thin eyebrows, and curiously wrinkled forehead. He had a small, high-bridged nose, which showed when the scarf slipped from it.

She unlocked the first box. The men neither moved nor spoke, just stood watching her; and the gun and knife threatened. She pressed the second switch, lifted the top of the box,

43

and started to work on the combination. As the tumblers clicked, the men pressed forward. She pulled the top of the safe up, then stood back, wearily.

'That's swell,' said the squat man. 'Get the bag, son.'

The other went into the hall and came back with a battered hold-all. The squat man took out the jewel cases one by one, the other opened them. The first case was the one Marjorie Addel had wanted. He grunted, and nodded satisfaction. Then he dropped all the cases into the bag.

'That's swell,' repeated the squat man. 'Now you don't have to worry. We're going to tie you up so you can't raise an alarm, but you won't be hurt. You— *What's that*?'

The front door bell rang.

It was as if time had gone back, and John—

Was it John? Had he lost his keys?

CHAPTER SIX

THE THIEF AND THE POLICEMAN

'THAT'S MAC,' the second man said abruptly.

Lorna's flare of hope and fear faded.

'Go and see,' ordered the squat man.

As the other hurried out, the squat man turned and gripped Lorna's wrist. He pulled her unprotestingly towards the hall. A third man came in hurriedly.

'The narks,' he said. 'Make it fast.'

The police!

'Where are they?' asked the squat man.

'Driving up.'

'How many?'

'How the hell do I know? Hurry!'

'We'd better,' said the man with the hold-all.

The squat man let Lorna go. One shout would warn the police, one scream, and—

The squat man drove his clenched fist into her face. The blow caught her on the side of the jaw. It seemed to lift her head from her shoulders. She felt another blow, blackness engulfed her, and she fell. She did not lose consciousness completely, but nothing was clear. There was a raucous throbbing in her ears.

The three men crowded together by the front door, and the squat man said unhurriedly:

'I'll take the front. You two go the back way. Meet in Putney – and hurry.'

'It's about time,' grunted 'Mac'.

He went through the flat, with the man who had the hold-all, to the fire-escape which led from the kitchen.

Footsteps sounded in the street outside; the squat man paused, listening, and heard someone enter the house. There was no light up here. He hurried down the first flight of stairs

45

as the sound of voices of the raiding police floated up. He reached the first floor landing, where there was a dim light, and hid in the shadows.

Tanker Tring and Bristow were the first among the police to reach the landing; two detective constables and two uniformed men came just behind them. They did not see the hiding man as they hurried upstairs – leaving one constable, who remained on the landing.

Bristow called out when he reached the top landing, and began to knock and ring at Mannering's door. The policeman on guard stood at the head of the stairs, looking downwards.

The squat man crept forward.

He drew within striking distance of the policeman without being noticed, shot out his left hand and tipped the man's helmet over his eyes. Then he brought the butt of his gun down on the nape of the policeman's neck. His victim fell, heavily. The squat man squeezed past him and ran down the stairs. As he reached the front hall, a door opened on his right, and a beam of bright light shone out. A woman stood in the doorway, shouting:

'What is it? What's the matter?'

A policeman stood in the street doorway. He turned quickly.

'It's all right, ma'am, you needn't worry. It—'

Then both of them saw the man with the gun. The woman stepped back, screaming. The cry was ear-splitting, carrying its alarm to the top floor.

The policeman drew his truncheon, and watched the squat man warily.

'Don't use that gun,' he warned. 'Don't be silly.'

The woman screamed again. Men moved, upstairs.

'Don't use that gun,' the policeman said, and drew a step nearer, holding his truncheon tightly. 'It won't do you any good.' He came forward steadily, his big figure blocking the doorway, the truncheon swinging in his hand. There were footsteps on the top staircase.

'Take it easy, now,' said the policeman. He looked relieved, as if he thought the greatest danger was past. 'We don't want—'

The squat man shot him twice.

The reports echoed about the front hall and the stairs, out

46

into the street. The policeman dropped his truncheon and clutched at his stomach. The squat man dashed past him, into the street. A police car stood immediately in front of the house, and the gunman jumped towards it; no one else seemed near. The blast of a police whistle came shrilly, so the police were stationed at either end of the street. The man jumped into the empty police car and let in the clutch. A policeman, blowing his whistle, ran towards him, but the car moved off towards the Embankment. Another policeman stood there, watching the police car. He couldn't see who was at the wheel until it was too late to jump on the running-board; it passed him in a flash, and turned right at the end of the road, towards Fulham. A little way ahead a small car was cruising; in it were 'Mac' and his companion.

The squat man drove close behind the small car, hearing the police whistles fading in the distance. The gun in his pocket was heavy against his hip. He drove on, the cars almost bumper to bumper. They reached New King's Road and turned up Harwood Road, through Walham Green. Near Lilley Road, the squat man put on speed and pulled up in front of the others. He stopped and jumped out, and climbed into the other while it was still moving.

No one spoke a word.

They reached Putney Bridge without being hailed. A little way along the High Street a high-powered limousine waited with a chauffeur at the wheel. The men in the little car stopped near it, scrambled out, left the little car at the side of the road and climbed into the limousine. It drove off towards Putney Hill, unmolested.

Tanker Tring's conscience and tenacity were having a night out. They had been responsible for his vigil in Green Street, and the police raid.

He was hammering on Mannering's door, and Bristow was ringing the bell, when the woman screamed downstairs. The other policemen with them turned. Bristow said: 'Go down, Tanker,' and Tring led the way, two followed. They stumbled over the unconscious policeman on the landing. The woman was still screaming, and they heard a man's voice, pitched on a low tone.

Suddenly, two shots rang out.

47

'The Devil!' roared Tring.

He leapt down the stairs, but stumbled at the foot; that was typical Tring luck. He pitched forward. The men behind had to jump out of his way. One lost his balance; the other went to the policeman who was lying on the floor, clutching at his stomach.

The car moved off as a police whistle blew outside. The men in the hall lost precious time; the injured man was groaning, obviously badly hurt. The woman had stopped screaming, and was leaning against the door, her face chalk white.

Upstairs, Bristow spoke sharply to the remaining men.

'You'd beter get this door down. Make a job of it.'

'Right, sir.'

'Be careful as you go in,' added Bristow, and turned and went downstairs.

He found Tring and one policeman bending over the injured man, the woman still leaning against the door, and another policeman standing helplessly outside. Bristow didn't speak, but went into the downstairs flat, and picked up the telephone. He called for an ambulance and a doctor, then put a call out for the stolen police car; unless it were left stranded within ten minutes or so, it would be stopped. He had never wanted to catch a man as much as he wanted to catch that gunman.

Tring, trying to help the wounded constable, straightened up when Bristow reached his side.

'Not much chance, sir, I'm afraid. It's Harris.'

'Where'd they get him?'

'Stomach,' said Tring, heavily. 'I've done all I can.'

Bristow saw the padded handkerchiefs over the wound; rough first aid. There was nothing more he could do. He went upstairs. According to Tring, Mannering had left the flat some time ago, but Lorna Mannering should still be inside. Thieves who had shot their way out might have killed her.

The door leaned on a broken hinge. His men were already inside the flat.

Lorna Mannering was sitting in an easy chair.

Her hair was a tumbled mass, pins and combs falling out, some loose strands on her shoulders, torn out by the roots. Her lips were red and sore, her face chalk white. A policeman was holding a glass of water to her lips.

She caught sight of Bristow – and tried to smile; it was pathetic. Then she sipped the water.

'What damn fool game is John up to now?' Bristow's voice was harsh.

'It's not – his fault.'

'Don't you believe it. What's he doing?'

'I – I don't know.'

She wouldn't betray Mannering; if she were dying, she would say nothing to harm him.

Bristow swung round and went through the other rooms. He saw the open settle, and searched inside. He inspected the safe and discovered how it worked; Mannering had done a good job, opening would have taken hours if his wife hadn't helped.

So she had resisted thieves, and they had turned rough.

Downstairs, a policeman was dying.

Bristow set his men to work in the room, with cameras and fingerprint equipment, then went back to Lorna. She was alone, with the glass by her side. There was some colour in her cheeks, but her eyes were hazy and bloodshot; she looked ill.

Bristow pulled up a chair to sit down. Tanker Tring entered the flat, heavy-footed, glowering.

'He's passed away, sir,' said Tring in a harsh voice.

'Sure?'

'There ain't no doubt. If I ever get that swine, I'll—' Tring broke off.

'We'll get him,' said Bristow. 'Keep an eye on the others, Tanker. We're in a hurry.'

There was one good way of getting Tring out of a room where he wasn't wanted; flatter him. Tring went promptly into the study. Bristow pulled up the chair and sat down. Lorna looked taut, defensive, defiant; he waited for her to speak. Her first words didn't surprise him.

'Who is dead?'

'One of our men.'

'Those shots?'

'Yes. You see how well your husband looked after you.'

She made no comment, he could question her all night and she wouldn't betray Mannering. Asking her to would be as pointless as banging his head against a brick wall.

'What were the men like?'

49

Her description was brief and vivid; the squat man's eyes and foreign accent, the tall man's small, high-bridge nose and curiously wrinkled forehead. Bristow made notes, then telephoned the Yard. Downstairs, a police surgeon had arrived from 'C' Division, and a police ambulance stood outside. Several newspapermen were at the door when Bristow went down.

The body was already in the ambulance, and the police-surgeon was waiting to see Bristow.

'Anything much to tell me?' Bristow asked.

'Nothing that won't keep. I want to get those bullets out pretty soon.'

'Send them to Ballistics Department and ask them for a rush job, will you?'

'Yes.'

'Anything we could have done to save him?'

'Nothing. Don't blame yourself.'

'I know who to blame,' Bristow growled.

'Who, Bill?' A lanky reporter, just within earshot, murmured the question.

'You be careful,' Bristow said.

'Give.' Other reporters drew near, hopefully.

'Mrs. Mannering was attacked but not seriously hurt. Motive, robbery. They've taken some jewels. We'd had warning and they shot their way out. For anything else, see the Back Room Inspector at the Yard. There can't be anything else tonight, and – no, you *can't* see Mrs. Mannering.'

'Was Mannering here?'

'No.'

'Any idea where we can find him?'

'You might have a look in hell,' Bristow said. 'You know your way around there, don't you?'

'Okay, Bill,' the lanky man said. 'You're sore. Who wouldn't be, after tonight? We'll do what we can.'

'Thanks.'

They went off, noisily.

Bristow looked up and down the street, saw no sign of Mannering, and went back to the flat. Two policemen were on duty outside. Lorna came out of the bedroom; make-up couldn't hide all traces of the attack, but she'd done a good job. Her eyes were feverishly bright, she moved as if with difficulty; that was from nervous reaction.

'Have a drink?' she invited.

'Thanks. When will John be back?'

'I don't know.'

'Where's your maid?'

'She'll be back late – she's gone to a dance.' Lorna was at the cocktail cabinet in the drawing-room.

'I'll help myself,' Bristow said. 'Sit down.' She was obviously glad to. 'I don't know who's the bigger fool – you or John. Why did you resist tonight?'

'It was worth trying. At least it gave you time to get here.' She watched him squirt soda into his whisky. 'Why did you come?'

Bristow sipped.

'A dose of the truth will probably help you, Mrs. Mannering. Sooner or later someone has to knock sense into John's head. You're as good with a hammer as anyone. We came because Inspector Tring had a funny idea – that a man called the Baron was coming out of his retirement. He—'

'*Inspector* Tring?'

'That's right.'

'Wonderful!' cried Lorna. Sitting, much of her tension had gone. 'John will love that.'

'He may have cause to regret it. Tring hung about here, saw your visitors – the girl first, the men afterwards. He was late in reporting the men, or we'd have been here earlier.'

Lorna murmured: 'He's so often late.'

'But he always gets there. He doesn't like jewel-merchants who make friends with ex-jail-birds.'

'Larraby?'

'That's right.'

'Poor old Josh! It's hard for a man to go straight once you've had him through your hands, isn't it?'

'It's hard to go straight when you've once been crooked. Being crooked becomes a habit. The habit always lands you in jail, and there's always a first time for picking oakum.'

'I thought we'd made progress, and convicts just stitched mailbags and broke stones,' Lorna said. 'Bill, you're just wasting your time. So is Tanker.' Her eyes were still too bright but she was in complete control of herself. 'You know as well as I do that you've more cause to thank John than hound him.'

'Thank him!'

51

'That's right. Remember the times he's caught your man for you.'

Bristow said evenly: 'Get this straight, Mrs. Mannering. Your husband asks for trouble every time he gets an urge to go chasing after crooks. You can't touch muck without getting soiled. He's helped us get our man sometimes, but he hasn't done it the right way.'

'He's caught them when you failed.'

'We catch up with them all, eventually. This hare-brained habit of pretending to be the great lone wolf detective puts him both sides of the law. You know what I mean when I say that if he gets caught on the wrong side, there'll be a lot of excavating done. Plenty of things he did in the past will be raked up. You'll learn all about being a grass widow.'

'He hasn't a black past, that's just your imagination.'

Bristow said: 'Well, I've warned you. Now, what happened before the attack tonight?'

She told him about Pudding-face and the call from Marjorie Addel, and the substitution of the paste gem for the real one. Bristow grinned at that trick.

'So you see, he's not such a fool,' Lorna murmured.

'He's too clever by half. I—'

A voice was raised in the hall, making Lorna break off and Bristow look round. The voice was raised again; it was Mannering, who said sharply:

'What's all this?'

'Nasty spot of trouble, sir, I'm afraid,' a policeman said.

'My wife?' The words were like bullets.

'She's okay, sir.'

Footsteps sounded, soon the door swung open, and Mannering came in. He ignored Bristow, and went straight to Lorna as she stood up. He took her hands and studied her face intently. He could see some of the marks, as well as the feverish brightness of her eyes and the puffy pinkness at the roots of her hair at temples and forehead.

He dropped her hands, and made her sit down.

'I shouldn't have gone out,' he said.

'So you expected trouble,' Bristow flashed.

Mannering took out cigarettes.

'So you're here. Late, I gather – after the damage was done.'

'We arrived before you did. What trouble did you expect?'

'None. I should have done. I didn't think it would come tonight.' Mannering gave an odd little laugh. 'I've been chasing over the countryside and getting lost, while here – forget it. What happened?'

Bristow told him.

'So we're right in it,' said Mannering, heavily. 'I almost wish I'd told you a bit before, but there was nothing for the police in this, until now. Tonight's visit from the lovely was a border line case. Just. I followed her as far as Guildford, but she knew Guildford better than I did, and shook me off.'

'Think she knew she was being followed?'

'Not at first. Her boy friend did.'

'Boy friend?' Lorna said, in surprise.

'She picked a man up not far along the Embankment. He'd been waiting for her – she only did the risky work. I think they tumbled to the fact that I was behind them when we reached the Kingston By-Pass. After that they kept trying to shake me off, but I held on as far as Guildford.'

'They could have driven through the town.'

'Not likely. They went to earth. As all they've got for their pains is a paste gem, they won't be very pleased.'

'Did you get a good look at the man?'

'No.' Mannering helped himself to whisky-and-soda. 'It wasn't Bray.'

'Bray?'

'Lorna's pudding-faced visitor. He's a jewel dealer in a small way, with a good reputation, as far as I know.'

'With rooms in Henrietta Street?' Bristow said.

'That's the man.'

'His reputation's all right,' Bristow said, 'but he's had some heavy losses lately. Did you know that?'

'I know he's not doing too well, and that he's been worried. I don't know how he got hold of a stone which looks like the Adalgo. Sit down, Bill. I'll tell you the whole sad story from the beginning.'

Bristow grunted.

Mannering told the story in greater detail than he had told Lorna, while Bristow listened, poker-faced. Lorna closed her eyes; she looked as if she were asleep, but didn't miss a word.

'Wouldn't you be interested in a paste diamond which looks

remarkably like the real Adalgo, Bill?' Mannering finished, 'Have a heart – say yes.'

'I didn't think you could get the rose tint in paste,' said Bristow.

'That's a new one on me, too.'

'Why did you put the real stone on show?' demanded Bristow.

Mannering chuckled. 'I was waiting for you to get round to that. It's simple – publicity. I told the trade that I had the Adalgo, wanting as many people as possible to know because I'd heard there were some rivals about. When the paste ones began to turn up, I put on the pressure – displaying it was a pretty touch.'

'It's a touch a fool like you would make,' said Bristow.

'Still sore? At least you can't accuse me of keeping material facts from the police,' Mannering pointed out amiably. 'There's no report of anything having been stolen so far, it was a problem for the trade rather than the police. As Tring was here, presumably you'd heard a whisper.'

'We hear plenty. We knew you were interested in the Adalgo business, and that you were having business callers here. I had Quinn's closely watched after you'd put the diamond in the window. Ever heard of smash-and-grab raiders?'

'No one's smashed or grabbed.'

'Not at the shop,' said Bristow, heavily. He pondered, still poker-faced; that concealed uncertainty, perhaps anxiety. 'What about Larraby?'

Mannering chuckled. 'The police are getting better and better!'

'The police have always been good. Why do you want to see Larraby in the morning?'

'Lorna wants him as a model.'

'*What*?'

'She thinks it a face worthy of paint, canvas and her modest talents,' Mannering said.

'I don't believe it.'

'It's true.'

'Come upstairs, I'll show you some sketches,' Lorna invited.

Bristow ignored her.

'Did you know who he was when he called at Quinn's?'

54

'Not until he'd told Carmichael,' said Mannering.

'He did that, did he?'

'He almost boasted of it. So wherever you look there's a blank wall. One is a most decorative wall – like Marjorie Addel. Know anything about her gown shop?'

'I didn't even know it existed,' Bristow said. 'I suppose you did the only thing you could with her. But—' he hesitated.

'If it weren't for this show, her visit wouldn't be a matter for police inquiry,' Mannering said. 'Let's look at facts. The men who came here tonight wanted the genuine Adalgo, thought they'd found it, and took the rest of the stuff as pin-money. They didn't believe the real one was on show at Quinn's. The diamond was the direct cause of the murder of your man. Marjorie Addel's interest in the same diamond puts her in the lime-light. Going to question her?'

'What do you think?'

'That a really good policeman wouldn't tackle Mistress Marjorie just yet.'

Bristow stood up. 'I know my business. Is there anything else you can tell me?'

'Nothing at all, Bill.'

'Is Larraby coming tomorrow?'

'Will you feel up to it in the morning?' Mannering asked Lorna.

'I hope so.'

'Good! If Larraby's up to no good, we'll have him under our eye. All reports of strange events will duly be laid before the police, William.'

'They'd better be. Mannering, I've been telling your wife that Tanker Tring's been promoted. He hasn't long to go in the C.I.D. and his promotion has put dynamite into him. Give him one big catch and he'll retire happy. You know what I mean.'

Mannering looked dazed.

'Tanker, *promoted*? Wonderful!' He hesitated, then said: 'I'll be seeing you.' He hurried out of the room, before either of them could say another word.

Bristow said slowly: 'I give up!'

'You should have done years ago, but why decide now?' Lorna said.

'He hasn't taken a look at the safe. He may have lost a

55

fortune. And he rushes out to see Tanker as if Tanker were all the world.'

'He's so much confidence in himself,' said Lorna sweetly. 'He knows he'll get the jewels back.'

CHAPTER SEVEN

A MODEL AND A PAINTING

'INSPECTOR!' called Mannering. 'Inspector Tring!'

Tring, in the hall, started up and glowered towards the stair-case. Mannering's footsteps rang out but he wasn't in sight. The shout had interrupted Tring's dark ruminations and came at a time when he had reluctantly discarded a theory that the robbery at the flat had been fixed by Mannering. The enticing theory might have stood up had Mrs. Mannering not been hurt.

'Well?' he called.

Mannering hurried down the bottom flight of stairs, reached Tring and took his hand.

'My dear chap! Wonderful! Congratulations!'

In spite of himself, Tring felt a glow of pride.

'Thanks,' he said. 'Ta.'

'It's the best bit of news I've had for years, Tanker, Everything comes to those who wait.'

'Maybe,' said Tring, and flashed: 'Everything comes to those who deserve it, Mr. Mannering, they all get their deserts.'

'So they should. Inspector, I'll never be able to thank you enough.'

Tring gasped. '*Thank* me?'

'Of course. If you hadn't kept your nose to the grindstone, my wife might have suffered much more. I say, Bristow tells me you're nearly due for retirement.'

'Supposing I am?'

'Retirement won't suit you, Inspector. You're far too active. And half the bad men in London will heave a sigh of relief if you go out of the game.'

'The retiring age,' said Tring, 'is the retiring age.'

'For the Yard, maybe.' Mannering drew him nearer. 'Think about this suggestion, Inspector. I need a good man, to keep an eye on the shop and look after me when I'm carrying jewels all over the country. There's a job waiting for you, for the asking. Of course, you may get better offers, but I hope not.'

Tring hadn't a word to say; just stared.

'Or if you prefer to wash up for your wife and grow cabbages, good luck to you,' said Mannering. 'You'd probably take to that better if you could pull off one big coup before you leave the force. You know, Inspector, this job may be your big chance. There's nothing like ending a distinguished career in a blaze of glory, is there? You've got your teeth into this one, don't let anyone take them out.'

Tring said: 'I've got my teeth in it, *and* in the right place.'

'Fine! If there's anything I can do to help, just say the word.'

Mannering pumped Tring's arm, and went back upstairs.

Tring waited until the flat door had closed, then pushed his bowler hat back and ran a hand over his forehead. Slowly, he shook his head.

'You're a caution,' he confessed *sotto voce*, 'a proper caution. But you can't pull the wool over *my* eyes. Corruption, that's what it is – bribery. You'd better watch your step.'

'Did you speak, sir?' asked a policeman.

'No, I didn't!'

'Sorry, sir.'

Bristow came down, and was morose on the way to the Yard.

'There's one good thing out of this,' said Tanker. 'We can watch Quinn's and watch this flat. Mannering won't be able to make a move without being seen.'

Bristow grunted.

'Aren't I right?' persisted Tring.

'We've watched him before.'

'He can't *always* have the luck.'

Bristow said: 'Tanker, you've always made a big mistake about Mannering. You've put everything that he's done down to luck. It isn't luck. He's got something which you and I haven't got and can't get. If you think we can stop Mannering from going on with this job, you're wrong. He's every right to investigate. He had the right before tonight, and it's ten times stronger now. Don't forget it.'

'He'll slip up,' said Tring stubbornly. 'We'll get him.'

'I'm worried about getting that killer,' Bristow said abruptly.

They finished the journey in silence.

A light shone beneath the door of Bristow's office when they reached it.

'Go and make your report, will you?' Bristow said.

'Yes, sir.' Tring plodded off.

Bristow went in. A lean-faced whippet of a man sat at his desk, smoking a pipe. His bright grey eyes sparkled, but good humouredly. He was Colonel Anderson-Kerr, Assistant Commissioner of the Criminal Investigation Department; a martinet.

'Hallo, sir. Don't get up,' Bristow greeted.

'Your chair,' said the other. 'What's all this about losing one of our men?'

'True I'm afraid, sir.'

'Mannering have anything to do with it?'

Anderson-Kerr knew what there was to know about Mannering, and accepted Bristow's view that the Baron as a cracksman no longer existed.

'This is one job where Mannering can't be blamed for probing on his own,' Bristow said. He lit a cigarette and talked, at length. Finally, he said: 'I don't think he knows any more than he's told me, and I don't think wild horses would stop him from investigating.'

'Do you want to stop him?'

Bristow gave a mirthless mile.

'I don't. I'd like to know more about the Adalgo business and I can't think of a more likely man to find out than Mannering. He knows the trade inside out. He's the most infuriating beggar – didn't even look at the emptied safe, but casually promised to let me have a list of the stolen goods in the morning. I let him have his way.'

'Why didn't he want to give it to you tonight?'

'He made the excuse that the full list was at Quinn's. I think he wanted to get rid of me so that his wife could take it easy. I wouldn't put it past her to tell him something she kept from me. They're hard to crack. Mannering's so often right, too.'

'About what, this time?'

'The Addel woman. If she's involved and we go after her at once, we'll warn her accomplices. We couldn't do more than take a statement at the moment. She might lie to us, and we could easily foul the trail.'

'What you mean,' said Anderson-Kerr dryly, 'is that you think Mannering can get more out of her than you, and you think he ought to be allowed to try.'

'I suppose that's it,' Bristow admitted.

The A.C. stood up.

'You're probably right. But we've got to get that killer. If Mannering suffers in the process, it's his lookout. Is the flat being watched?'

'I've two men on duty there.'

'I'd give Mannering his head but make sure you know where he's going,' Anderson-Kerr said. 'Get home now, Bristow, you look all in.'

Mannering heard Judy moving about the apartment, lay still and studied Lorna, who was sleeping on her side. It would be a pity to wake her. He glanced at the bedside clock and started to get out of bed, to stop Judy bringing in the morning tea.

Lorna stirred.

She looked rested; when she opened her eyes, they were quite clear. He stood watching her, as recollection flooded her mind, and saw the way her body tensed.

'Slept well, my sweet?'

'Eh? Oh, yes.'

Judy tapped.

'Come in,' Mannering said. He took the tea tray at the door. 'Thanks, Judy.' He went to Lorna's bed, put the tray on it and began to pour out. 'Head ache?'

'Not too much. What's the time?'

'Five past eight.'

'Larraby's due at nine.' She sat up and took her tea.

'Put him off, and take it easy.'

'No, I'll be better up and doing.'

'Going to take a bath?'

'Yes, run the water for me, will you?'

He shaved in the bedroom. Lorna was still in the bathroom when he'd finished, keeping very quiet. He fidgeted for a few minutes, then went in to her. She was standing with the towel round her shoulders, examining her forehead; her hair was tied in an untidy bun at the top, to keep it from being wet. A few damp ends fell to her shoulders and clung to her neck.

'Is there *no* privacy?'

Mannering closed the door.

'None for an abandoned woman like you. I had visions of you unconscious in the bath. Take it easy today, my sweet.'

'I keep seeing visions – of having to identify you on a mortuary slab. I think I should faint right out. I – John! It's cold!'

He dropped the towel to the floor and put his arms round her.

'I'll put that right. Listen, my sweet. I love you. I hate myself for having let you in for that show last night. It was unforgivable. Look at me.'

She had to look in the mirror, for he stood behind her; their cheeks were close together.

'Forget it, John.'

'Not in a lifetime. Just say the word, and I'll drop the Adalgo case.'

She said: 'I half believe you would.' She laughed, slipped away from him and picked up her robe. 'And you'd be ten times as moody as I've been lately if you did. Darling, I hate these jobs but there's something fascinating about them, and nothing will ever keep you out of them. If it weren't this it would be another. Hurry and dress, I want to be ready for Larraby.'

He kissed her.

At breakfast, she was gay and seemed fully recovered. Judy, nervous and excited after being told of the attack, had prepared a monumental breakfast; Lorna ate well.

'You'll do,' Mannering said. 'Now, business! Bristow is arguing with himself whether to let me have a lot of rope, for a hanging – and probably thinks I'll get more out of Marjorie Addel than he.'

'Well, you're better looking.'

'That probably doesn't weigh with him.'

'It would with her. She will deny everything,' Lorna said.

'Don't forget the piece of paper she signed in her excitement. Marjorie and the boy friend are mixed up in this, and I think she'll lead the way to others. There'll be some fun and games when they discover that they haven't the Adalgo and practically all the other stuff in the safe was paste.'

'Was it?' Lorna's eyes sparkled. 'I thought—'

'I'd moved most of the good stuff, there were some odds and ends in the safe, that's all. Hardly enough to worry the insurance company. Bristow let me put him off until this morning, that's why I think he wants to encourage me to go on. It's almost a pity not to disappoint him.'

'Wicked!'

The front door bell rang.

'That'll be Josh,' Lorna said.

'Mr. Larraby has made a conquest,' Mannering said dryly.

It was Larraby. He had shaved and his face shone, but otherwise he was exactly the same. He was carrying a copy of the *Morning Cry*, and was grave as he entered the dining-room. He raised the paper a little, to draw attention to it, looked at Lorna keenly, and then turned to Mannering.

'I felt that I ought to keep the appointment, Mr. Mannering, although I shall understand if Mrs. Mannering would rather not do any work this morning. I have read about the affair here last night. I – I am *really* grieved.'

'Thanks,' said Mannering. 'But it wasn't your fault.'

'It certainly wasn't, Mr. Mannering. *I* shall never again take anything that is not mine. I've never shown any inclination towards violence, I assure you – I hate the thought of it. But that doesn't stop me from being deeply sorry. And something else has occurred to me since I read this account.' He held the paper up again, and Mannering, studying him, felt the effect both of his manner and of his appearance; Lorna had been right about his looks. 'I know I'm a branded criminal, Mr. Mannering. I am still on my ticket and have to report daily to the police station, and tell them of any change of address or means of livelihood.'

'Well?' said Mannering.

'And as the police are here – I saw two downstairs – and you are involved, by coming here I might put you to some inconvenience. The police would possibly—'

'They know you're to sit for Mrs. Mannering, and they can think what they like. What's on your mind, Larraby? Want to back out?'

'Oh, no, sir!'

'Have some coffee,' said Lorna quickly.

'Well—'

It was soon evident that Larraby was hungry.

Just before nine-thirty, Lorna took him upstairs. When Mannering went up, half an hour later, Lorna was absorbed, and Larraby sat like an image; he did not even move his eyes to look at Mannering.

Bristow didn't telephone.

Mannering made a list of the stolen goods, gave them to one of the policemen outside, fetched his *Talbot*, and drove slowly towards the West End. He wasn't followed.

He drove to Lander Street, which was not far from Quinn's. A single gown was in the window of the small shop, black with a touch of white at the waist and the neck; a simple effective creation. Would the girl be here? Or would she hide, fearing a visit from him or the police?

A slim, pale woman approached when he entered. Her black hair was plaited and wound about her head, she looked immaculate.

'Good morning, sir.'

'Good morning. Is Miss Addel in?'

'She is not here just now, sir, but I am expecting her at any moment. Is there anything I can do for you, until she arrives?'

'Has she been in yet?'

'She telephoned to say that she would not be in until after eleven o'clock, but that she would not be much later.' The dark-haired woman was aloof but unsuspicious. 'Would you care to wait in the office?'

'May I stay out here?'

'Just as you like.'

Mannering sat on an imitation Louis Quinze chair. Like the owner – if Marjorie Addel were really the owner – the shop had a touch of quality. The pale blue carpet had a thick pile, the silver-framed oval mirrors, set in walls of duck-egg blue bordered with silver gilt, gave the small shop an air of spaciousness. Two or three model gowns were draped on stands on small rostrums, but no other gowns were in sight. A room led off to the right. At the back of the shop were two closed doors, one of which presumably led into the office. The dark-haired woman went in there, moving as if the carpet were air and she too superior to walk on *terra firma*.

No one came in during the next ten minutes.

Where was the staff? He could hear no one, except for the assistant; the place was deserted. The woman came out.

'Can I take a message?'

'No, thanks.' Mannering lit a cigarette, and rose. 'Perhaps I will go into the office, after all, if—'

A car stopped outside. Mannering looked up, hoping that Marjorie Addel hadn't yet arrived. He had lulled suspicion by staying out here; now five minutes in the office might pay good dividends.

An elderly woman came to the door. The sleek woman glided forward, and as she passed him, Mannering murmured:

'Shall I be in the way?'

'If you *would* prefer to go into the office, sir, that will be quite all right.'

'I will,' said Mannering. It would take a lot to disturb that woman's poise.

The office was small, light, luxurious. He sat down at a small, walnut desk. The customer came in, a loud-voiced woman, a type he heartily disliked. She wanted an afternoon gown. *Salons* were so difficult. It was nonsense to pretend that she had an awkward figure to fit. She did not suppose that she would be able to find what she wanted here . . .

The dark-haired woman ventured to disagree politely, was sure she could find exactly what *modom* wanted. And *modom* certainly did not have a difficult figure to fit – it was ridiculous to say so. *Modom* and the assistant went into the room next to the office, the door closed. The sound of voices continued subdued by the walls; *modom* was being difficult. Did she know she would turn any gown into a sack?

Mannering glanced into the top drawer of the desk, found only business notes, then looked at the blotting-pad. He shifted it this way and that. There were several brown stains on it, and some bright red, some green. He began to trace the brown marks with a pencil; they were not ink; the others were.

Dried blood looked very much like this.

He pushed the chair back and looked at the cream fur rug in front of the desk. There were several tiny darkish stains on it. He bent down, and touched the rug; it was damp. He stood up and went to the wall; from there it was obvious that parts of the rug had been washed; these places were highly whiter than the rest. He went down on both knees, ran his fingers about the long fur. For a few moments he saw nothing; then he moved a tuft to one side, and, on the actual skin, was a brown spot half an inch across. He touched it; it was the same caked matter as the stain on the blotting pad.

Blood? They'd want to wash bloodstains away.

He felt a rising tide of excitement.

The voices still came from the fitting-room; he was safe from interruption there, safe until someone else entered the shop. He ran through the desk, and found nothing of interest; then he pulled at a drawer which was locked.

Modom was still complaining.

Mannering took out a knife, slipped it between the desk and the lock, and eased the lock to one side; it opened almost at once.

There were several papers in the desk. The top one was a letter, and the paper was headed:

Bray and Co.,

Dealers in Precious Stones,

11a, Henrietta Street,

W.C.2.

Pudding-face was certainly no stranger to Marjorie Addel. Time had suddenly become precious; this place had its secret.

CHAPTER EIGHT

THE BODY IN THE STOCK-ROOM

THE letter was in Bray's handwriting which Mannering knew well enough, and was dated the previous day. No one was named, and there was no envelope. Bray had promised to be at the shop that evening, 'as arranged'; so the letter had been sent to someone on the staff. Marjorie Addel hadn't appeared to know Bray by name.

Bray – a jewel-merchant in difficulties, if Bristow were right. Bray had probably been relying on the commission he would get for the sale of the single diamond to tide him over immediate difficulties. He'd given Lorna the impression of being agitated and in a hurry, in a rather hesitant fashion – that was like Bray.

He had promised to return in the evening; what had kept him away?

Modom was talking raucously.

He crossed to the door and went down on his hands and knees. Looking along the floor, he saw patches of the part of the parquet flooring which had recently been washed over; near the edges it was polished, near the rug it was dull; the rings made by the floorcloth stood out clearly.

The small window behind the desk had recently been washed. He examined it closely. The paintwork was scraped, as if sandpaper had been rubbed over it, in several places. If blood had been smeared there and dried, sandpapering to remove traces would occur to anyone with a practical turn of mind.

He could see no trace of blood near the door to the salon.

He put on his gloves and opened the window. It led to a tiny courtyard. There was a door, marked '*Addel & Co.*' opposite him – access to the courtyard was from another room. The window of the dressing-room ran almost at right-angles to that of the office. He could see the shadows of the two women in there; one had her arms above her head, and the voices were still. Keep trying, *modom*!

The cement floor of the courtyard had a damp patch in the middle, but was dry at the sides; there had been no rain lately.

Mannering opened the window wide, and climbed out; it was a tight fit. He went to the door; it was locked. He examined the lock with a swift, expert glance; there were thousands like it.

He closed the window behind him, opened his knife and worked on the door. All the windows overlooking the courtyard were of frosted glass; he wouldn't be seen unless one was opened. A breath of the past stole over him; excitement came with it. His fingers moved swiftly, surely.

The door opened.

He put the knife away and stepped into a dark passage; ahead was a flight of stairs. They creaked as he went up. It was gloomy here, and he could not see marks on the staircase. At the top, he opened an unlocked door and light shone on boards which were still damp from washing.

This was a store, cum-workroom. Large built-in walnut cupboards lined it, and there were several rows of dresses covered with plastic material, tables, sewing machines. There was little room to move. The floor had recently been washed, familiar damp patches reached one of the built-in cupboards, but the floor was dry in front of the others.

The cupboard was locked. He opened it, almost mechanically, not thinking of the task, only of the mystery here. Mystery? Why wasn't the staff on duty?

To prevent them from finding out – what?

The lock clicked back. A row of dresses was in front of him, but the door, a double sliding one, still covered half of the cupboard. He slid both sections in the other direction.

A man's body swayed forward and would have fallen had Mannering not put out a hand.

He held it upright.

He'd asked for it; and he'd got it.

The man's head and shoulders were covered with a pale canvas drape. Bloodstains showed on a dark grey waistcoat; Bray always wore dark grey. Mannering eased the canvas up gently; it was in loose folds and not difficult to move. The body lurched to one side, and he grabbed it.

Then he saw the face; the round, pale pudding of a face.

He pulled the canvas back again, propped the body up and slid the door to.

He'd asked for it—

If he reported this to Bristow, Marjorie Addel would soon be at the Yard, and might not come out for a long time. He wanted desperately to see her. If he didn't report it to Bristow, he would probably see the inside of the Yard before he wanted to.

Why not tell half the truth; tell Bristow about the bloodstains? He could lock the doors and cupboards as easily as he had picked them, and he had left no prints. But getting downstairs and into the office before the dark-haired woman had finished with *modom* became urgent. He locked the cupboard door and the door at the top of the stairs. *Modom* was still talking, and her arms were above her head again. He fastened the outer door, glanced at the notice of *Addel & Co.*, and went to the office window. He pulled it open gently. He could see no one inside. He put a leg over the window-sill, and a woman's voice came:

'*Oh!*'

She was in a corner, out of sight.

The damage was done, it was pointless to back away. Mannering squeezed himself through quickly, waiting for the woman to scream. She didn't but he could hear her heavy breathing.

Marjorie Addel was standing by the safe, which was wide open. She had been agitated last night; now terror showed in her blue eyes.

He closed the window, smoothed down his hair, and said amiably:

'Oh, hallo!'

She seemed to be fighting for breath.

'All right, Miss Addel. I'm not going to run off with your money.'

'You're – John *Mannering*.'

'That's right.' Mannering took out cigarettes. 'Did you find your friend last night?'

'*What were you doing out there?*'

'Looking round the yard. It's a nice, clean tidy little yard.'

What did she know?

'You had no right there.' Her middle name should be 'Naïve.' 'Why did you come here?'

'To see you. As you were out, I looked about.' He offered his case; she ignored it. He smiled amiably. 'I'm full of strange ideas. I thought you might be hiding from me.'

'Why, why should I hide from you?' she demanded.

'You might think I want the diamond back.'

She was calmer now, and moved from the safe to the desk. What had terrified her? Him? Or the thought of what he might have seen. If she knew about the body, would she have calmed down so quickly?

'You're lying to me.'

'Never!'

'Why did you come here?'

'To see a lovely lassie.' Mannering backed to the desk and sat on the corner.

Modom was still talking. Marjorie Addel, dressed in the same simple frock as on the previous night, and the same light coat, had a strained composure which made him wonder whether she was fooling him; could anyone of her age be so unsophisticated?

He said solemnly: 'I wanted to make sure that you had found your friend and returned the jewel to him.'

'I – did.'

'Good.'

'He is going to get in touch with you soon,' she added. Was there slyness in the way she looked at him?

'I see,' said Mannering, and the body of Bray seemed to press against his arms. 'What's his name, Miss Addel?'

'You know that well enough.'

He moved swiftly towards her, took her by the shoulders before she could dodge, held her tightly, his fingers pressing hard into her flesh.

'That's not the point. Do you know him?'

'Of course I do! Let me go.'

'What's his name?'

'Let me go! You've no right—'

He began to shake her, gently, to and fro. She opened her lips to shout, but no sound came. Her hair began to move about, a lock fell into her eyes and she shook her head to get it away, so that she could see him. Her lips trembled, the pink flesh of her cheeks quivered, she tried to resist but couldn't prevent him from moving her; as the rhythm of the shaking increased, her teeth began to chatter.

She kicked him on the shin; it hurt.

'Not bad,' he said. 'There's more in you than there looks, my darling. Now let's have the truth, or I'll shake it out of you.'

'If you don't let me go, I'll scream.'

'Go ahead. Scream.'

She didn't.

Mannering said: 'So you don't want a fuss, my pretty. I don't know what you do want, but I know you'll probably get some nasty surprises before you've finished. Either you're as bad as they're made or you're a simpleton. Both kind have been hanged in the past.'

'*Hanged?*' she gasped.

'That's right.' He moved one hand, stretched the finger and thumb round her pale throat and pressed lightly; she caught her breath. 'Oh, I'm not going to choke the life out of you, I'm trying to make you realize what it feels like to be hanged.'

She said: 'I think you're mad.'

He let her go. She backed away, rubbing her right shoulder. She didn't sit down, and as she looked at him, she seemed more mature, more wary; as if the physical shaking had jolted her mentally, and she was now terrified of him.

'Yes, I think you're mad. Who's talking about hanging?'

'Do you read your newspapers?'

'I – I've been too busy this morning.'

'A policeman was killed last night.'

'What has that got to do with me?'

She didn't look relieved, just wary; and had she known about the body in the workroom, she would surely have shown relief when he talked about a policeman.

'He was shot by the thief who wanted the diamond you took.'

'You mean – at your apartment?'

'That's right,' said Mannering. 'Death comes easy once you've started killing.' He rubbed the surface of one of the brown spots on the blotting pad. 'Do you know what that is?'

'Ink.'

'Do you use brown ink?'

70

She didn't answer, and he bent down, ran his fingers through the long-haired rug and uncovered a brown spot.

'Know what that is?'

She shook her head, but she didn't seem scared, now, she looked at him as if he had taken leave of his senses; would she be able to act like that if she knew what the stains meant?

He said: 'It's blood.'

'*Blood*?'

'Your hearing's good. The stuff that oozes out when you cut yourself, or when you get shot, or when someone sticks a knife in you.'

'If you don't stop talking like this, I'll—'

'Well?' he barked.

'I'll call for help.'

'Yes, you need help,' said Mannering. 'Don't forget, that's blood.' He picked up the telephone. 'You don't happen to remember the number of Scotland Yard, do you?'

'I—'

'Never mind, I've got it. Whitehall 1212.' He dialled, and kept glancing at her. She licked her lips. The lock of hair fell into her eyes again and she brushed it away impatiently. 'Think up a good explanation – say you killed a cat.'

'You're crazy!'

'That's right. Hallo . . . Superintendent Bristow, please . . . Yes, I'll hold on.'

Marjorie Addel came towards him; he thought she was going to try to snatch the telephone away, but she stood quite still. She was – lovely. He'd known that from the beginning; there was a ripe beauty about her, which was more mature than her years. The dress was cut so that no one could make any mistake. Her curving eyelashes swept her cheeks, her complexion was perfect, her lips were parted and her teeth were white and even; and appealing?

She didn't speak.

Bristow said: 'Who's that?'

'Mannering. Bill, I think you ought to come to Marjorie Addel's place, in Lander Street. Discoveries of importance. Strike the medal for me on the way here, will you, and make it snappy.'

'What—'

The girl moved, snatched the receiver from Mannering, pushed him back, and cried:

'Is that Scotland Yard . . . This *is* Marjorie Addel . . . Yes, but he's no right here, he broke in . . . Yes, *broke* in . . . He's talking a lot of nonsense about blood, I don't feel safe with him.'

She banged down the receiver.

Mannering said. 'Not bad, my pretty, there's much more in you than you wanted me to know, isn't there? You've ten minutes, at most, before Bristow arrives.'

'That's ten minutes too long!'

'I don't think you quite get it,' Mannering said. 'You're on the spot. Both you and your boy friend.'

'Who?' That thrust hurt her, she lost a lot of confidence.

'The boy friend, who left you to do the dirty work last night, and then rode off with you. I followed you as far as Guildford. Didn't you know?'

'It was – *you.*' Yes, she was badly hit by this, she backed away from him. 'Paul—' Her colour ebbed.

'So he's a Paul, is he? I don't recommend gallants who let their ladies take all the risk. You're not going to get out of this easily. That is blood.'

She said: 'I thought – it was – a police car.'

'You didn't think fast enough. If you tell me the truth—'

'I've told you the truth!'

'Oh, no. Bray didn't ask you to come and collect that diamond, he'd know that I wouldn't hand it over to a stranger. Someone else thought that one up. He probably doesn't know yet that I palmed you off with a paste gem.'

She raised her hands: 'No,' she whispered.

'Yes.'

'It *wasn't* the diamond?'

'It was worth about five pounds.'

She said: 'I didn't dream—' and broke off, her hands clenching and unclenching at her breat. 'Paul must be told, Paul—'

'Why? Who is Paul? Why did you lie?'

'The police mustn't know about *Paul,*' she said, and suddenly clutched his arm, pressed herself against him. 'You mustn't mention Paul. Say what you like about me, I don't care, but don't drag Paul into it. The police mustn't—'

She dropped his arm, and swung round.

She snatched her bag from the desk and pushed past him to the door. He did not stop her, but followed quickly. The door of the fitting-room opened and *modom* and the dark-haired woman appeared. Marjorie Addel brushed past the customer, who reddened with anger as she staggered against the assistant.

'I'll be back, Zara,' Marjorie said, and rushed out of the shop. She turned right, waving to a taxi, which went by.

A man on the other side of the road hurried in the same direction as Marjorie Addel; he was a Yard detective officer. The girl stopped to wave at another cab as Mannering caught up with her and he gripped her shoulder. She tried to push his hand off. Passers-by stopped, a man said in a nervous voice:

'Now, what's all this?'

'Let me go!' cried Marjorie. 'Taxi – *taxi*!'

The detective-sergeant ran into the road. A car jammed on its brakes to avoid him. Other cars were pulling up, a crowd gathered swiftly and the D.O. was on the fringe. The man who had spoken nervously, weedy-looking and middle-aged, touched Mannering's arm.

'You'd better let her go.' He looked round for moral support from other members of the crowd.

'I will do as I like with my own sister!' snapped Mannering in an angry voice, and the nervous gallant backed away, non-plussed.

Mannering picked Marjorie up bodily, swung round and strode back to the shop. She was too startled to protest or struggle; but she was no lightweight. The D.O. was trying to force his way through the crowd.

A green Morris pulled up near the shop. Inside it, Bristow and several other men saw the girl, helpless as a babe, beginning to pummel Mannering's chest.

Mannering kicked open the door. *Modom* stood aghast, even the woman Zara was shaken out of her calm.

'Marjorie!'

'Be quiet,' said Mannering. 'She isn't well.'

Majorie's fist caught him on the nose.

Bristow was already at the door. *Modom* had *never* been so insulted, she would *never* buy anything from *this* place of violence. Eager, excited faces pressed against the window.

Bristow reached the door, with Tring. By then, Mannering was at the office door. He put the girl down, but still kept a grip on her arm. He whispered:

'Where's Paul? Tell me or 'll put the police on to him.'

How desperate was she to keep Paul out of the reach of the police?

'Hurry!'

Bristow said sharply: 'Mannering.'

The girl whispered: 'Paul Harding, The Lees, Guildford. If you tell the police, I'll—'

'What's this, Mannering?' Bristow was just outside the door; had he heard? 'taken up kidnapping?'

Mannering eased his grip.

'Hallo, Bill. Not kidnapping, just a little persuasion to make Miss Addel realize that she shouldn't go away before you arrived. She got excited.'

'Oh, *did* she?' growled Tring.

The woman Zara, had managed to get *modom* out of the shop. She came towards the office, agitated and fighting to keep her composure. She pushed past Tring; the doorway of the little office seemed jammed with people. The assistant saw the letter on the desk, face uppermost. She looked pale and shocked, but the fire flashed in her eyes.

'Will you tell me what all this is about?'

'Now—' began Bristow.

'Oh, this man Mannering is impossible!' exclaimed Marjorie. 'I have an appointment I'd forgotten, and wanted to go, and he wouldn't let me.' That was quick, clever. She was talking to Bristow, ignoring the other woman. 'Will you make him leave the premises?'

'Soon. Who is this woman?'

Zara was at the desk.

'Zara? My sister-in-law.' Marjorie stamped her foot; quite a little actress in her own right. 'It's outrageous! This man—'

Mannering said: 'Look, Bill.' He pointed to the brown stains on the blotting pad and rug. Bristow examined them closely, Tring went down on his knees to look at the carpet.

Marjorie Addel stood back, her breast heaving. Mannering was by her side, and pretending to watch the policemen. Actually, he was watching the sister-in-law, who was edging towards the desk. She looked over her shoulder, and saw two plainclothes men who were standing in the shop. She turned her back on them, and her right hand moved.

Bristow and Tring seemed interested only in the carpet.

Zara picked up the letter from Bray and slipped it into the neck of her dress.

Bristow looked up.

'Yes, that's blood.'

'Now have a look at the window,' said Mannering.

CHAPTER NINE

THE REPORTER AND A PHOTOGRAPH

'WHAT does all this mean?' demanded Zara. Two spots of colour burned on her cheeks; she had plenty of nerve – as much as Marjorie; two little actresses in their own right.

Bristow said: 'I'm sorry, Miss Addel, but we shall have to ask you and your sister-in-law to wait here, while we look round.' He spoke from the window, which he'd pushed open. 'May I have the keys or is the storeroom open?'

'It's locked.' Marjorie pointed to the desk. 'The keys are in the second drawer.'

'What right—' began Zara.

'Zara, don't be difficult, he's a policeman.'

Zara whipped round her. 'They have no right to search here!' The two spots of colour were livid; they looked as if they hurt her, and her eyes were like glass. Nothing that was found was likely to surprise her.

'Please do just what you think is necessary,' Marjorie said.

'Thank you.' Bristow took out the keys and slammed the desk door shut. He climbed out through the window, and Tring followed. A detective-sergeant stood in the office doorway, blank-faced.

'Mannering,' Bristow called.

'Coming, sir.'

'You needn't come out here,' Bristow said, at the window. He kept his voice low, so that the women could not hear. 'What put you on to this?'

'I've shown you.'

'Did you break in?'

'I was asked to wait in here and got as far as the yard, then sweet Marjorie arrived. So I had to show myself. I'd have liked another half hour alone.'

'What has she had to say for herself?'

76

'A lot of hysterical nonsense.'

'I mean Miss Addel.'

'So do I.'

'Not much hysteria about her,' said Bristow. 'Don't talk to either of them.'

'No, sir,' said Mannering humbly.

Tring was at the workroom door, trying the keys. Mannering drew back. Inside, Marjorie was calmness itself; a remarkable change, unless she was a practised Circe. She joined her sister-in-law, who couldn't keep still, and kept talking about angry customers and ruin; the red spots didn't fade.

Marjorie said little.

Now and again, the men in the shop called to someone outside. Inside, the waiting was getting on the women's nerves. Marjorie began to show it and looked as if the other's agitation worried her. She didn't once try to speak to Mannering.

He felt the nervous tension, went to the window and looked out.

Bristow appeared; a pale-faced Bristow, who strode across the yard.

'Have you seen it, Mannering?'

'Seen what?'

'Never mind. Let me come in.' Bristow climbed through and stood watching the woman. Zara leaned against the desk, as if she would fall, but Bristow concentrated on Marjorie Addel.

'Well?' he barked.

'Will you tell me what all this mystery is about?' cried Marjorie. 'It's driving me crazy.'

'Will you tell me what a murdered man is doing in your workroom?'

Zara screamed: *No!*

'Murdered,' echoed Marjorie. Was that trick of repeating a word deliberately used to gain time? 'A murdered man. I don't – I don't understand. I – it's not true. It can't be true!'

Bristow said: 'How well did you know Arthur Bray?'

'Bray?' Her voice sounded blank.

Zara groped along the desk, reached the chair and sat down. Bristow didn't seem to notice her, but little missed him.

He said: 'Come with me, Miss Addel, please.'

'Why? Where?'

'To see the man.'

Was Bristow persuaded that she knew more than her sister-in-law. The old trick of confronting a suspect with the body often worked, but why not try it on the two of them?

Marjorie said: 'Very well.'

She didn't lack nerve; she wasn't so naïve now. Was this the cunning of desperation, had the threat of danger to her Paul sharpened her wits?

She went out, through the window, in front of Bristow; Tring was still outside. Zara sat in the chair, her hands clenched in her lap. The letter hidden by her dress showed in faint outline; the dress had all the cunning of design of Marjorie's, they were beauties in their different ways. This woman's eyes were dark, her complexion almost sallow; olive, almost. She wasn't English and her name wasn't English, but except for its almost pedantic form, her voice wouldn't betray that she was a foreigner.

The shop door opened. A young man wearing an old raincoat and a battered trilby came in, dodged past the constable on duty, and said:

'Where's Mr. Bristow?'

'You can't come in here, sir.'

'Not to see Mr. Bristow? Why, hallo – excitement this morning.' He could just see Mannering. 'The great John!' He was Forsythe, a reporter from the *Morning Cry*. 'Hallo, Mannering! Big development from your trouble last night?'

'Certainly not,' said Mannering, 'I'm a spectator.'

'Oh, yeah?' Forsythe had a merry face, fair hair which was thin at the front, and a first-class reputation. He grimaced at Mannering from the door. 'Let's have the truth, old man – it's about the Adalgo diamond, isn't it?'

'You'd better ask Bristow.'

'Don't give us any trouble, Mr. Forsythe,' said the plain-clothes man. 'Clear out.'

'I'll see you later,' said Mannering.

Forsythe beamed. 'That's a promise. All right, sergeant. I'll go quietly.' He went away from the office, but stayed in the shop. Two men from other newspapers came in, the three stood in a group, talking in whispers.

During the interlude Zara had not spoken, but watched Mannering closely. She was still watching him, her eyes like black diamonds. Her back was to the policemen.

At last she spoke, in a hoarse voice:

'Are you – *the* John Mannering?'

'I think I'm your man.'

Tring called out: 'Clark!'

The plainclothes man hurried to the window.

'Come here,' Tring called.

Mannering was alone with the woman, and he went to her.

She said: 'Will you help Marjorie?'

'If I can and if she deserves helping.'

'She does. You must believe that.'

'Are you really her sister-in-law?'

'Oh, yes.'

'What about the help you need yourself?'

'I do not matter.'

Did that mean she was protecting Marjorie?

'You know that they'll search you at the police station, don't you?'

'That will not matter, either.'

'I should get rid of Bray's letter before they search you,' advised Mannering. 'It's addressed to no one, and any finger-prints on it will probably have faded by now. Take it out and screw it up and drop it in the waste-paper basket.'

'You – saw me?'

Voices sounded in the courtyard; a door slammed.

'You haven't much time,' Mannering said.

She snatched the letter from her dress, crumpled it up and thrust it into Mannering's coat pocket. Tring appeared, but hadn't seen what she had done; no one in the shop had seen. She snatched her hand away. Before Mannering had a chance to take the letter out, Tring climbed through the window.

'Not bad,' Mannering said.

'What's that?' Tring demanded.

The woman turned away from Mannering, and stepped towards Marjorie, who came in with Bristow. She was very pale, and had nothing to say. Her eyes were lack-lustre; was that from shock or pretence?

'It's true,' she said. 'It's true.'

Bristow took both women away, for questioning. The police took possession of the shop.

Marjorie begged him to help Paul; Zara begged him to help Marjorie. In his pocket was a letter Zara had been frightened that the police should find. A pretty mix up; and there was more, the bait of Paul Harding's address: *The Lees, Guildford.*

Marjorie had kept her head well; too well?

Mannering went thoughtfully back to Chelsea.

Judy let him in, and said that Lorna was still in the studio. Mannering went whistling up the rickety stairs. Lorna glanced round at him, and Mannering felt her glow of satisfaction; all dark thoughts and brooding had been swept away by her work. Larraby had gone – but Larraby was there, on canvas. Mannering stood looking at the portrait, while Lorna wiped her hands on an oily rag.

'Well, well,' Mannering mumured.

'Do you like it?'

'It's perfect.'

'It's only half-finished, but it ought to be all right.'

'It's got him, body and soul,' said Mannering. He went a little closer, and then drew back. 'Mind, body and soul,' he amended. 'Has he seen it yet?'

'No. I sent him out to get some lunch and told him to be back at half past two.'

'You're going to work yourself to death,' said Mannering, as she went to the wash-basin to wash her hands. 'Judy's complaining that lunch is getting cold.'

'I'm almost ready. Lorna took off her paint-daubed smock. 'I'll have to sign that with a diamond!' She laughed. 'I wouldn't have missed Larraby for the world.'

They went downstairs. Judy brought in a chicken *en* casserole, and started to serve.

'We'll manage,' said Mannering.

'Very good, sir.' The girl went out, trim, prim, tiny.

Lorna said: 'John, what a selfish beast I can be.'

'You said it.'

'How have you been getting on?'

'Oh, uncovering an odd murder or so.'

'Only or so?'

'Just one, to be exact.'

She put down her fork.

'You almost sound serious.'

Mannering talked, leaving nothing out. Before he had finished, the chicken was cool on their plates. Judy looked in, and bobbed out again. They finished the course in silence, and Judy brought in canned raspberries and cream.

'You're fated,' Lorna said at last. 'Fingerprints?'

'Not mine. Bristow may fancy that I'd seen the body before, that's the only danger.'

'I hope it is.' Lorna finished her sweet slowly. Then she threw up her hands. 'Isn't it wonderful? Two beauties to protect now, plus a young man. I can see it working out very well, darling. The police are watching you. You're keeping something back from them for the sake of a pair of pretty blue eyes. Before you know where you are, you'll be fighting Bristow openly. Why must it always work out like this?'

'The spice of life,' murmured Mannering.

'The vinegar. You won't go too far without telling Bristow, will you?'

'I will not.'

'I don't believe you. What happened to the note from Bray?'

'It's still in my pocket.'

'How nice! Supposing Bristow had the bright idea of coming here with a search-warrant?'

'The letter isn't addressed to anyone at Lander Street,' Mannering pointed out. 'Bray came here several times and was due here last night, so there's no reason why he shouldn't have sent me a confirming note. I'm not a bit sure that it's any use as evidence.'

'There may be prints on it.'

'I'll soon find out,' said Mannering.

After a pause, Lorna said: 'There are times when I understand why Tring hates you so, darling.'

Mannering chuckled. 'Our Tanker's having a wow of a time. Coffee?'

Larraby was back on the stroke of half past two.

'Come up when I call, will you?' Lorna went ahead; to brood for a few moments, then throw a piece of cloth over the unfinished canvas until Larraby had taken up his position again; no sitter here ever saw a half-finished portrait.

'Like the life?' Mannering asked Larraby.

'It's just as good as a holiday,' said Larraby. 'It's – it's a new life. Mr. Mannering, I hesitate to ask for anything else, but if afterwards you can think of a way of helping me to rehabilitate myself, perhaps find me work, I'll—'

'I will'

'Larraby!' called Lorna.

The little man's footsteps were firm on the staircase.

Mannering watched him out of sight, then went into the drawing-room. Larraby was a persuasive type; was his manner natural, or artificial?

Mannering took out the letter, held it close to the window, and then took a tiny bottle of grey powder from a writing-table and sifted it over the paper. A few faint prints showed, tiny fragments; the police might find them useful. Zara had been wearing cotton gloves, and on paper like this, prints soon faded.

A car pulled up outside. He saw a battered trilby on the man who got out.

Mannering went to open the door himself.

'As arranged,' said Forsythe. 'May I come in? Thanks. I tried to get round before lunch, but crime seems to be flourishing this morning.'

'Where?' asked Mannering.

'In most parts of London,' said Forsythe. 'Three smash-and-grabs, an attempted murder – beer-and-passion variety – and a spot of bother at a Communist meeting.' He laughed. 'Thanks. Mannering offered cigarettes. 'You're in good company.'

'Yes,' said Mannering dryly.

'Yours is the tit-bit of the show, though,' Forsythe went on. 'Murder and robbery here last night – I see you've still got a Robert on the doorstep – and the carved up corpus at Addel's this morning. A ripe piece, Marjorie Addel.'

'Ripe's the word.'

'What's the word for her sister-in-law. Exotic?'

'Mysterious?'

'Do you think so?' Forsythe was anxious.

'I was asking you.'

Forsythe grinned.

'It's a waste of time trying wordy warfare with you, John. I've just come from Bristow. He's up to his eyes in work and more like a clam than ever, which means that he's on delicate

82

ground. I gather from his Eminence Tanker Tring that harsh things are being said about you at the Yard.'

'Again?'

'And again! You've stuck out your neck with the Adalgo. The thieves didn't believe the real stone was at the shop, of course – perhaps they think they got it last night.'

'They didn't get it,' said Mannering. 'You can print that.'

'Thanks,' Forsythe said. 'Which reminds me, we're giving you a lovely piece of free personal publicity.'

'No, thanks.'

'You've got it. We sent a cameraman round to Quinn's this morning. He took a beauty of the Adalgo in all its glory. I had a word with the masterly Carmichael – where do you find 'em?'

'Carmichael's been in the trade for years.'

'If you'd said centuries it wouldn't surprise me. And there's that chalk-faced boy with him, Simon. John, supposing there were a raid on Quinn's, what good do you think those two museum pieces would be?'

'Quinn's *is* a museum.'

'Seriously, aren't you taking a risk?' Forsythe tapped the ash from his cigarette, and looked up with a crooked grin. 'You may not think so, but you'll read all about it in the *Cry* in the morning. Open invitation to smash-and-grab – that's the line. The Editor has decided that you're to be the star for this story, and I've had to do what he tells me. Sorry. But you're warned.'

Mannering laughed. 'Thanks. You don't want a statement from me, you're doing pretty well on your own.'

'Oh, come,' protested Forsythe. 'We say that Quinn's isn't protected well enough, so you ought to say something about it. How does this go: "Mr. John Mannering told a *Cry* reporter that he had every confidence in his staff and in the precautions taken to protect this treasure house from the depredations of burglars"?'

'Mr. Mannering told a *Cry* reporter that he had no statement to make,' corrected Mannering firmly.

'Oh, well. Were you first at the scene of the crime in Lander Street?'

'I went to buy my wife a new dress, and the police came while I was there.'

Forsythe put his head on one side.

'That's interesting. Oh, that's most interesting. And you were so anxious to buy your wife a dress that when Marjorie Addel rushed out of the shop, refusing to sell to a man with such a reputation, you chased her, picked her up and carried her back. *Most* interesting.' Forsythe paused. 'Have you ever thought much about tourists in London?'

'I've often felt sorry for them.'

'There was one in Lander Street you won't feel sorry for,' said Forsythe dreamily. 'He was there with his little Leica, and I saw him with the Leica and heard he'd got a kick out of snapping you carrying the Addel beauty. I've paid him twenty pounds for the copyright. Don't say I haven't warned you.'

'If you think you're going to blackmail me into making a statement by threatening to publish that picture, you're mistaken.'

'Not even whitemail?'

'I'm colour blind.'

'Oh, well. It's a good picture. Your wife ought to like it.'

'She knows all about the Sir Galahad act. It's no use, Teddy. I'm not making a statement to you or anyone else, yet. When and if I make one, you shall have it first.'

'I'll believe you. You'd better mean what you say, or that photograph will be splashed.' He laughed. 'I'm holding it myself. If I let the News Editor see it he would want a front page splash, but I'd rather get the story. Can I ask a few questions, off the record? Did you go to the shop this morning expecting to find trouble?'

'No. I fancied that Marjorie Addel was up to no good, because she'd been to see me here. When I went to the shop she hadn't arrived. I was shown into the office, and saw the blood. It struck me as odd.'

'Odd! You ought to write for the films. Who showed you into the office?'

'The mysterious exotic.'

'Zara Addel,' mused Forsythe. 'She wouldn't have done that if she'd known that blood was splashed all over the place, would she? Most people know that you can smell blood better than a bloodhound. Pity. I was hoping Zara had done something she was going to regret.'

'Do you know her?'

'One hears this and that. No one knows her well, but she's

been a bit high-and-mighty with one or two calf-lovers who've met her at the shop and then bought gown upon gown for imaginary girl friends. Zara's dark eyes capture young hearts. When the suitor thinks all is well because she's all melting at the shop, and suggests a trip further afield, she slaps faces. Some think it's her way of doing business, others that she's just not of a romantic turn of mind, and such advances surprise her. Whether you like her or not, you've got to admit that she's got plenty. You know what I mean – the latent lure of the hot blooded South and all that kind of thing.'

'Mixed with naïveté,' Mannering suggested.

'Just the word. Not really of this world – except where business is concerned.'

'What do you know about Marjorie Addel?'

'We've dealt with her occasionally. Zara's the power behind the scenes, and Marjorie's one of the best woman designers in the trade. Your wife's bound to know of her. Well, I must be getting along. I won't use that snapshot unless you fail me over the exclusive story. Oh, I nearly forgot. We've dug out a bit about the history of the Adalgo, but we may as well have it right. Diamond of fate, wearers get stabbed to the heart, only rightful owner a Queen. Care to check?' Forsythe took a sheet of paper from his pocket.

Mannering read it through.

'Not bad.' He made several pencil alterations.

'Can I say you gave us the information?'

'You'll say it anyhow.' Mannering gave the paper back. 'Do you know if there's any prospect of an early arrest for the policeman's murder?'

'Not a hope. The car they escaped in was stranded, no fingerprints, no nothing. Any ideas?'

'I never have ideas.'

'Modest Mannering! Well – thanks.'

Mannering saw him out, and returned to the study.

The flat was quiet. The settle-safe was closed. He glanced at it, imagining the scene when the squat man had forced Lorna to open it. Murder, intrigue, illogical beauties, Larraby, legend – all were tied up with one gem: the Adalgo. The squat man thought he had it; Marjorie Addel's Paul thought he had it.

What was Paul Harding like?

He'd find out.

The adalgo was living up to its reputation, but why were those paste replicas in existence? Why had so many people been convinced that they had the diamond? Two or three fakes, two or three mistakes, could be coincidence; there was no coincidence about this. Because he was believed to have the Adalgo, Bray had been brutally murdered, with two or three bullets in the stomach – as the policeman.

The same kind of crime often meant the same murderer.

Why not?

He had the real stone, for possession of which bullets were being freely exchanged; no wonder Lorna felt frantic.

But he'd find out, on his own. He'd always worked alone, and would again. Out of the past, the old familiar compulsion gripped him. In the days of the Baron he'd been compelled to walk alone, trusting no one; he trusted no one now. Could he trust Lorna? There might come a time when her nerve would break if he told her everything that came to his mind in days like these; and there was danger, bearable alone but not when shared; he'd shared too much danger with her. The police? They were watching, lynx-eyed, in the hope that he would make a slip, would twist his words and misconstrue his actions. Marjorie—

He could trust no one completely; but the truth was there, for the finding.

The telephone bell rang, and kept ringing.

He took off the receiver.

'Carmichael here, sir. I am sorry to worry you, but—'

'That's all right. What's the trouble?'

'I really think you ought to come here if you can. A young man who gives his name as Paul Harding is in the shop. He is very angry about the Adalgo diamond. He – er has made somewhat wild and scandalous charges against you, sir. I have been able to calm him only by promising him that you will come at once.'

CHAPTER TEN

A YOUNG MAN AND HIS MANNERS

MANNERING parked the *Talbot* near Quinn's, and walked briskly to the shop. Tanker Tring was at the corner, behaving like an ostrich by ignoring Mannering. One policeman in uniform stood in Hart Row.

The diamond was there in all its beauty.

More people than usual were looking at it. The reward of publicity.

Mannering stood watching, and knew that he was being watched. A girl looked round, saw him, and exclaimed:

'That's him!'

'That is *he*, darling,' corrected an elderly woman. 'And whom do you mean?'

'Why, John *Mannering*!'

A dozen people turned and stared; Mannering beamed and went in, while at the corner Tring scowled.

The shop was very dark.

Carmichael stood at the far end, with a tall young man; Carmichael raised a hand in eager welcome. Behind him, Simon stood like a pallid, black-clad ghost.

Paul Harding came forward, like a dog from a leash; trinkets and furniture shook.

He was young, a good looker, and well-dressed. His thick, brown curly hair refused to lie flat. Aggressiveness glowed in his eyes and showed in his manner. He looked a fighter, and undoubtedly was in a fighting mood.

'Are you Mannering?'

'Yes.'

'Where the hell have you been? I want to know—'

'Come into the office, and tell me what you want to know.' Mannering put a hand on the young man's arm; he was trembling; Marjorie couldn't have been more agitated. He let himself be ushered into the office.

Carmichael closed the door.

'I've waited for you for nearly an hour,' Harding snapped, as Mannering took a book out of a cupboard. 'You've the damned nerve to stand there fiddling about as if – as if – as if I didn't matter a damn!'

Mannering smiled amiably. 'Do you?'

'I'll show you whether I matter! You palmed off a fake gem on Miss Addel last night. The real one's in the window. Before I leave here, I'm going to have it.'

'The trade value is ten thousand pounds.'

'I know what it's worth, but you've no right to it. I'll make a full report to the police unless you let me have it.' He put his hand in his breast-pocket and pulled out a jewel case. He flung it down on the desk, and it burst open. The paste stone fell out and rolled along the table. '*That's* yours.'

'They're both mine.'

'They're not! The real stone—'

'You know, you and your Marjorie learned in the same bad school. What makes you think that you can come filibustering in here, shouting wild accusations, and then march off with a ten thousand pound diamond? It's time you grew up.'

Harding's hands clenched.

'You've got the nerve to talk to *me* about filibustering! You've no right to that stone. You should never have been allowed to have it. It wasn't Bray's to sell.'

'He didn't sell it.'

'I know he didn't, you had it on approval. You'll take it out of the window and give it to me, or I'll send for the police.'

Mannering took out his cigarette case, selected a cigarette with great care, and pushed the case across the desk. Harding didn't notice it. Mannering sat down, slowly.

'Mannering, if you—'

'You weren't so fond of the police last night, were you?'

Alarm touched grey eyes which were as bright as Marjorie's.

'What the hell do you mean?'

'What I say. You thought they were following you, and you dodged them. I was in the car behind that "M.G."'

Harding gulped, but fought on.

'That doesn't matter. The police have nothing on me. They'll have plenty to say about your keeping the stone which Bray sent you. They—' Harding paused, and then rested clenched fists on the desk and thrust his face forward. He made a palpable effort to speak calmly. 'Look here, Mannering, I'm not fooling. I mean to have that diamond. If I have to go to the police, I'll go to them. It isn't yours. You've admitted that. I don't want to make trouble, but I'll go the whole hog if you make me.'

Mannering said:

'Sit down, Harding. I like that tone much better.' He held out the case again, and Harding accepted both cigarette and light. Here was a man scared out of his wits but fighting hard, knowing what he wanted, facing risks which he hated. The desire for the diamond obsessed him. He was afraid of the police, but used them as a threat. Nothing mattered but getting the Adalgo.

Did he know about Marjorie's arrest?

Could he have kept silent about it, if he did?

'Look here, Mannering—'

'I'm coming to it. How much does Marjorie Addel mean to you?'

'That's my business. I'm here—'

'I know why you're here. Are you engaged to her?'

'No. Will you give me that diamond, or—'

'Take it easy. Marjorie's having a spot of bother with the police.'

Harding started back; the cigarette dropped from his mouth.

'She's at the Yard, being questioned.'

Harding muttered: 'At – Scotland Yard?' The news had knocked him silly.

'Yes. Want to help her?'

'Help her?' Harding sounded stupid. 'I don't see – Mannering. *Mannering*! You told the police about her visit last night, because a few of your lousy stones were stolen. You've done this to her. Why, I'll break your neck!'

He struck at Mannering's face. Mannering caught his wrist as Harding swung another blow, then gasped as Mannering twisted. He was half way out of his chair, and couldn't move.

The colour drained from his face, which was only a foot from Mannering's. Perspiration rose in little blobs on his forehead. He had the sense not to move.

Mannering let him go, and pushed him back into a chair.

'If you and the girl would behave like ordinary human beings, we'd get somewhere. Bray was murdered last night or this morning.'

Harding caught his breath. 'Murd-ered.' He had Marjorie's trick of echoing words.

'At Marjorie's shop.'

'At – Addel's,' gasped Harding. 'Bray—' he paused. He swallowed hard, and then stood up slowly. 'It's not true, it can't be true.'

'The body was found in the workroom by the police, and Marjorie and her sister-in-law are now being questioned. Marjorie says she didn't know Bray. Obviously you did. Isn't it time you told me what you knew of him?'

'It – it doesn't sound – feasible.'

'It's the second recent murder over the Adalgo diamond. Anyone interested in the stone is going to be questioned by the police. Your turn's coming.'

'It's dreadful,' Harding muttered. 'Dreadful.'

What had really shocked him most? Bray's death or Marjorie's danger?

At last, Harding said in a dull voice:

'This is all true isn't it? Bray is dead?'

'Yes.'

'They can't think that Marjorie or Zara had anything to do with it.'

'They can and they will until they know the truth. Both women will probably be detained for the time being. That's why Marjorie needs help. She needs it from someone who will keep a cool head. I've promised to do what I can.'

'Will – will you—'

'What I can do depends on knowing the truth.'

'I – I'm sorry I lost my head just now,' Harding muttered. 'I can't expect you to give me much of a hearing, after that. But this—'

'Supposing you tell me what you know about Bray, and how you came to meet him,' Mannering suggested.

There was no fight left in the man.

90

'It – it's simple enough. My father's a collector of precious stones. He hasn't got many, he's not what you'd call wealthy, but he's got a few very good diamonds. About six months ago, he bought the Adalgo. It was sold at – at rather a low price. Like a fool, I thought that he'd bought it under cover.' Harding raised his head, defiantly. 'I expect *you've* bought gems under cover before now. Every collector has. I thought – well, thought it had been smuggled into the country, and that he hadn't paid duty on it. That's why I was nervous about the police last night.'

'I see,' said Mannering expressionlessly.

'I had a heart-to-heart talk with the old man this morning,' said Harding, wearily. 'He told me that I was crazy. I must have been! He'd bought the stone at a private sale, there was nothing wrong about it. The previous owner didn't realize what it was – its history, I mean – and put too low a price on it. There's nothing wrong in that.'

'Nothing at all,' Mannering agreed, heavily.

'Then my father had a bad run in his business, and lost a lot of money in one or two speculations. He had to realize on some of his collection. He did a lot of business with Bray, who often found him rare stones. He asked Bray whether he could sell the Adalgo. Bray said he knew you were interested, and brought it along.'

'I see,' said Mannering. 'And then?'

'One of those thousand-to-one chances came off,' said Harding. 'My father put a deal through his New York brokers a few weeks ago. It's come out a winner. Oil. He decided to cancel the sale of the Adalgo, and tried to get in touch with Bray. Bray wasn't at his office. I said I'd come and see you, and if you had the thing, get it back.'

'Fair enough, up to that point,' Mannering said. 'Next?'

'A rather queer thing happened, Mannering.'

'How do you mean, queer?'

'Well, we were leaving the house – Marjorie was with me, and my father was alone in the house – when a man stopped us in the drive. I'd never seen him before. He was a tough customer, and put the wind up me. He told me he'd seen Bray, and knew Bray had offered you the Adalgo. He said he knew the Adalgo had been smuggled into the country, and would make trouble if he wasn't squared. I would have liked to have pushed his face in, but he caught me on the raw – I was already nervous about the diamond. I told him to come back and see me in the morning – anything to get rid of him. Then Marjorie and I drove to London. I don't mind admitting, Mannering, that I had cold feet – oh, not for myself but for the old man. He's sick, and I didn't want anything to go wrong. Can – can you understand me?'

'Go on.'

'I was anxious to prevent you or anyone else learning that my father owned the Adalgo,' went on Harding. 'That's why I was so nervous about the police. The long and short of it is that Marjorie said she would go and try to get it from you. We – we decided to put one across you.'

'Nice thought!'

'We knew a bit about your reputation,' Harding went on heavily, 'and we didn't think that any ordinary story would fool you. Marjorie's a bit of an actress – amateur – and we decided that she should put on an agitated girlish act, well – you *are* a bit of a ladies' man, aren't you?'

Mannering drew a deep breath.

'I *see*. Marjorie was to appeal to the Old Adam in me?'

'Yes. Everything would have been all right, I think, but – but when she got to your flat, she was so nervous she forgot Bray's name.'

'Well, well!'

Harding gave a weak grin.

When she told me about it afterwards, I nearly split. I thought she had got the diamond then, you see, we couldn't tell paste from the real thing. The way she told me how she tried to remember that name, and kept waiting for you to ask her – she was sure you wouldn't let her have it without naming Bray – was damned funny. Well, you know what happened. We thought she'd pulled it off, and drove home. I realized we were being followed, and being a bit worried about the police—'

'Why were you, just then?'

'Well, the man who'd stopped me had said he would get a reward from the police if I didn't pay him to keep quiet. I was pretty edgy. I've been busy lately. My nerves aren't what they might be,' added Harding. 'Well Marjorie did a bit of weaving about Guildford, and we shook you off. If we'd known it was you—' he broke off, and shrugged his shoulders. 'But *Bray*. It's damnable! He always said he was worried about handling that stone. He said there was blood on it, and always would be. Besides—' Harding broke off.

'Yes,' encouraged Mannering.

'I don't know how much I ought to tell you,' muttered Harding. 'The police—'

Mannering said: 'Cards on the table, Harding. If this is something the police must know, I'll tell you. If it can be kept from them, I'll hold it back. Don't make the mistake of thinking you can play ducks and drakes with the police. They're good. But you've nothing to worry about if you're told the truth. The diamond wasn't smuggled.'

Harding stood up abruptly.

'Oh, what the hell! I suppose the police will find out, anyway. My father went out after we'd left the house last night. He saw Bray. They had a pretty fierce quarrel — I don't know what it was about, probably because Bray hadn't the diamond. It was at Bray's office. You can see why I'm worried, can't you?'

CHAPTER ELEVEN

MR. MANNERING AND THE DETECTIVE

IT all sounded so beautiful. If he'd had to sit down and work out a story to fit all that had happened, Mannering couldn't have done better himself. All the i's were dotted and the t's crossed. That was, if he could believe in two people in the early twenties being so dumb. That curious quality of naïveté penetrated through everything that came to the surface in the case. Even in the acting story; and he didn't doubt Marjorie's histrionic ability. They'd actually believed that Mannering would hand over a diamond they knew to be worth a fortune . . .

Even they couldn't have believed that.

But they had; Marjorie's shock when he'd told her about the fake had been real shock.

Could Harding be so desperate, simply to get the jewel back for his father? Was that motive enough? Not by a hundred miles!

He'd told that tale well, made it almost convincing – perhaps too convincing; the last touch had been masterly.

'What the hell am I going to do?' demanded Harding. 'If I tell the police—'

A bell rang softly; it was the telephone from the shop to the office. The ringing sound was so low-pitched that it could be used when anyone was entering the shop, without the caller knowing.

Mannering lifted the receiver.

'Yes?'

Simon's husky voice sounded in his ear.

'We thought you would like to know, Mr. Mannering, that Superintendent Bristow is outside – or rather he is just stepping into the shop.'

'Thanks,' said Mannering. 'I'll see him in a moment.' He replaced the receiver, seeing that Harding was watching him intently; but Harding could not possibly have heard the Simon message.

'The police have come to see me,' Mannering told him. 'Do you want to make a statement?'

'No! No, of course not.' Harding clenched his fists. 'Look here, you haven't sent for them? This isn't a trick to—'

'Oh, be your age!' said Mannering. He was having too much of Harding-Addel tantrums. 'They don't know you, do they?'

'Not as far as I know. There's no reason why they should.'

'Then there's no reason why you shouldn't be a customer leaving the shop,' Mannering said. He stood up, and opened the door. 'Hurry. Yes, we'll look after all that for you,' he added in a louder voice, and shook hands. 'Goodbye.'

'I do appreciate all your trouble,' said Harding with commendable steadiness. 'When shall I see you again?'

'I'll tell you later – call me here or at home.'

Mannering ushered him out, to see Bristow waiting halfway along the shop.

There was no time to dwell on young Harding's story, no chance to check where it corroborated what he already knew. The visit from Bristow meant that the heat was on; Bristow would keep it on, giving him little chance to relax; and when with Bristow, a single mistake might prove fatal.

If Bristow knew who Harding was, for instance.

Carmichael went forward to open the door for Harding, and Mannering approached Bristow, who gave the youth a long, calculating stare, then turned to Mannering. So that trick was won. Bristow was looking a trifle drawn but was as spruce as ever. There was a fresh gardenia in his buttonhole; that was Bristow's favourite flower, and it was an unhappy day when he failed to get one.

'You're just in time for tea, Bill,' greeted Mannering, and led the Superintendent into the office. Simon, as if by magic, brought in tea.

Bristow sat in Harding's chair. He wasn't sure of himself, which meant that he wanted something.

'Well, Mannering. I've asked you not to do too much on your own, haven't I?' His voice was flat.

'And I haven't.'

'You knew Bray's body was in that room,' Bristow accused.

'My dear chap! I can't see through a brick wall.'

'You'd been upstairs – the lock had been picked. I've had it down and inspected it, and the marks are fresh. Why must you go crazy?'

Mannering murmured: 'I didn't go crazy that way, Bill. But if I had, I would have called you just as quickly as I did.'

'Oh, you knew he was there. One of these days when you do a job that – oh, forget it! Why did you chase the girl out of the shop? If you'd let her get away, we would have picked her up and had a much stronger case.'

'I didn't want her to panic,' said Mannering.

'Why not?'

'Haven't you seen her eyes?'

'Don't be a fool. What had you been saying to her?'

'I warned her that she would be in trouble over the Adalgo stone, and that you would ask her many questions,' Mannering said. 'As she was bound to know that soon, I didn't see any harm in it. The bloodstains shook me. The office and yard had been covered in blood, and I thought you ought to know about it. Surely you can't complain about that. Any news of Bray's murderer?'

Bristow leaned back; in his manner there was a promise of frankness, a 'we're old friends, John, let's work this out between us' look.

'Not yet. He was killed in that office, there isn't much doubt about that. He was carried up to the stock-room, and the murderer tried to rub out the traces. I'm not sure whether either of the women partners knew anything about it. According to her statement, Miss Addel was away from the shop all the evening, but—' Bristow hesitated; he was going to try to pull a fast one. 'You know as much as I do, I expect. She stayed the night at that house in Guildford.'

'Which house?' asked Mannering.

'The one she told you about.' Sly Bill Bristow!

Mannering chuckled. 'She didn't tell me about any place at Guildford, Bill. You may be surprised, but I spent ages trying to persuade her to be frank with you, and all I got for my pains was a kick in the shins. Did she tell you about that?'

'A kick?'

'A hard one.'

'Oh,' said Bristow, who knew he'd failed. 'Well, you probably asked for it. She spent the night at Guildford, and came back late this morning.'

'With friends?'

'You'd better try to find out for yourself. She told you that she knew Bray, didn't she?'

Mannering looked blank.

'I told you that she didn't seem to know him. What's the matter with your memory today?'

Bristow leaned forward and smiled a little wanly; he was preparing another catch question, and looked as innocent as Marjorie Addel.

'To tell you the truth, John, I'm tired. I've had a run of late nights, and I'm not feeling at my brightest. A good night's sleep would put me right. Sure she didn't mention Bray to you?'

'Quite sure.'

'She still insists that she doesn't know him,' said Bristow, with a fine disregard of consistency. It was when he appeared to be illogical, tired and losing his grip that he was most dangerous. 'Yet the man was killed there between the time they shut up at six o'clock last night, and midnight. He'd been dead about twelve hours. Say between nine and nine-fifteen.'

'Medical evidence?'

'That's what the doctor says. What did you think when you saw Bray?'

'But Bill, I haven't seen him since he died. You wouldn't let me – remember?'

'How well did you know Bray?'

'Casually. We didn't do much business.'

'Did you like him?'

'Well enough to be sorry he's dead, and to hope you find the murderer, but not well enough to risk my neck.'

'I hope you mean that. Did Bray ever speak to you about a collector named Harding?'

Was that a trick question or just for information? Bristow stifled a yawn as he put it.

'No.'

'Do you know a collector of that name?'

'I've never met one. There isn't one of importance, or I'd know him.'

'He collects in a small way,' Bristow admitted. 'He saw Bray at Bray's office last night, about nine o'clock – a little after nine.'

'Sure?'

'Yes.'

'What's your game, Bill? Bray must have been killed between that time and midnight, not between six o'clock and midnight.'

Bristow didn't seem to hear that. Harding and Bray had a fierce quarrel. People in the next office to Bray's heard them. Harding, who lives at Guildford, was recognized. A man who read about the murder told us about Harding's visit.'

'Oh,' said Mannering. 'Praise the press!'

'You followed Marjorie Addel to Guildford. You know she went to Harding's place, don't you. You knew that she's in love with Harding's son. You knew she stayed there all night, and that was why she was late at the shop this morning.'

Mannering said: 'Did I, Bill?'

Bristow growled: 'You think you're clever but you're a fool.' He stood up. 'Harding is being questioned now. We've got him, and we're looking for his son. The son's an officious young upstart, by repute, and may think that you can help him better than the police. If he comes to you, you'll tell me at once.'

'Well, well,' said Mannering. 'You couldn't have known much sooner.'

There were limits to reticence; Paul Harding's visit had to be mentioned now.

'Meaning what?' Bristow demanded.

'He was here just now.'

'The man I saw going out?'

'Yes.'

'I see,' said Bristow, slowly, ominously. 'You allowed him to go without telling me who he was. You had him here before I could get at him – a man who's urgently wanted. Ten minutes ago you told me you'd never heard of a jewel collector named Harding. Now you have the impudence to admit that his son was sitting under my very nose when I came in the shop.' Bristow's voice was low-pitched, angry. 'I've told you time and time again that one day you'll go too far, and this time you've done just that. For years – for eight years – you've gone your own sweet way, you've made a monkey of me a dozen times, laughed in my face because you've always had an answer and an alibi, but

98

this time you've gone over the line. You may have stopped lifting jewels, but you haven't stopped trying to teach the police their job. Now you're going to have a chance of watching them at close quarters. You're coming with me to the Yard for questioning. You'll have to think up something very smart before you get away. You've deliberately withheld a wanted man, but you won't have a chance to do it again. Come on.'

Mannering put his head on one side, and stood up slowly. He took out his cigarette case, and lit a cigarette. Bristow turned to the door. He touched the handle as Mannering lit the cigarette.

Then Mannering gave a sudden, deep, hearty laugh.

It made Bristow snatch his hand away from the door and swing round.

'What's funny?'

'My dear chap! Not you – you were wonderful. I shall remember that to my dying day. *I'm* funny!'

Bristow snapped: 'Perhaps your wife will think so.'

'Come, Bill!'

'Stop stalling. We're going places.'

'Whenever you've a warrant, William.' What was this? Super bluff or sober action? Had Bristow come to take him to the Yard, and played a cat and mouse game until now? 'It's still funny,' Mannering said. 'In this job, I've tried to keep things warm for you. Never again – I was a damned fool not to work on my own, working with you blunts what mind I've got. How the blazes did I know you wanted young Harding? I needn't have told you about the bloodstains, not about Marjorie Addel. You might not have known that Bray was dead for days – for weeks. Isn't it funny?'

'Maybe it was, until you let Harding walk out on me.'

'How was I to know that you wanted him?'

'You could guess.'

'So you're that good. Forsythe and other bright newspapermen would have fun out of that – a man arrested because he didn't guess the next police notice. Have the papers mentioned that Harding was wanted?'

Bristow didn't answer.

Mannering rubbed his hands together briskly.

'Come on, Bill. Let's go. You won't feel proud of it later.'

'I'm not paid to feel proud.'

'You're paid to do your job. Why don't you do it? You ought to know what young Harding looks like – you ought to have recognized him. Not so good, Bill, is it? A wanted man walks past you without any attempt at disguise, and you let him go.'

'Why did you lie to me about knowing his father?'

'I don't know a collector named Harding. I know an impetuous young man who says his father collects precious stones, but that's the best I can do for you. Bill, you make one crazy mistake with me. Aways at your elbow and at the back of your mind is the nonsense notion that I was once the Baron. If you could get that out of your head, you'd be a wiser man – and you'd know when to ask me for help. Do you know what's at the bottom of this job? Of course you do – the Adalgo diamond. Do you know who has, or did have, copies or similar stones? You don't? I *do*. I'm probably the only man in the country who can help you in this particular case. And will I help? Just ask me! Come on, let's go. I'll call my attorney from the Yard.'

Bristow didn't move.

'Aren't you anxious to let Inspector Tring have his great triumph?' asked Mannering. 'Or are you worried in case I find a way to give Forsythe the story? It won't look too good, but you're not paid to look after your reputation, you're paid to get results. Remember?'

After a long pause, Bristow said:

'I'll give you an hour to put on paper all you know about the Adalgo, the fakes and the simliar stones, all that Harding told you and all you know about the girl and that dress shop. If I catch you out in a single lie, I'll charge you with complicity and hold you until the inquiry's over. Is that clear?'

Mannering sat on the corner of the desk; he felt warm.

'All right, Bill,' he said slowly.

'Mind you put everything down. Give the statement to Tring, who's outside, as soon as it's ready.'

Bristow went out, and closed the door with a snap.

He'd asked for trouble again and it had lost no time in coming. He was the fool. The only way to work was on his own, telling Bristow of the *trivia*, sops to keep him quiet. He couldn't run with the hare and chase with the hounds, and should have known it. Bristow snatched at everything he said, built it up, exaggerated it, read sinister significance when there was none.

Bristow thought he had him – right there. Mannering pressed his thumb against the desk, and laughed.

'All right, Bill!'

He pulled a writing pad in front of him and wrote swiftly, brief, numbered notes. He omitted only two things; the first discovery of Bray's body and the fact that Marjorie had given him Paul Harding's address. There was risk in the second omission. If Paul were detained, the girl might blame it on to Mannering and tell the police everything, out of spite. But that would make her a fool and where Paul and the Adalgo were concerned, she wasn't a fool – just a mixture of fierce intensity and naïveté with a mind of her own and a determination as great as Harding's.

He didn't know the truth and wasn't near it, yet; nor was Bristow.

He signed the two closely written sheets with a flourish, tucked them into an envelope and hurried out. Simon loomed out of a corner.

'I shan't be back, Simon.'

'Very well, sir.'

The crowd of sightseers had grown, before long it would be a seething mass of people, young, old, eager, blasé. He heard the murmur of their talk through the muted loudspeaker. He opened the door and two schoolboys rushed forward, waving autograph books and pencils.

'*Please* will you sign, sir?'

Tring was on the other side of the road.

'You really ought to get that chap to sign,' said Mannering. 'The man with the bowler. He's one of the big men at Scotland Yard.' He signed two books; three others were thrust in front of him. The first lad, with a heartfelt: '*Thanks, Mr. Mannering*,' scurried across the road to Tring.

By the time Mannering had finished, Tring was surrounded, looking puzzled and tipping his hat to the back of his head.

Mannering joined the little group.

'Be a sport, Inspector!'

'*Please*, Inspector,' piped a treble voice.

'Now look here—' began Tring.

'It won't do you any harm, and look at the pleasure it will give them,' said Mannering brightly. 'Sign away – I'll let you use my pen, if you like. Oh – I nearly forgot. Give this to Bill Bristow for me, will you?'

He thrust the statement into Tring's hand, and hurried off. From the corner, he saw Tring signing autograph books; there was a lot of good nature in Tring, who hated only one thing: the Baron. Hate? It wasn't too strong a word. He must not under-estimate Tring's motivation – this deep-rooted desire to pull off a coup which he'd dreamed of for eight years.

When Mannering took his car from the parking place and drove off, Tring was still signing.

Mannering weaved in and out of the traffic, taking short cuts here, detours there; he did not see a police car behind him, and doubted whether one had been there; they would follow him by radio if they really meant business. Well, he meant business; Lone Wolf Mannering!

He was in the same mood when he reached Green Street. Two plainclothes men were near the house. He waved to them, left the car outside and hurried up the stairs. He let himself in.

'Up or down, my sweet?'

Lorna did not answer. No move came from the kitchen. This was Judy's daily hour or two off, and Lorna often went for a riverside walk after an intensive day's work; she had put every-thing she had into Larraby's portrait.

It was surprisingly easy to forget Larraby; and that might be dangerous.

Someone moved in the drawing-room.

'Lorna!' Mannering's voice sharpened; why hadn't she called out? He pictured a squat man with a gun.

The drawing-room door began to open.

Mannering went swiftly to the open door of his study; he was keyed up on the instant, ignoring the fact that the police were downstairs; anyone expert could have hoodwinked them, to get inside.

Then he saw Larraby.

Larraby paused in the doorway, looking round nervously. Mannering showed himself.

'I *am* sorry, Mr. Mannering,' said Larraby, rubbing his eyes. 'Mrs. Mannering asked me to stay here and give you a message, and I dropped off to sleep. Sitting in the same position and hardly daring to blink is a bit tiring. I *am* sorry.'

'That's all right,' said Mannering. Why had Lorna left the man alone in the flat? Fool! He'd promised to send Simon along, and had forgotten to; he was careless even about Lorna. But there were limits to the trust which should be put in Larraby.

'What was the message?' he asked.

'Mrs. Mannering received a telephone call about four o'clock,' said Larraby. 'She was a little irritated, but it was obviously important. She did not tell me the nature of the telephone call, but I think she was a little apprehensive.'

Mannering said sharply: 'Yes?'

'She said that if you got back before she did, she would like you to 'phone a Mr. Leverson, of Wine Street. Aldgate,' went on Larraby, and stifled another yawn. 'I *am* sorry that I dropped off.'

'Forget it.'

Had Larraby been asleep or was he foxing? Could any man who'd been in the trade and in jail, talk so calmly of Flick Leverson, showing no sign that he knew of the man who had been the biggest jewel fence in London?

Leverson was probably the only man who could prove the identity of the Baron; and certainly the only man who could be trusted not to use that proof.

A call from Leverson often meant a warning of trouble.

Mannering went to the telephone.

CHAPTER TWELVE

THE BEGGAR AND THE BOY

MANNERING could hear the ringing sound, but there was no answer from Leverson's house. Larraby stood a little way off, watching with his tired, sad eyes. The *brrr-brrr-brrr* began to get on Mannering's nerves. He banged down the receiver.

'Exactly what time did she leave?'

'A little after four.'

'And she was in a hurry?'

'She was certainly anxious not to lose much time,' said Larraby. 'She gave the impression that something of great importance had happened, Mr. Mannering. She was more excited, I think, hardly frightened – just eager. I said apprehensive, that's true, but – no, she *wasn't* frightened – except of getting wherever she was going too late. She actually said: "I mustn't be late," several times.'

'Thanks.' Mannering dialled Leverson's number again.

Lorna knew the old fence well, and would recognize his voice, would know if it were a phoney call. Why should it be phoney? There was no reason to think it had been, but plenty for being alarmed. Leverson was as much of the past as the Baron.

The *brrr-brrr-brrr* went on and on.

He put the receiver down again, and Larraby said:

'No answer, Mr. Mannering?' A fatuous question; everyone was fatuous. Could Larraby have lied?

'Not yet. You'd better get home.'

Larraby looked at him gravely.

'Before my big mistake I had a pleasant little home at Harrow,' he said gently, 'and my wife and daughter used to be fond of me. I was certainly most fond of them, Mr. Mannering, and I loved my home. I threw them away.'

Lorna had rushed off to Leverson, so it was urgent business.

Larraby was talking in his soft voice and somehow compelling attention.

'My wife and daughter have a strict code of behaviour, and I shocked them. They haven't found it possible to forgive me. I like to think that one day – oh, I'm sorry. I – I was dreaming about them when you arrived, that's why they're on my mind.'

'They'll come round,' Mannering said.

If he were caught and jailed, Lorna would live in a hell of his making; Larraby's wife had made a hell for him.

'I hope so. Perhaps if I were to re-establish myself, with a regular job, a respectable job—' Larraby broke off. 'What am I thinking of! Goodnight, Mr. Mannering, goodnight! I will be here at nine in the morning, as Mrs. Mannering asked.' He scurried to the front door, and his hand was on the knob when Mannering said:

'Wait, Larraby.'

Larraby turned. 'Yes?'

'Where will you sleep tonight?'

'Please don't worry.'

'I'm not worrying. Is it a doss-house?'

'Well—'

'So it is. Haunt of vice, den of thieves, a proper place for an ex-convict to sleep, eh? Like it there?'

'I hate it!'

'Don't go back.'

'But—'

Mannering said: 'Don't go back. Come over here.' The little man approached him slowly, almost nervously; Mannering felt bleak and looked it. 'Larraby, I've taken a chance on you. You know what's on, don't you?'

'That there is trouble—'

'A conspiracy to steal the Adalgo. Didn't you know it?'

Larraby said slowly: 'I hope only one thing, Mr. Mannering, that you never allow Mrs. Mannering to wear that diamond. I've studied its history – there is a book in the drawing-room. Call it superstitious, call it what you like, but—'

Mannering gripped his shoulder, and knew that it hurt. Larraby neither flinched nor avoided his eye.

'Know anything about the conspiracy?'

'I do *not*,' said Larraby.

'For some crazy reason, I believe you. The police don't. No one in their right senses would, but I believe you. If I'm wrong, you'll go back to jail and there won't be any rehabilitation after that.'

Larraby said: 'I would rather kill myself than betray you.'

It was absurdly melodramatic; and it rang true.

Mannering let him go.

'All right. Buy yourself another suit, get lodgings somewhere near here, there are plenty of places. Don't worry about your future, just about your soul.' He took ten pound notes from his pocket and stuffed them into Larraby's. 'And throw away that tray of matches.'

Larraby didn't speak; he closed his eyes, turned abruptly and went to the door.

Footsteps sounded on the stairs; not Lorna's, but a man's. Mannering went to the telephone and touched it. The footsteps drew nearer; they were of a man in a hurry. Larraby opened the door.

A man said: 'Larraby! What the hell are you doing here?'

That was Paul Harding.

Larraby drew back, startled.

Mannering picked up the telephone, dialled Whitehall 1212, and listened. The ringing sound echoed in one ear, Harding's heavy breathing in the other.

'*This is Scotland Yard, can I help you?*'

'I called to see Mr. Mannering,' Larraby said.

'*Tell Bristow Paul Harding is at Green Street.*'

'So you did,' breathed Harding.

'*Very good, sir.*'

The telephone went *ting*! as Mannering put down the receiver. He'd lost nothing, betrayed nothing; the men outside would report Harding's arrival, and perhaps were already on the telephone; this was a thing he could safely and usefully tell Bristow.

'Yes, I did,' said Larraby. His voice was thin with emotion. Fear? Anger? Disappointment. '*Good* afternoon.'

He disappeared.

Mannering picked up the receiver and dialled Leverson's number. The *brrr-brrr* began, soft, insistent. Harding came in and banged the door. He reached the study, and drew back sharply, a brooding aggressor.

'Who are you calling?'

'My wife.'

'Oh.' Harding came into the room. 'What was that man doing here?'

'Help yourself to a drink.'

'I don't want a drink. What—'

'You've never wanted a drink so much.'

'What was that man doing here?'

'My wife is painting his portrait.'

'Good Lord! She must be hard up for a model! The man's a rogue – didn't you know?'

'No.'

'He was sent to prison for—'

'I know that one. A single jail sentence for a single crime doesn't make a man a rogue.'

'Nonsense! My father never trusted him.'

'They've done business together, have they?'

'They did, at one time. Still, if you know about his past it's none of my business.' Harding lit a cigarette. There was no answer from Leverson. Mannering put the receiver down. 'We'll go in the next room.'

'I had to come to see you again, Mannering.' Harding became subdued again. 'I hope I haven't chosen a bad time, but—'

'The time's all right. Whisky?' Mannering stood by the cocktail cabinet.

'Thanks.'

'What's the trouble?' Mannering asked.

'You remember I told you about my father's quarrel with Bray?'

'I don't forget that easily.'

'Those damned police had the nerve to detain him for questioning! They only let him go half an hour ago. I called home, they told me about it then. He'd just telephoned to say that he would be back later in the day. And he'd left a message for me, Mannering.' Harding took a gulp of his whisky-and-soda. 'It's – fantastic! He asked me to ask *you* if you'd go to see him.'

'Oh, did he?' said Mannering heavily.

'Yes. Will you?'

It wasn't really as complicated or crazy as it seemed. There was a simple solution to all this, the odd pieces of the puzzle would fall into place.

'Will you? I know I behaved like a fool, but—'

'We can't blame your father for that. Yes, I'll go. What does he want?'

'I just picked up the message, that's all. You'll go as soon as you can, won't you?,

'Yes.'

'Thanks. Then I'll be off.'

'I shouldn't go just yet,' said Mannering.

'Why not?'

'The police saw you come in.'

'I'm not worried about the police!'

'Blow hot, blow cold. Love me, love me not; "I fear the police, the police can go to hell." '

'They're worried about you,' said Mannering.

'What the devil do you mean?'

'I saw Bristow at Quinn's, remember? He told me that he wants a chat with you.'

'And you've sent for him!' Rage flared up again. 'That's who you telephoned. You've told him I'm here! Why, I'd like to break your neck!'

'You were seen to come in.'

'You've given me away! You – *now* I know what a foul swine you are,' bellowed Harding. 'And Marjorie trusted you, she—' He choked, turned on his heel. and made for the door.

Before he reached it, the bell rang.

'Love me, love me not.'

'Is that – your friends?' Harding managed to put a sneer into his words.

'Probably.'

The bell rang again.

'Aren't you going to answer the door?'

'There's no hurry. So your father's been released.'

'The fools should never have detained him.'

Mannering said:

'You want help, Marjorie wants help, your father wants to see me. You don't give a damn for the police and shake as with palsy when they come for you. What's the truth?'

Harding didn't answer. The bell rang again.

Mannering shrugged, and opened the door – to Tring.

'Hallo, Tanker! Got over the writer's cramp?'

'Took your time letting me in, didn't you?'

'There's always plenty of time. Do you know Mr. Paul Harding?'

'I'll be glad if you will come along with me, to make a statement,' Tring said laboriously. 'I am Serg – I am Inspector Tring, of New Scotland Yard.'

He took out his card, but Harding brushed it aside.

'Are you arresting me?'

'No, sir.' Tring was formal. 'We would like you to make a statement, that's all.'

'Do I have to go with him, Mannering?'

'No,' said Mannering, 'but I should, if I were you.'

Tring, preferring not to voice agreement with Mannering, said nothing. Harding's face was set and angry. He wanted to talk to Mannering, or else to make a fool of him.

'Oh, all right,' he growled.

'Thank you, sir,' said Tring. 'Goodnight, Mr. Mannering.'

He turned, and ushered Harding out of the room.

Mannering crossed to the window. Tring appeared in the street first; his car stood outside the house, with a police constable by it. Harding got in, and Tring followed clumsily. The door slammed.

Mannering caught sight of a familiar figure on the other side of the road as he turned away.

There was a burned out house, only the shell of which was standing, nearly opposite; behind one of the walls stood Josh Larraby, invisible from the street. The little man appeared to be standing on tip-toe, so as to watch Harding.

Larraby watched the car disappear, and then stepped cautiously from his hiding place. He looked up at the window, caught sight of Mannering, smiled and hurried towards the Embankment. The policeman on duty watched him.

Why was he so interested in Paul Harding?

What did the two really know about each other?

Mannering took up the telephone and dialled Leverson's number. *Brrr-brrr, brrr-brrr.* The ringing sound mocked him. Lorna had been dragged by the hair across this room, probably over the very spot where he was standing, and in spite of the warning, in spite of the danger, he hadn't sent Simon here. But the police had been outside all the time, it wasn't so easy to fool them as he'd told himself, Lorna ought to have been safe.

Had Larraby told the truth?

He was caught with a sudden surge of fear, swung round, thrust open every door in the apartment, looked in the cupboards, even lifted the seat of the settle. Then he approached the attic staircase. His breathing was uneven, he was near panic. He went up, slowly. The hatch was down and locked from the outside, as Lorna usually locked it. The bolt stuck when he pushed it. He pushed harder and caught his finger on a splinter. He winced, flung the hatch back, and thrust his head and shoulders through.

If Lorna—

Larraby's portrait stood on the easel without a canvas cover; it was an uncanny likeness, and more than a likeness. The studio was empty. Mannering laughed, unsteadily, climbed in and looked in the store cupboard, with its tidy stores of paint tubes, chalks, crayons, pencils and brushes. He kicked aside several pieces of webbing, used for packing.

Of course she wasn't here.

What had got into him?

Doubt about Larraby, chiefly; he knew that.

He stood and studied the portrait. There was something Lorna hadn't caught; Larraby's expression, when Mannering had gripped his shoulder downstairs; that intense, almost desperate denial of bad faith. Larraby had persuaded Lorna that he could be trusted or she wouldn't have left him here alone; a known jewel-thief, given the freedom of a place full of *objets d'art*, some of them priceless. Larraby had a way with him — and Larraby had been watching Harding and knew just how to conceal himself.

Mannering went out, and crossed to a policeman on duty over the road.

'Constable—'

'Yes, sir?'

'Did you see my wife leave?'

'Yes, sir, I did.'

'Remember what time it was?'

The constable hesitated, then took out his notebook, flipped over a few pages and said in a flat voice: 'Three minutes after four o'clock, p.m.'

'Thanks.' So Larraby had his time right.

Mannering half-turned, then said: 'Was anyone with her?'

'Not when she left the house.'

'Did she meet someone?' Perhaps Leverson had come to see her and they'd gone off together.

'She met a reporter,' said the policeman stolidly. 'I don't know his name.'

'Youngish chap, battered trilby, soiled raincoat, who's been here before?'

'That's the man, sir.'

'Did they go off together?'

'In his car, yes.'

'Thanks,' said Mannering. 'You're good.'

'I can understand you being worried after the other night, sir.'

Mannering said: 'Yes.' He was more worried than he wanted to admit, and the news of Forsythe's visit only slightly reassured him. He hurried across to his car. Larraby and Harding, Tring and his own patchwork thoughts, had delayed him an hour, he ought to have been at Leverson's house long ago. He drove fast through the thinning evening traffic, towards the East End, Wine Street and Flick Leverson.

The past sat beside him.

Leverson, the tall, silvery haired, one-armed fence, cultured, mellow, incomparable judge of precious stones, known by the police but never caught, was a man with a mind which made Tring seem addle-pated and Bristow second rate. But it wasn't fair to compare them or anyone with Leverson, who stood head and shoulders in any company. The one thing Mannering did not know about him, was the real reason why he had turned 'bad'. But that was a nonsense word to use about Flick; he was a man to trust and a man to love.

Lorna knew he could be trusted implicitly.

The Baron had gone to Leverson in the early days, selling his loot; through Leverson, who had identified him, he had seen a picture of himself as he had been. The calm, friendly voice and the insistent questions: 'Are you sure you ought to be doing this, Mannering? Oughtn't you to give it up? It isn't your field – oh, you're brilliant at it, but it's a spendthrift brilliance.'

'Not bad, coming from you,' Mannering had said.

'Never mind that. I always had a kink, but you haven't. You

were hurt and took revenge out of society, but no hurt ought to rankle for so long. What kind of a life will it be for Lorna?'

He'd won; and hadn't taken long to win.

Soon afterwards, Leverson himself had retired; but a dozen times he had been mentor, friend and confidant, amused at the Baron turned detective, amused at the irony of Bristow working both with and against him; a job like this would appeal to Leverson. But – why had he suddenly called Lorna? What did he want? He probably knew a lot about the Adalgo, would guess that Mannering had it in the window to attract attention, but why—

Mannering turned into Wine Street, a wide thoroughfare with neat, tall, red brick houses on each side, gateway to the slums of the East End.

The first person Mannering saw was Larraby.

CHAPTER THIRTEEN

THE FENCE AND THE DIAMONDS

MANNERING pulled up and Larraby approached. Another car turned into Wine Street, but neither of them appeared to notice it.

'Well? What's this?'

'Mr. Mannering—'

'I thought you didn't know Leverson.'

'And I did not, sir. But I made inquiries after I left Chelsea, and learned who he was and where he lived. I thought perhaps you would come here, and hoped that I would be able to help.'

It sounded plausible. Mannering opened the car door and got out.

'Have you seen the police car at the end of the road?' asked Larraby.

'Yes,' said Mannering. 'And the policemen in it have seen you.'

'I've nothing to fear from the police now,' said Larraby. 'What are you going to do, Mr. Mannering?'

'We'll see.'

Was Larraby's explanation too plausible?

Mannering rang the front door bell; there was no answer.

As he stood on the doorstep, with Larraby behind him and the police watching from the corner, the past came upon him again. He had first come here by night, with jewels for which he asked a heavy price. Fantastic years!

Forget the past, and deal with the present!

He rang again. There was no sound inside the house.

'It is – puzzling,' Larraby murmured.

Mannering said: 'Stay here, will you?'

He walked towards the farther end of Wine Street, to an alley at the back of the house, approached by a narrow service road. He did not glance round, but knew that one of the policemen from the car was following him. He wished it were dark.

The gate which led to the small back garden of the ex-fence's house was closed. Mannering thought he saw the policeman at the end of the alley. The windows were closed. He went up to a long, narrow one, which was in Leverson's small dining-room. The curtains were drawn, and he could not see inside.

He tried the window, but it was locked; so was the back door.

The gate in the alley opened, and a plainclothes policeman appeared, a young, fair-haired man.

'Excuse me, sir.'

'Hallo?'

'Have you any right on these premises?'

'Yes,' said Mannering, 'the right of a friend of the owner.'

The man said: 'Oh.'

Mannering stood on tip-toe and peered over the net curtain at the kitchen window; no one was in sight.

'Did you expect to find someone in?' asked the detective.

'Yes,' said Mannering. 'Obviously no one is, so I'll go back.'

They went back together. The detective returned to his car, and Larraby stood quietly outside the house.

'No sign of anyone, Mr. Mannering?'

'Nothing. We'll go back to the flat.' But he didn't want to go back, he wanted to get into that house.

A two-seater car turned into the street, and Forsythe was at the wheel. News? Mannering was sick with anxiety. The reporter pulled the high-powered car up with a squeal of brakes, and waved.

'Hallo, hallo! I thought I might find you here, as you weren't at the flat, and—'

'Where did you leave my wife?'

'Eh? Why, here. No trouble, is there?'

'She isn't here now. I haven't been able to get an answer by telephone since half past six.'

'Well, I expect she's on her way back,' said Forsythe reassuringly. 'I tried to make her tell me why she was coming, but clams run in the family. She's all right. Can you spare me half an hour?'

'Just now, I want to find my wife.'

'My dear chap! Leverson's an old friend of yours, and he's pretty sound,' said Forsythe. He grinned. 'A truly reformed character! There are several things I'd like to talk to you about, Mannering – including one that will surprise even you.'

Mannering only wanted one surprise: to see Lorna come out of that house.

'What is it?'

'The police have released the two charmers.'

Mannering said sharply: 'Sure?'

'I am a fact-finder by trade. Odd, isn't it? They've also questioned a man named Harding and his son, and let them go. They won't give the Press a statement. Any new slant from you? You know the line – the police won't play, so we play with the police.'

'You're smart enough to think up new slants for yourself,' Mannering said. 'You met Lorna in Green Street, didn't you?'

'Yes. She wanted a cab, so I offered her a free lift. She was uncommunicative, but pleased, I gathered – very pleased. I guessed you'd sold the Adalgo, or something. I thought you'd sent for her, knowing how you can play on the emotions, and—'

'I didn't.

'You're really worried, aren't you?' Forsythe observed, frowning.

Another car turned into the street; Bristow's old green Morris. It looked antiquated, but had a supercharged engine, and was as deceitful as its owner could be. Bristow paused to have a word with the men in the other police car.

'Teddy, do something for me,' Mannering said quickly. 'Go back to the flat and wait for me.'

'Damn it, with the police on the doorstep—'

'If there's a story, you'll get it.'

Forsythe frowned. 'It would have to be some story, John. All right. Where's the key?'

Mannering gave him one. Larraby, who had heard all this, started to speak, but stopped himself.

Mannering said hurriedly: 'My wife and the maid ought to be back by now. There might be a message from one or other of them. Off with you, before Bristow comes.'

'May I go with Mr. Forsythe?' asked Larraby.

'Why not?'

'Come on, if you're coming,' said Forsythe.

The engine roared, and Larraby got in. The small car moved at speed, and Forsythe waved to Bristow, getting no response.

Bristow's car pulled up, by Mannering.

'You're very interested in Leverson's house, aren't you?' asked Bristow. 'Quite like old times.'

'Yes, isn't it? Are you interested, too?'

'I am,' said Bristow. 'What are you doing here?'

'Lorna paid a visit, and hasn't returned.'

Bristow nodded, as if that satisfied him, and went to the door, and rang and knocked. A young detective-sergeant was with him, other police looked on. Bristow waited for less than five minutes, then turned and nodded to the sergeant.

This visit had been arranged beforehand; Bristow knew plenty, probably much more than he would reveal.

The sergeant went to the window and examined it closely, then began to fiddle with the catch with a knife. Mannering could have opened that window in half the time, but at last it banged up.

'In you get,' said Bristow to the sergeant.

'I hope you've got a search-warrant,' Mannering said.

'I've got all that's needed.' Bristow waited while the sergeant climbed into the house. 'You've shown some sense. If my man hadn't been watching you, you'd have been inside, I'll bet.'

'How could I get in?' Mannering was in no mood for fencing with Bristow, who made no comment.

The sergeant, a tall and dark man, opened the door from the inside.

'All okay, sir.' He sounded proud.

'Go through and make sure the back yard's covered,' said Bristow. 'Report at once.'

The sergeant hurried off and Bristow stepped into the gloomy hall. Mannering followed him, half expecting to be told to stay outside, but Bristow let him come. Except for the sergeant's footsteps, the house was silent.

The sergeant soon came back.

'Everything's all right at the back, sir. Shall I go upstairs?'

'We'll all go. Start searching down here and keep together,' said Bristow.

There was no one in any of the downstairs rooms, and Bristow led the way, and the sergeant brought up the rear, as they went upstairs. Their footsteps were muffled by the thick carpet; the whole house was hushed.

Bristow knew the house well. He turned to the big front room, Leverson's study. It was a treasure house of antiques, almost a miniature Quinn's.

Bristow pushed open the door.

'Mannering, you'd better—' he began, and then stopped short.

Mannering banged into him.

Bristow steadied himself and went slowly into the room. Mannering looked over his shoulder.

He saw Flick Leverson's white hair, smeared with red. The old man was lying face downwards in a corner of the room. Mannering's heart thumped enough to suffocate him, but there was only Leverson. Lorna wasn't here.

In a low-pitched voice, Bristow said:

'It's a good thing you didn't come in before, Mannering.'

He went forward slowly, so that Mannering could see Leverson clearly; the fence had an ugly wound in the back of the head, and the side of the head was cracked right in.

Bristow said, without turning round:

'Sergeant, go downstairs and telephone the Yard. You know what we want. Don't use the telephone here, go outside.'

'Right, sir.' The sergeant hurried off, no longer proud, but breathless.

Mannering said in a harsh voice: 'So Flick's gone.' It was inane, but words didn't matter. In the red mess of Leverson's head, he saw a picture of Lorna.

'Yes,' said Bristow. 'Don't touch him. Don't touch anything.'

They stood quite still, looking at the man on the floor and at several glittering jewels near his pale, outstretched hand.

CHAPTER FOURTEEN

THE SUPERINTENDENT AND AN IDEA

MANNERING went down on one knee beside the dead fence. The contrast between his peaceful pale face and the silvery hair curling at the temples, and ugly, oozing gash, made Mannering's eyes sting. He still saw that mind picture of Lorna.

'Don't touch anything!' Bristow barked.

Mannering groped in his waistcoat pocket, took out a pair of silver tweezers, and said:

'This won't damage anything.'

Bristow wasn't feeling so good, or he would have ordered him out. Mannering gripped the big diamond between the ends of the tweezers and gently drew it from Leverson's grasp. There were several other jewels; he'd died protecting them.

'Is it real?' Bristow demanded.

Mannering took the diamond to the window. It had a faint red tinge, and, photographed, would have been identical with the real Adalgo. He turned it round and round. The light was poor but a real diamond would have scintillated more than this did.

'Paste,' he said. 'I'd better look at the others.'

'There could be fingerprints,' Bristow said, and his voice was hard.

'If there are, I shan't smear them.' Mannering took another gem from the fence's hand; a second trickled out and rolled along the floor. All three looked alike. There were two others, still in Leverson's palm, more difficult to prise free.

'Well?' Bristow demanded.

'All paste.'

'Seen them before?'

'Yes.'

'Where?'

'These were taken from my flat the other night.'

118

'So Leverson—'

Mannering said: 'Don't say it.' He stood up, and Bristow backed sharply away from him. 'Don't say it. Flick wasn't in the market for hot stuff. He could no more prevent people offering him jewels than you can help taking the oath in court. He hadn't bought for years, and you know it.'

'He had these.'

'Would Flick have bought paste?'

'I suppose you're right,' muttered Bristow.

'I am right. He was offered these, held them, and telephoned me. He knew I'd been robbed, knew what had been taken. I was out, so Lorna came rushing over to see him – did you know that?

Bristow didn't answer.

'Lorna was thinking it a triumph – and it's quite a line on her squat-faced gentleman, if you see it straight. Don't get any other crazy ideas, Bill, such as thinking that Lorna could have done this.'

'I'm not that crazy.'

'After what I've seen of you today, I'm ready to believe you'd think anything,' Mannering said. 'Have you had any report about Lorna?'

'No.'

'That's what policemen are for,' Mannering said bitterly. 'To hang about Green Street, hang about Quinn's, follow me all over the town, but when there's trouble – no policeman. What brought you here?'

'I heard—' began Bristow, and then shut his mouth like a trap.

Mannering said: 'All right, Bill, keep your secrets. Just think this one out. My wife's missing. Not all the bright policemen in Scotland Yard are going to stop me from finding her.'

Bristow lit a cigarette. Men came up the stairs and into the room, one carrying a camera and tripod, another a black case, a third a small vacuum cleaner; they would go over the room for prints, sweep up the dust, analyse it, go through all the motions of investigation.

'Take it easy,' Bristow said. 'This job had an ugly streak from the beginning, this isn't the ugliest. I had a squeal, that Leverson had this stuff.'

'Squeal from whom?'

'I don't know and wouldn't tell you if I did.'

Mannering said: 'I can tell you. The thieves. They passed them over to Leverson, knowing he'd send for me, then squealed to you, thinking you'd come and catch us together. You brought half the Yard, hoping to catch me in conference with a man who could give you—' he broke off. 'Oh, forget it.'

Bristow said: 'You'd better go. I shouldn't have let you come.'

'Your one concession to decency,' Mannering said, and went out.

After he had been back to the Yard and made out his report, Bristow went to the Hampstead house of the Assistant Commissioner. It was near the Heath, a small house of distinction, standing in its own grounds, two garden walls bordered by open, sparsely tree-clad land.

Mrs. Anderson-Kerr was throwing a party, and there was music and much laughter. Bristow found it trying as he sat in the library, waiting for Anderson-Kerr.

It was half past nine.

Mannering had left Wine Street hours before Bristow.

The Superintendent had never known Mannering in a worse mood; and never, he admitted, with such justification for one. And Mannering didn't know everything.

Anderson-Kerr, in tails and big white tie, came in.

'I'm sorry I had to keep you. Sit down.' He indicated a chair. 'Whisky, as usual?' He poured out. 'You probably need that. I've had nearly as much as is good for me tonight.'

'Thanks,' said Bristow, morosely.

'Well, what's new?'

'You know everything about Leverson's murder,' said Bristow, settling back in his chair; the whisky warmed him but didn't raise his spirits.

'Yes, I had your message about the paste diamonds. It was worth taking a chance on.'

'I wish we'd taken it hours earlier,' Bristow said, savagely. 'There are a dozen fences in London whose death wouldn't matter a damn, but Leverson – well, that's hardly the point.' He checked himself. 'He was battered about the head, and probably had the real as well as the false diamonds which were taken from Mannering's flat. The real ones were gone. It's reasonable enough to think that he did telephone Mannering, as reasonable that Mrs. Mannering would hurry to see him. All reports tally, including Larraby's, who told Mannering where his wife had gone. They agree that she was excited and on edge; as she would be if she knew that the diamonds had been found.'

A door opened, a girl's gay laughter sounded.

'She was followed to Wine Street and away again,' went on Bristow. 'Mannering always prefers to play solo on a job like this. I tried to stop him. Whether I would have been wiser to—'

'Don't worry about that.'

'Right. Our man lost her in the Soho side streets,' said Bristow. 'It was a pretty obvious trick. There was a taxi at the end of Wine Street. Mrs. Mannering took it, and our man says that he *thinks*—' Bristow sneered that word – 'that there was someone else in the cab. He followed the cab as far as Soho, and then got caught up in a traffic block, and was shaken off. He took the number of the cab, but it's not registered with us, it's a pirate. Someone was waiting in the cab all right. It was planted there for Mrs. Mannering, and that she's been—' he paused.

'Kidnapped,' Anderson-Kerr said for him.

'What else can it be?'

'Can you guess why it happened?'

'From the time Mannering first bought the real Adalgo diamond, it's been on show. It is again today. I've made quite sure that it is the original stone – Mannering wouldn't make a mistake of that kind, anyhow. I think the murderers are after the real stone. They've only just realized that Mannering still has it, and will put high pressure on him through his wife.'

'I suppose it could be,' said Anderson-Kerr, after a pause. 'Why had Mannering been so keen about the fakes and similar stones?'

'I don't know. Probably just for the hell of it. There may be a motive he hasn't yet told us.'

'How are you going to find out?'

Bristow said slowly: 'He's worried out of his wits about his wife. It wouldn't surprise me if he doesn't prove more amenable than usual. If I try the heavy hand with him again, he might crack. I've been paving the way. I gave him a scare in Quinn's this afternoon, he's not quite sure which way I'm going

121

to jump. He's worried that we'll dig up evidence that he's the Baron. I think I'll wait until morning, and then have a go at him.'

'And if his wife turns up?'

'I doubt whether she will. I think he might get a message from or about her, and go off on his own. If he does, and we watch him, we might pick up enough to high pressure him in earnest.'

'*Agent provocateur*, Bristow?'

Bristow grinned, in spite of himself.

'We make a habit of giving Mannering a chance to hang himself,' he said.

'Well, do as you think best. Rules don't help much with Mannering. Did you find anything useful at Leverson's house?'

'Nothing except the paste gems,' said Bristow. 'There's nothing in the house on our stolen goods list. Oh — there was one small thing. Leverson's maid was sent for by a relative in Watford — or she was supposed to be. Leverson gave her the afternoon off. Her relatives hadn't sent for her, and she rushed back. It was a bad show. She's hysterical, but when she calms down she may be able to give us some information. There wasn't a single fingerprint, nothing at all to help us, any more than there was at Mannering's flat. We can't get a line on the man with the small high-bridged nose and the wrinkled forehead, either — he certainly isn't known to us. Wherever we look, there are dead ends.'

'What about the Harding family and the two Addel women?'

'I'm following them up.'

'Sure we were wise to let them go?'

'I think so, sir,' said Bristow formally. 'We couldn't hold either of the Hardings. I hoped to trap them into some kind of admission, but it didn't work. Marjorie Addel was at Guildford last night, according to young Harding and a servant at Harding's house, that gives her an alibi. She says she didn't want her Paul worried, that's why she kept his name back. Says she panicked when she tried to run off this morning. She's certainly well worth watching. Zara Addel was with friends last night, and we haven't been able to shake her story or their evidence. We didn't have much to hold them on, I think they're better free and being watched.'

'You're probably right. It's costing us a lot of men.'

'It's a triple murder job, now.' Bristow was bleak.

'Yes. Yes, all right. Anything you want from me?'

'We'll probably have to arm our men,' said Bristow. 'I'm not happy about them chasing after this mob with their bare fists. I know the Home Office doesn't like it, but—'

'I'll arrange it. What's Tring doing?'

'Eating his heart out,' said Bristow. 'He's afraid Mannering will slip through his hands again. He's quite sure that Mannering is still active as the Baron, nothing will shake that out of him. He's so intense in trying to justify his promotion that I almost wish—' he broke off. 'No, I don't! He's watching Mannering tonight, with another man.'

'And all radio cars are warned to look out for him?'

'Yes. If it were any other man, I'd say he hadn't a chance to get out of our sight, but—'

Anderson-Kerr said: 'He's our evil genius, I know.'

The telephone bell rang. Outside in the hall, the girl laughed again. The music welled up, light and lively, stamping footsteps sounded, as the quick, pulsating rhythm of the Conga began. The 'party' would probably file through the house . . .

'Yes, he's here,' said Anderson-Kerr and handed Bristow the telephone. 'It's Tring.'

Bristow grabbed the receiver.

'Thanks . . . well, Tring?'

'He's done it,' cried Tring, 'he's done it again! Went to Quinn's and then to his flat, and since then we haven't set eyes on him. No radio reports, no nothing. I could cry.'

'Don't cry – find him,' snapped Bristow.

CHAPTER FIFTEEN

THE BARON AND THE LOCKED DOOR

MANNERING flung open the door of his flat and Larraby and Forsythe appeared from the dining-room, two jack-in-the-boxes.

'Any news?' Mannering asked.

'Not a squeak,' said Forsythe. He had a glass of beer in his hand. 'I helped myself.'

'That's a habit,' Mannering said. 'Everyone is taking everything they can lay their hands on. Any word about the Addel women or the Hardings?'

'No.'

'Mr. Mannering—' began Larraby.

Forsythe said: 'Hold it. John, what's under your skin? You're too jumpy, by far.'

'I haven't jumped half far enough. Why aren't you at the telephone?'

Forsythe said: '*Hum!*' and turned towards the instrument. 'My news room?'

'Yes. Flick Leverson, retired jewel and art dealer, savagely murdered in his Wine Street home. Head bashed in. Police on the scene within half an hour or so – very smart work, butter Bristow as much as you like. Jewels were stolen. One was found clutched in the dead man's hand. No one else was at the house.'

Larraby cried: '*No!*' His voice was husky.

'I'll deal with you in a minute. Bristow's in charge of the case. Leave me out, if you can. And for light relief, tell the story of Inspector Tring, newly promoted, signing autographs like anything for schoolboys outside Quinn's.'

Forsythe was already dialling his office number.

Mannering said to Larraby: 'Why were you at Leverson's house?' It was one thing after another, punch after punch into a feather pillow. He couldn't even hurt the pillow, and he wanted to hurt someone.

'I've told you,' Larraby said.

'Tell me again.'

'I discovered who Leverson was, because you had agitated me over Mrs. Mannering's disappearance. I wanted – I want – to help.'

'That's what you say.'

Larraby burst out: 'It's what I mean. Have I got to have threats and innuendo thrust down my mouth every time I see you? If I have—' his voice trembled, his eyes were glassy. 'If I have, I'd rather—'

'*Shut up!*' hissed Forsythe.

'I'd rather starve!' cried Larraby.

He swung out of the room, banged into a hall chair, recovered himself and pushed the chair aside. When he reached the front door, he was nearly in tears. He pulled at the catch and fumbled it, pulled again savagely, and was halfway out when Mannering caught him up.

'Josh, don't—'

'What do you think I am? A worm? I won't stand for it, from you of all people. You're worse than the police! All you do is—'

'Take it easy.'

'To hell with you!' cried Larraby. He wrenched himself from Mannering's grasp and ran to the head of the stairs.

Behind Mannering, Forsythe was still talking.

Mannering said aloud: 'It's getting worse.' He closed the door and went into the drawing-room, where Forsythe was saying: 'Yes, I'm going straight over. Cover the Yard. I won't be – here! Hold on, I've a juicy bit. Outside Quinn's this afternoon, Detective Inspector Tring of N.S.Y. was seen—'

Mannering took the receiver from him, and said into the mouthpiece: 'Cut that last bit,' in a passable imitation of Forsythe's voice, and put the receiver down.

'I apologize for believing you,' Forsythe said.

'A change of heart, not fact. What do you make of Larraby?' Forsythe considered, for some time.

'Nice little chap, singing paeans of praise for the Mannering menage. I should say that he's fallen for Lorna hook, line and sinker, and that you're not far behind in his esteem. He's all right. Odd little cuss, of course, very conscious of having fallen from grace, pathetically grateful for your kind heart and all that. Where is he?'

'Recanting. He formed the wrong opinion of me.'

'Oh,' said Forsythe. 'John, take it easy. I don't like that look in your eyes. You're not even sure that bad men have carried your wife off.'

'For a reporter, you take some convincing,' Mannering said. 'Spread the word that she's missing, will you? No, I do not blame you for taking her to Leverson's, don't be a fool. If you meet Larraby outside, tell him I'd like to see him.'

'Emphasis on like?'

'Please.'

'I'm on my way,' said Forsythe. 'If I get a whisper of news, I'll tell you. Will you be here?'

'I may be.'

'Wherever you are, good luck,' said Forsythe.

The front door bell rang. Mannering's heart turned over, and he stood with his teeth gritting together. Forsythe went and opened the door, so that Mannering could see into the hall. If this were Lorna, if—

Forsythe opened the second door.

'*Oh!*' exclaimed Judy.

It all had to happen now.

'All right, my pet,' said Forsythe, 'I'm an invited guest. I – hallo, Josh! Still here? The Boss would like to see you.'

Judy came in, fresh and pretty, her eyes rounded with curiosity; Larraby came in timidly.

'Wait a minute, Josh,' Mannering said. 'Judy, I don't want you at the apartment tonight. Go out, stay with some friends, and leave your address written down in the kitchen so that I can tell you when to come back. Is that clear?'

'Why, yes, thanks *ever* so. Are you going away?'

'Don't argue. Pack what things you need and hurry.'

Mannering went into the study, beckoning Larraby. The man's eyes were red-rimmed, there was dullness in them, as well as a drawn look on his face; he looked older and more careworn, his calmness had gone, his voice was unsteady.

'Mr. Mannering, I'm sorry I lost my temper.'

'We'll call it quits, Josh. Will you try to answer some questions without assuming that I'm accusing you of lying?'

'Anything.'

'Why did you watch young Harding?'

'You don't know that?' Surprise took the tremors out of the man's voice.

'I don't.'

'But his father was the owner of the Mace collection, which I stole,' said Larraby. 'I recognized the son at once. And – I never trusted the old man. I must say that.'

'Why not?'

'How can anyone explain that kind of feeling?'

Mannering said: 'I see what you mean. What about the young one?'

'He isn't a man I like but I had less to do with him than with his father. Both, naturally, were vindictive. I suppose I shouldn't blame them.'

'Listen, Josh. You know what's happening and you know this flat may be visited again. I'm going out. Will you stay here, in case there's a message from my wife?'

'Gladly.'

'Thanks. Make yourself at home, raid the larder, and make your first job seeing that girl off the premises. I don't mind risking your neck but I won't take chances with hers.'

'The police—'

'The next visit might be from someone the police won't have in mind or be worried about. I haven't anyone in mind, either. I just know that—'

The telephone bell rang.

Mannering tensed himself. Larraby swallowed hard, and moved away. Mannering took the receiver up slowly, and said:

'Yes?'

'John,' said Lorna. '*John.*'

Mannering sat down on the arm of a chair, slowly. Lorna had uttered two words, and told him that everything he feared was true.

Larraby went out.

'So they've got you,' Mannering said.

'I'm all right. They haven't hurt me. John, don't let this make any difference to—'

She broke off; he thought he heard her cry out. His hand gripped the receiver until it hurt. There was no time to have the call traced, no point in calling Larraby. He'd let her down and he would never be able to undo that.

A man spoke quietly.

'Mannering.'

'Yes.'

'I want the Adalgo.'

'I thought you might.'

'And I am going to get it.' There was a trace of foreign accent in the voice.

'Are you?'

'Without any funny stuff from you,' the man said. 'Do not try to be clever.'

'I don't see anything funny in this.'

'That's as well,' the man answered. 'Go to Guildford High Street and wait under the big clock until someone speaks to you. He will ask you if you want your photo taken. You understand that?'

'Yes.'

'Tell him you'd rather have your portrait painted – that will make you think of your wife, won't it?'

'Yes.'

'Then do what he tells you,' the man said.

Mannering took an old, wide-brimmed felt hat from the bottom of a cupboard, put on a blue gabardine raincoat, twisted a blue scarf round his neck, and left his bedroom. Larraby was in the study, under orders to wait there for half an hour. Mannering put out the kitchen light and opened the back door. He went softly along the iron platform of the fire-escape which jutted out from the wall. There was no escape at the house next door, but there were large windows and large window-sills. It was too dark for him to see whether police were watching from the back; if they were they'd watch the gate leading to the service alley.

He leaned forward, gripped a window sill, and swung off the iron platform. It clanged faintly. He hung, at full stretch, from the sill, groping with his feet until he touched the one below it. He stood firmly but with only the front of his feet on the sill. He crouched down until his hands gripped the stone, lowered himself gently, and repeated the trick at the next window. He didn't think of the possibility of falling.

He dropped lightly to the ground.

He crossed the garden, climbed two walls, then entered the alley from a narrow gate. Outside 11a, he saw a shadowy figure on his lonely vigil. Mannering walked firmly towards the street, then into the main road, took a bus to Victoria Station, and walked to a lighted shop in a side street – a games and trick shop where he knew exactly what he wanted. He bought a make-up outfit in a small case, and slipped it into his one empty pocket; the other pockets were already full.

Next, he went to a garage.

An hour after leaving Green Street, he was at the wheel of a powerful car, his hat pulled low over his forehead, the scarf round his neck. He drove past policeman after policeman, without any one of them looking at him twice.

On the open road, he drove fast.

At Guildford, the big High Street clock said 10.15. He drove to the parallel street, at the side of the town, to the Public Cloakrooms. Once in a locked compartment, he took a wash-leather bag from his pocket, felt its contents, tucked it away and then took it out again, as if he couldn't resist it. Inside the wash-leather was cotton-wool; inside the cotton-wool a diamond so fiery, so beautiful, that the tiny compartment seemed bright. He stared at it, and put it away, in an inside pocket. In his waistcoat was one of the paste replicas; the last he had.

The first was the real Adalgo; the paste gem was now at Quinn's.

He took a small mirror from his pocket and hung it on the hook inside the door, then opened the make-up case. The light was poor.

He worked greasepaint into his face, daubing it on heavily at his eyes and lips, without *finesse*. He took a spongy piece of thin rubber from his breast pocket; it looked like a torn piece of latex. He put it into his mouth, and he worked the rubber over his teeth, taking his time. His own white teeth were completely hidden by a yellowish film. He put rubber cheek pads into his mouth, which made his face look round and plump. Anyone who saw him at close quarters would know that he was disguised; that was all. He wasn't Mannering to look at; he didn't feel like Mannering.

He was the Baron, with a house to burgle and at the end of it, a wild happiness of relief or the dark shadow of the consequences of failure.

He kept the gabardine coat on, and felt in the big pockets. A tool-kit, folded in canvas, was an old friend. He unfolded it, hitched up his undercoat and tied the kit round his waist.

Gloves – with their cotton fingers and palm piece – and he had nearly everything. He touched his hip pocket, and felt an automatic pistol. Carrying a loaded gun was a risk the Baron had seldom taken.

He was warm when he went out.

He drove a mile outside the town, and left the make-up behind the hedge near an Automobile Association call-box, from where he could easily find the spot again, then returned to Guildford. He parked the car in a by-road, and walked up the steep hill to the clock. He stood there for five minutes; no one approached him.

A policeman walked past, looking at him casually.

Mannering lit a cigarette.

A man standing a few yards off glanced at him curiously, then walked past. He had a small, high-bridged nose; and he wore his trilby hat on the back of his head, showing a deeply lined forehead.

The man walked to and fro, several times, and then paused.

'Good evening,' said Mannering.

The man said: 'You Mannering?'

'No password?' Mannering sneered.

The man ran his finger along his chin, and drew nearer.

'Would you like your photograph taken?'

'I'd prefer to have my portrait painted. More effective, I'm told.'

'You talk too much,' the other snapped.

'But I say the right words,' said Mannering.

'You're *not* Mannering.'

'Ask the next man if he wants his photograph taken in a dark street.'

'How do I know you're Mannering?'

'Perhaps this will convince you.' Mannering put his hand to his pocket and drew out the paste gem.

'Gimme—'

'Later.' Mannering put the replica away.

'Okay, you win. Don't get too clever, and follow me.'

The man led him to a sleek car parked at the top of the High Street; no one else was in it.

'Get in, Mannering. And watch me.'

Mannering climbed in and sat next to the driver, and the other put a gun into the dashboard pocket in front of him, well out of Mannering's reach. They went along the London Road for half a mile, then turned right. Mannering kept an eye on the driving mirror; they were not followed.

In this residential part of Guildford, Mannering had lost Marjorie Addel two nights before; he recognized some of the turnings. Was he being taken to Harding's house? Wasn't that too obvious a rendezvous?

'Good looker, your wife,' the driver said.

'I'm glad you think so.'

'Nice figure, too. If you want to keep her that way, behave.'

Mannering didn't speak.

They turned into a wide avenue. Houses stood in their own grounds on either side, and the starlit sky made a benign background. The powerful engine purred softly; the car slowed down, and the driver put out his indicator.

They turned into a short drive.

The grounds were thick with bushes and trees, hiding the lower part of the house. One light shone.

The driver said: 'Nice face *and* figure, don't forget.'

'I won't,' promised Mannering.

He fell heavily against the driver, knocking the man's hands from the wheel, then drove his clenched left fist into his nose. The car lurched. Mannering grabbed the handbrake as tyres squealed and grated on the gravel. Then the front wheels hit a grass verge, and the nearside wheels left the ground. Mannering, flung forward, banged his head on the windscreen, then settled down in his seat. The car righted itself with a dull thud and a creaking of springs.

The driver was holding his nose and groping for the gun. Mannering pulled his hand away, then hit him on the side of the jaw. The man hit back, caught Mannering in the neck, and started a shout. Mannering gripped his throat and pressed his thumb tightly against his windpipe. They sat, twisting and turning in silent, deadly struggle.

A car horn blared in the road. Headlights flashed along the trees and on to the struggling men. The car and the light passed.

Mannering's right knee was wedged painfully between the seat and the brake.

Mannering kept his hand round the sinewy throat, feeling the gulping intake of breath; tighter, tighter. The struggles became weaker. The man's hands dropped to his side. Mannering let him go, made sure he was out, then freed his knee. It was burning; but it could have been much worse. He had damaged that knee years ago, and had put it out again.

He climbed out; his knee carried the weight all right. He went to the driver's door, opened it, pulled the man out to the gravel, then dragged him head first towards the trees. They'd dragged Lorna, like this – but by the hair. He paused to rest; the man was breathing unevenly.

Mannering took a length of cord from his coat pocket, bound the driver hand and foot, gagged him with his own handkerchief, and left him behind the bushes.

He went along and studied the drive closely. There was a circular carriageway past the front door, and he was close to it. He got into the car, fidgeted with his gloves, and pulled at the self-starter. As he did so, he watched the house.

The starter squeaked; the engine ticked over quickly.

Mannering backed towards the road, and a car came along, bathing him in its headlights. A man walking along the pavement called out:

'What do you think you're doing, backing out blind like that?'

'Sorry.'

'I should damn well think you are.'

'Sorry,' repeated Mannering. Was he to fail because of a fool who'd had a fright? The man went on, and Mannering swung the car into the road, drove towards the end of the road, stopped at the corner. The nameplate on the wall of the corner house read: *Bingham Street*. Marjorie Addel had not mentioned Bingham Street when she had given him Harding's address; just said: *The Lees*.

He parked halfway between the corner and the house, pointing towards the London Road. He checked the petrol gauge; according to that the tank was half-full. He got out, leaving the door unlocked, and walked to the gate from which he had come. His knee was warm, not painful. The name of the house was painted on in white letters, just visible in the light from a street lamp a few yards away. It was *Green Ways*.

So it wasn't Harding's.

He turned into the drive, and went to his victim; the man was still unconscious but his pulse was beating steadily. Mannering went through his pockets and stuffed everything he could find, except money, into his own pocket. The next door house was ablaze with lights and the sound of radio music came clearly from it; noises off were an advantage.

The single light still shone inside this house.

It came from the hall, and was dim because the door had thick frosted glass in the top panel. There were no lights in either of the downstairs rooms facing the drive; his good luck. A grass path ran right round the house, and muffled his footsteps. Used to the poor light, he could see obstacles in his way; stones, a rambler and a jutting wall.

There was no light at one side of the house, and none at the back, but when he reached the far side he saw a crack of light from a curtained window. He approached it cautiously – and stubbed his foot against a dark stone on the path. It moved and dropped noisily to the gravel. He stopped quite still.

He could hear voices.

None was raised in alarm.

He walked to the window, alert for any sound. His toe was hurting, and his right knee becoming painful; he would not be able to put much weight on it. He stood outside the window, and peered up. It was open an inch or two at the top; that explained why he could hear the men talking. There were heavy curtains and a narrow crack of light in the middle. No one could see out, any more than he could see in.

He walked softly past.

At the back, there was still no light. He turned the handle and pushed the door, but the thousandth chance that it was open failed him. He took out a flashlight and examined the lock.

It was a new one.

Then he heard a sound inside the house. He switched off the

flashlight, on the instant. The sound was repeated, a man was walking towards him.

A light came on and blazed out from a window, two feet from where Mannering stood.

CHAPTER SIXTEEN

THE BARON AND THE WINDOW

THERE came the sound of splashing water, and a metallic noise; a man was filling a kettle. He began to whistle a popular tune. There was a *pop* as the gas was lit, a clatter as the kettle went on.

Mannering stepped cautiously away from the window. He could see a corner of this room and an open door. Light shone so brightly that he could be seen against it from next door. The whistling continued, merging with the radio music, from the kitchen of *Green Ways*.

On the grass path, Mannering walked quickly towards the unlighted side of the house. The shadows of bushes moved gently, as if men were walking there; it was the wind. There were faint night sounds, close by.

He reached the far side of the house and felt the windows with his gloved hands; the flashlight wasn't needed for this.

He felt the top of the tools round his waist; he knew each, by its handle. He drew out a glass-cutter with its tiny splinter of diamond, and there was a tube of thin glue, wrapped in a cloth. With the cloth, he smeared glue over the middle of the window, then pressed a square of thick brown paper over it, smoothing it down. He worked as swiftly as if he were in daily practice.

People came along the street – heavy steps and light. A man spoke, and his words carried clearly above the sound of music.

'Do you know whose car this is?'

'Sorry, no. Goodnight.'

'Goodnight, sir.' The couple walked on, but the first speaker remained.

So a policeman was within earshot.

Mannering turned to the window and pressed the cutter against the glass, it gave off a faint squeaky note. He made two diagonal cuts, one above and one below the square of paper.

The policeman walked past and his footsteps faded.

Mannering cut the glass again, twice, then drew back. He fingered the corners of the paper, and touched a piece of tape, stuck firmly to it. He pulled the tape gently, one hand touching the paper.

The glass came away with the paper.

He eased it away, then put it by the wall, out of reach of the window. He put the tools away, cleaned the touches of gum from his gloves with spirit from a tiny spray, and paused.

The music sounded like a triumphal march.

He put his arm through the hole and felt the window catch, then groped cautiously. He identified a thin strand of wire – the wire of the burglar alarm. It would raise a din if the wire were cut, but not if he moved it gently. He eased it away from the catch until it hung loose.

The catch was strong, probably had a spring which would make it shoot back and strike the window loudly. He held the finger of his left hand against the catch, and pushed with his right. The catch stung his finger as it moved.

He pushed the window up; it made a faint sound.

He climbed in and went straight across the dark room, feeling his way. There was a crack of light beneath the door, presumably from the hall. The door wasn't locked.

He peered into the hall; it was empty. He went to the front door, unfastened it, leaving it on the latch; a quick getaway might depend on trifles.

He crossed to the other side of the hall, and to the room where he had heard voices. Men were talking, but he couldn't catch the words. He went to the back of the house; there was no light on in the kitchen; the man had finished his tea-making.

The murmur of voices made the only sound now.

He looked quickly in all the other downstairs rooms, which were empty, then went upstairs. The thick carpet on stairs and landing muffled his footsteps. He glanced into four of five rooms which opened from the landing; all were empty bedrooms.

He opened the fifth door cautiously and heard someone breathing. He stood tense, ears strained. Yes, someone was in here. He felt for the key, which was on the outside, and took it out.

Bed springs creaked; and his heart jumped.

There was a sigh, as of a man or woman waking up; a woman? The springs creaked again, and then the breathing steadied.

A woman? *Lorna.*

He stepped inside. A faint light came from the windows of the house next door. He could see the shape of the bed, the bedclothes and the pillow.

Lorna's dark hair was not against the pillow; whoever lay there was fair.

He went nearer, hearing the woman's even breathing. He made out her features, vague yet unmistakable. This was Marjorie Addel.

He hated her because she wasn't Lorna.

He went out and locked the door, and slipped the key into his pocket. The girl had not stirred. He went up another flight of stairs, and looked into three attic bedrooms and a bathroom; all were empty.

He went downstairs.

The door of the room where the men had been talking opened. As he reached the first floor landing, on his way down, a door opened. A squat man left the room, and another called from inside:

'That won't make him hurry. Don't waste your time.'

'I'll be back,' said the squat man.

He was dark and good-looking – an Italian, Spaniard or Southern Frenchman. A *squat* man with powerful shoulders, a deep chest and firm tread. A *squat* man; no other word could describe him so well.

He walked to the front door as Mannering watched.

The squat man paused at the door, then opened it and went outside. He didn't stay long, but hurried in and locked the door. He started to speak before reaching the room.

'I thought I told you to lock the front door.' His voice was easy on the ear, with a faint accent; a Latin accent, which Mannering had heard over the telephone.

'So I did,' another said.

'Don't lie to me.'

'But, Lopey—'

'I said don't lie to me. I've just seen it with my own eyes.' He went into the room, and closed the door on a phrase: 'Mannering hadn't better be much longer.'

The door was closed; *but it wasn't locked.*

Mannering reached it, touched the handle, opened it a fraction; the squat man could hardly have sat down.

'You didn't think he'd come, did you?'

'You will be quiet while I talk to the lady,' said the foreigner.

Lorna!

'Do you think he will come? Yes? He had better come. We will, perhaps, send him some – what is the word? Bait, yes.'

Mannering heard a gasp; heard Lorna.

He opened the door another half inch, and took out his gun.

'You will be sorry if he does not,' went on the squat man. 'I am told that you paint beautiful pictures.' He laughed. 'With your lovely hands, yes. This one? You are right-handed, yes? Now if I bend it a little more, the bone would break. You wouldn't do very much painting for some time if that happened. You would do none, if you lost all your fingers. Do you think just the little finger would bring your husband along?'

Lorna did not speak.

Mannering pushed the door wide open and went in, with the gun in his right hand.

'Nothing will bring Mannering,' he said. His voice was hard, metallic, unfamiliar. 'I've come in his place.'

CHAPTER SEVENTEEN

THE MAN AND HIS WIFE

A TABLEAU of three rigid figures faced Mannering. Lorna, sitting forward on a wooden chair, one hand stretched out, hair dishevelled and face white with pain, eyes dazed but beginning to glow; for Lorna wasn't fooled about his identity. The squat man, one hand almost touching Lorna's, was twisted round in an odd position as he stared at the door; the third figure was a big, ungainly brute with thick wet lips, a low, receding forehead and massive chin.

The brilliant eyes of the squat man flickered. He straightened up and his hand moved slowly towards the inside of his coat.

'So you have come instead of the gentleman,' he said softly. His hand kept moving, almost imperceptibly. 'Welcome, my friend.'

'Take your hand away.'

'My friend! I—'

'Take it away and keep both hands in sight. That goes for *you*, too,' Mannering said, and nodded.

'Sure,' the brute gasped. 'Sure!'

Lopey lowered his right hand – then moved it, like a dart, inside his coat and towards his shoulder. He jumped to one side, and Lorna put out a leg. He fell over it, hit the floor with a crash, and was still moving when Mannering reached him. Mannering dipped his hand inside his coat and drew a snub-nosed automatic out of a shoulder holster. He slipped it into his pocket and backed away.

The brute was licking his lips and breathing wheezily.

Mannering said: 'Get out, Mrs. Mannering. Unlock the front door and wait for me on the porch.' No one in the world, not even Lorna, could have recognized his voice as his. She almost seemed to doubt who he was.

He snapped: 'Hurry! Mannering's not paying me by the hour!'

She stood up, steadied herself against the back of the chair, and passed him; she didn't hurry; he thought it was because she couldn't, was too stiff from sitting on that chair.

Lopey rolled over.

'Listen, pal—' began the brute.

'You tell your story to the fairies,' Mannering said. 'Turn round and face the wall.'

The man gulped and obeyed, slowly. Lopey began to sit up; he'd banged his head and was dazed. Mannering turned the gun round in his hand and struck him sharply on the temple with the butt. He dropped back, with a grunt; there was no foxing about the way he fell.

'Listen—' the big man twisted his head round to see what had happened. 'I never—'

'Later,' said Mannering.

The man spun round and jumped at him. Mannering smashed his left fist into the big jaw, but it was like hitting concrete. He brought his knee up into the man's stomach, and that was more like a feather pillow. The gasp of agony was shrill, the man staggered to one side. Mannering struck him on the nape of the neck with the gun; he pitched forward and hit the wall with his head.

Mannering turned – and his right knee gave under him, pain streaked through his leg. He gasped and stood upright, clenching his teeth. After a while, he moved more cautiously, and bent over Lopey. He went through the man's clothes, putting everything on the chair Lorna had been using. Watch, wallet, comb – he had black, glossy hair with a natural wave, he was like a handsome man whose head and face had been crushed into a concertina. The quality of his clothes were good and the cut was foreign; certainly not Savile Row. The padded shoulders were square but they didn't exaggerate the real size much, Lopey had the chest and shoulders of a bull.

Mannering's knee throbbed. He didn't find what he wanted – the diamonds which had been taken from his flat, or any diamonds.

He ran his hands over Lopey, prodding, probing, and found something flat and hard, not in a pocket, but sewn into the coat.

He made a cut with his knife and ripped the lining open. Inside was a small paper packet. As he unfolded it and diamonds winked up at him, a glory of light and colour. He paused only long enough to examine them; they were the real diamonds which had been stolen from his flat.

He went towards a bookcase in the corner, and as he reached it, heard a movement outside. He swung round, gun at the ready.

Lorna whispered: 'Are you there?'

Relief ran through him, like warmth on a cold day.

Lorna stood on the threshold.

'Yes, I won't be long.' His voice was still harsh and unfamiliar, he was living the part. 'All quiet outside?'

'A policeman is standing near the big car. Is it yours?'

'Yes. We'll manage without it.'

He spared a moment to look at her. Colour was back in her cheeks, she'd smoothed down her hair. She was wearing gloves, and massaging the little finger of her right hand. He shot a malevolent glance at the squat man. 'Did you know that Marjorie Addel was here?' he asked.

'We can't try to get her away!'

'Why not?' asked Mannering. 'And if it comes to that, why should we?'

'She's been drugged.'

'Sure she's not kidding?'

'She got here just after me. I was in a room upstairs and I heard the two men talking. They were to give her a shot, to keep her quiet.'

'She may be coming round now,' Mannering said. 'We ought to try—'

'We can't!'

'All right, we'll leave her,' he decided. There were limits to folly. 'You can tell Bristow about the drugging later, that should put her right with the police.' He moved several of the books in the bookcase and dropped the diamonds behind them. 'Bristow ought to find that hiding place without much trouble,' he added. 'As you're here, call the Guildford Police, just tell them there's been a burglary. They should arrive in ten minutes, we'll leave the door open and make them a present of Lopey and his friends.'

'Friends?'

'There's another trussed up in the garden,' said Mannering. 'Keep your gloves on, there's no need to say you used the telephone.'

Lopey and the brute were still unconscious, and not likely to come round for some time. Mannering took cord from his pocket and tied their wrists, lifted Lopey and dumped him behind a chair in a corner of the room. If the police were delayed and the two men came round, they would have little chance of freeing each other.

Lorna was at the telephone.

Ought he to leave Marjorie?

'I'm going upstairs,' he said.

The girl was still in the room. Mannering switched on the light, and she turned in her sleep, muttering, but did not open her eyes. She looked almost sulky. One bare arm lay over the side of the bed, and in the crook of the elbow was a small red puncture; so dope had been injected.

Her handbag was on the dressing-table. It contained the usual oddments of make-up, all expensive; there were no letters.

Mannering hurried downstairs, leaving her door unlocked. Lorna was coming from the drawing-room.

'They're on the way,' she said.

'Let's go.' That was Mannering's 'own' voice, and there was a lilt in it.

'Dare we use the car?'

'If the luck's with us.'

They went across the hall towards the front garden. Mannering's knee hurt badly. He was trying to persuade himself that the watchful policeman would ignore them if they walked away; the man was interested only in the owner of the big car. Mannering took Lorna's arm and squeezed, but neither spoke.

They reached the drive as a car came along the road with headlights full on.

It swung out, then turned towards this house. One moment welcome darkness was about them; the next, they couldn't escape the light.

Mannering whispered: *'Come on!'*

He pulled at Lorna's arm and they ran out of the beam of the car lights. His knee screamed. They reached a corner of the garden as the car swung round the circular carriageway. Mannering glanced over his shoulder, and saw two men jump from the car almost before it stopped; and come towards them, knowing they were there. Police?

Lorna's breathing was short, panting. They reached the wall, and the two men were separated from them by shrubs and trees. Rough grass near the wall made them stumble, and jolted Mannering's knee again. The men plunged behind them, noisily, but no police whistles sounded; would the police work silently?

There was a thick hedge near the wall.

'Over you go,' Mannering said. He lifted Lorna by the waist and raised her to the top of the hedge. His knee bent beneath him, and he stifled a gasp of pain. Torches were shining towards him, and strange, spiky shadows appeared.

There were still no shout or whistle of alarm; these men weren't policemen.

Lorna scrambled down to the street, and he climbed up the hedge; that wasn't easy. When on the other side, he wouldn't be able to run; he would have to use the big car, policeman or no policeman.

As he reached the top of the wall, he looked back.

The two men in the grounds both had torches, and one beam shone fully into Mannering's eyes.

'There he is!' a man cried.

Another man slipped, the flashlight swivelled round.

It shone on Larraby! – a different Larraby, with his hair smoothed down, and a trilby hat on, but – Larraby.

Mannering had only a swift glimpse of him as the torch wavered wildly. Then a different voice came, from the gate.

'What's going on here?' The policeman was back.

The flashlights blacked out, as Mannering dropped to the ground in a hush. His knee gave out again, and he gasped.

'What is it?' Lorna asked sharply. 'What is it?'

'My old pal, the knee,' said Mannering. 'We'll have to make for the car.'

He forced himself to run; pain stabbed through his leg like red-hot needles. The red glow of the borrowed car's rear-light seemed a long way off. He went past the drive-gates and saw a flashlight pierce the gloom, shining on the uniformed police-man, who was on the ground; a man – Larraby? – stood over him, with an arm raised. Mannering shouted:

'*Police!*'

He passed the gates before the men looked up.

Lorna was already at the wheel, the car door was open. As he climbed in, she let in the clutch, and the car moved off.

'Which way?' she asked.

'Straight on. Headlights.'

She switched them on, and a white blaze carved a light in front of them.

Near the corner with the main road, two cars swung towards them. Mannering saw police uniforms, four or five of them in each. One of the cars slowed down. A man shouted, and the driver of the second car waved out of the window.

Lorna swung the car towards London.

Mannering watched the driving-mirror tensely. Neither police car had turned yet.

There were no others cars on the road.

'Make for the High Street,' he said. 'Straight on.'

He sat nursing his knee, damning it and himself. He'd made a mistake in calling for the police, and—

Had he? What would have happened to Marjorie Addel if he hadn't?

He thought of Larraby, and forgot his knee, until they reached the top of the High Street.

'Second right, and then left,' directed Mannering.

There was some traffic about, and a policeman stood at the kerb; he looked at the car as it passed, but made no move to stop them. In the road which ran parallel to the High Street, Mannering said:

'This will do. I've another car farther down.'

Lorna pulled up, and Mannering got out but nearly fell. Lorna took his arm firmly and reassuringly, and he hobbled towards his hired car. A few passers-by looked at them curiously, because he was so obviously in pain. Another policeman drew near, and stopped:

'You hurt, sir?' the law asked.

Mannering forced a grin.

'Old trouble, trick knee,' he said. 'My car's farther down. I'm all right.'

'Let me give you a hand,' offered the law.

Lorna began: 'No, I—'

'Thanks – thanks very much,' said Mannering. 'Save me leaning on my wife. Supposing you go and start the car, darling?' He used the harsh voice.

Lorna hurried off, and the policeman's supporting arm was sturdy.

'Yes – old knee joint trouble,' Mannering said. 'Twisted me knee coming out of a show. Careless of me. I'll be all right – and you're very good.'

'Glad to help, sir.'

The car seemed a mile off, but at last Lorna reached it. They made their way slowly, passing hundreds of people, some curious, some oblivious. Mannering's heart was thumping, but his lips quirked. What could be better than a police escort, at a time like this?

Lorna looked out of the window.

'Here you are, sir,' said the police. 'Back or front?'

'Oh, front, I think. More leg room.' Mannering put his hand to his pocket and touched coin; then he drew it away; a coin might have a fingerprint on it, there was danger in that. You've been very good,' he said. 'Number XL5. I won't forget XL5.'

'Only too glad to help, sir,' said Constable XL5.

Lorna started the car; the policeman closed the door, and stood watching them as they drove off.

Mannering said little, and Lorna drove fast; she did most things well. Thoughts fought one another. Had the police caught 'Lopey' and the brute and the man in the grounds? Had they caught Larraby – he could not think clearly about Larraby. Would the diamonds be found and Marjorie rescued? And – had he left anything at all, to show who had broken into the house? Motive wouldn't matter, if he had left any clue.

It was always like this; a frenzy of fears.

How would they explain Lorna's escape?

That was the most pressing problem, and Bristow would—

He exclaimed: 'Fool!'

He had forgotten that he still had on the make up.

Constable XL5 had surely *noticed*.

145

Mannering laughed. He'd twisted his knee 'coming out of a show.' What could have explained make-up more convincingly?

'Let's laugh later,' Lorna said.

CHAPTER EIGHTEEN

THE LADY AND THE LIE

AT Green Street, Lorna helped Mannering on one side, a policeman from downstairs supported him on the other. Mannering was past enjoying the irony of helpful policemen.

Judy opened the door.

'Judy, I told you—'

'I had to come back, sir, my friend couldn't put me up for the night.'

'Where's Mr. Larraby?'

'I haven't seen him, sir. Have you had an accident?'

'It's all right, Judy,' said Lorna. 'Telephone for Dr. Kennedy, and tell him that Mr. Mannering has put his knee out again.'

'Yes – yes, ma'am.' Judy hurried off.

Lorna led the way to the bedroom, the policeman went out, Mannering hobbled across the room and sat down on the edge of his bed. He was past talking, could only grit his teeth and glare at his knee. His face was chalk white. Between spasms of pain, he tried to think. If Bristow came now, how could he fool the man? He wasn't up to a battle of wits. There was Lorna's account of her escape to fix; he must think up something good.

Lorna was speaking; he had to concentrate to hear her.

'Stop worrying,' she said. 'Let me get your shoes off.' She went down on her knees, unfastened his shoes, pulled off his socks. He plucked at his collar and tie, but there was no strength in his fingers.

Judy entered the room.

'Is there *anything* I can do, ma'am?'

'Come and help me,' said Lorna.

They put him to bed, and he caught a glimpse of the swollen and discoloured knee. The doctor would lose no time, but would Bristow? He had probably heard already of the affair at Guildford, and would jump to the truth.

The front door bell rang.

'Bristow,' he muttered. Perspiration stood out on his forehead, and the veins on his neck were thick.

'He'll be in bed, idiot, it's probably the doctor,' said Lorna. She gripped his shoulders and forced him to look at her. 'I told you not to worry. If Bristow comes, I can handle him.'

She would try; she hadn't turned a hair since he'd found her, hadn't complained or relaxed.

'Don't tell him a story I can't corroborate.'

'Don't *worry*.'

She kissed his forehead.

'Listen to me. That house was raided, and your captors alarmed. They neglected you, gave you a chance to get out.' He paused, gripping her hands. 'No – not good enough. How – how did you and I meet?'

'I telephoned you—'

'But Judy might have been here, she'd know—' Mannering gritted his teeth.

Then the door opened and Judy said:

'The doctor, sir.'

Mannering looked at Judy, not at the doctor, a youngish man with a fresh complexion, athletic figure and amiable eyes.

'Judy, what time did you get back?'

'About an hour ago, sir. I—'

'Now don't worry about anything, Mannering,' said Dr. Kennedy. 'You're not looking too good.'

Lorna said, 'Judy wasn't in when I telephoned you, John.'

Mannering relaxed; damn this pain, he couldn't think even of the obvious. 'No. No,' he said. 'I – but – I'd have been seen, I—'

Kennedy looked puzzled. Lorna glanced at him knowingly, brows raised.

'He's put his knee out for the third time this year, and had to walk some distance. He's a bit light-headed.'

'Oh. Now go easy, Mannering—'

No one seemed to understand, not even Lorna. Of course, she was right to stop him from saying too much in front of Kennedy, but why didn't she understand how easy it would be for Bristow to disprove a story which wasn't absolutely water-tight? They could make up a convincing one together but if Lorna told one and he another, the damage would be done. Once Bristow proved that he had forced entry, the door to jail would be wide open. Bristow had been almost vindictive in this show; Tring certainly was. Past and present merged together in a nightmare of uncertainty, while the doctor prodded and probed at his knee and the waves of pain filled him with nausea. It was no use, his mind was hazy, he would have to leave it to Lorna.

The doctor was saying something briskly. The doctor was rolling up the sleeve of his pyjamas jacket; there was a sharp prick. The doctor spoke again, soothingly. Lorna stood by with her hand on his forehead – a cool hand.

She was smiling, reassuringly and confidently; but her face was going round and round.

There were voices; followed by a sharp ring of a bell. The front door – this was Bristow, Bristow was here. Mannering tried to ease himself up on his pillows, but they pressed him down. The bell rang again. The bedroom door opened, and he saw and recognized Judy. She said something; he could not catch the words but he thought he heard 'Bristow.'

Kennedy left him. Kennedy and another man were talking in the doorway. Lorna leaned over him, as if to stop him from seeing who was at the door, and whispered:

'Leave it to me, darling. Leave everything to me.'

Bristow stood in the drawing-room, stiff, aloof. The gardenia in his buttonhole was wilting; he looked tired, but Lorna didn't like his stony expression. He'd obviously called at the Yard after a report from Guildford, and had not lost a minute getting here. Tring was in the hall, looking at her without friendliness as she entered the drawing-room.

'Well, Mrs. Mannering?' Bristow was abrupt.

'Well, Superintendent.'

'I want to see your husband.'

'If you disturb him, I shall make an immediate complaint to the Home Office. Dr. Kennedy made it clear that John, in severe pain, was given an injection of morphia. In spite of that, you tried to force your way into the room and to question him.

Bristow lit a cigarette.

' "Forced" is a bit strong. What's the matter with Mannering?'

'He has put his knee out.'

'At Guildford?'

Lorna said icily: 'I've been to Guildford. I understood that the police were watching me, but that didn't help much. It certainly isn't to their credit that I wasn't murdered. You're hardly covering yourself with glory.'

'Mrs Mannering—'

'Don't Mrs. Mannering me! If you want a statement, you'll have to change your manners.'

Bristow bit his lip.

Tring, near the door, stared, wide-eyed; *Mrs.* Mannering was usually quiet and reasonable. Bristow was looking pretty sick.

'Well?' Lorna's voice was sharp.

'I am sorry that I have given you cause for annoyance, Mrs. Mannering,' said Bristow formally. 'I shall be glad if you will make a statement, and—'

'I'll begin now. I was at home, working, protected by policemen back and front, when—'

Bristow said: 'Now, look here—'

'Don't you like my statement?'

Bristow said slowly: 'I don't know which of you I'd rather deal with.' He laughed, quite suddenly and unexpectedly, actually patted her hand. 'All right, all right, dress it up as you like. Mind if I have a drink?'

'Help yourself.' A friendly Bristow was more dangerous than a hostile one, but he had a welcome trick of laughing at himself when things wouldn't go right.

'Thanks. Did John get you out?'

'I got out.'

'Did they do you any harm?'

'Only damage to my opinion of the police.'

'Let's leave out that one,' Bristow said. He measured whisky. 'Drink for you?' Lorna shook her head. 'I know what happened and I shall probably be able to prove it, so the nearer you stick to the truth, the better. How long were you at Leverson's house?'

'Not long.'

'What did he want?'

'He'd been offered the jewels taken from here, and the seller said he would meet Leverson late in the day. Leverson thought that John might prefer to keep the appointment. I was coming back to tell John when I was caught – I didn't think of a pirate taxi. The police might do something about that.

'We will.'

'One of the men who robbed the apartment was in the cab – the squat one. He held a handkerchief over my face until I blacked out. I woke up as we ran into Guildford. He blindfolded me and I didn't see the house we went to.'

Bristow said: 'Hm. Go on.'

It had been easy, so far; but Bristow was ready to pounce if she made one false move.

'The others called him "Lopey," don't ask me what that means. He wanted to know where the Adalgo diamond was, and I said I didn't know.'

'Did you know?'

'I didn't. He didn't get rough, but talked about breaking my fingers, even sending one to John. You let some some nice people roam about, don't you? Something prevented him from forcing the issue then, thank God, and I was left alone in a room. Someone broke in. I managed to get out, and climbed over the garden wall – it had a nice thick hedge in front of it, look at my stockings.'

Sheer nylons were holed and laddered, and her legs were covered with scratches.

'All by your little self,' said Bristow.

'I am a grown woman, and I don't like the thought of losing my fingers,' Lorna said coldly. 'I took to my heels and ran. There was another man running away, I saw him in the garden. Dozens of men seemed to be about. I turned a corner and bumped into John.'

'*Aren't* the fates kind.'

'You'd expect him to look for me, and expect him to try Guildford, wouldn't you?'

'It wouldn't surprise me if he went to the moon disguised as a Martian. Go on.'

'That's all. John ran with me, we didn't want to get mixed up in the free fight that was going on. He slipped off the kerb and put his knee out. You know he's had trouble with it before.'

'I know he has a wonderful wife,' said Bristow, and sounded as if he meant it. 'Why did you telephone the Guildford police?'

The trick questions always came so glibly.

'Telephone? I was so anxious to get out of that house I couldn't have talked sense to anyone. What happened at the house? Half the Guildford police force seemed to be there when I left.'

'Ask John what happened,' said Bristow.

'You love that old story, don't you? I suppose you won't tell me about it, but you may as well. We have friends on newspapers, you know.'

Bristow said: 'I know that, all right. That bright specimen Forsythe was there on our heels. He's nearly as slippery as John.' Bristow still seemed good-humoured. 'He could tell you that we found your missing diamonds, two unconscious men—'

'*My* man? Lopey?'

'Not a squat one, if that's what you mean. A gorilla and a man who answered the description you gave of one of the men who came here. Forsythe can also tell you that this chap had gone to meet Mannering in Guildford, and was met by a stranger. He thinks. He doesn't know how John loves grease-paint! Forsythe can tell you that we found Marjorie Addel, doped and just coming round, but he can't tell you what she said to us.'

'Pity,' said Lorna. 'Was anyone hurt?'

'One policeman had a head wound, but not serious – he was keeping an eye on a car he didn't recognize, hoping to pick a winner. You'll sign a statement to the effect of the one you've just given?'

'Yes.'

'John's had better square with it,' Bristow said.

'Well, I'll have plenty of time to tell him about it, won't I?' Lorna asked sweetly. 'Or are you going to leave a man in his bedroom?'

Her heart nearly betrayed her as she spoke, it was thumping so hard. If Bristow left a man, it would be because he had some evidence to justify it; if he didn't—

'Not this time,' Bristow said. 'Relief for you, isn't it?'

152

'I'm more than sorry, I love strange men about the house,' said Lorna. She turned away, to hide her expression. 'I hope there isn't much else. I'm tired.'

Bristow said slowly: 'There's one other thing. Only a fool would let you take risks like this, Mrs. Mannering. Tell the fool that he's wasting his time and is storing up trouble for himself. And tell him—'

He broke off.

'Yes?'

'Never mind,' said Bristow gruffly.

The telephone bell rang. Tring shifted about the hall, Lorna looked at the instrument, Bristow watched it with his head on one side. Then he said: 'Goodnight,' went out and closed the door.

He hadn't any evidence against John, he was just guessing; and he could guess right a thousand times and do nothing about it. That didn't matter so much as the obvious fact – he was glad that he had no evidence.

The bell kept ringing.

Lorna took off the receiver slowly.

'Hallo.'

'*Mrs.* Mannering?' It was Forsythe, and the relief made his voice shrill. 'Why, that's wonderful! John was in a hell of a stew.'

'I know.'

'And he found you! I shall always believe in miracles after this. I've just come from Guildford, there's quite a story. Want it yourself, or shall I speak to John?'

'Leave it to the morning, will you? John's asleep.'

'Like an innocent babe, I bet! But—' Forsythe's tone changed. 'It's the very devil. I'm dreadfully sorry, you know, we all liked what we knew of Flick Leverson.'

Lorna caught her breath. 'What's happened to him?'

'You don't *know*?'

'He was all right when I left him.'

'Oh,' said Forsythe. 'Is John asleep or unconscious? He couldn't forget to tell you that. Leverson was killed. Nasty business. *Is* John all right?'

'Yes,' said Lorna. 'Yes, he's fine. I won't stop now.'

She put the receiver down and went slowly into the bedroom.

Mannering looked pale and drawn. They'd made a little cage for his knee, to keep the bedclothes off it. That injury would probably stop him from getting up tomorrow; for days.

It *must*.

She knew that it wouldn't.

CHAPTER NINETEEN

THE INVALID AND A SURPRISE

MANNERING woke up feeling low and sorry for himself, but the pain in his knee was much easier, although the swelling was worse and the compress about it was uncomfortably tight. He yawned – then suddenly stretched out and felt inside the pocket of a waistcoat, on the bedside chair. He found what he wanted.

He brooded for a while.

Lorna and Judy re-bandaged the swollen knee before breakfast. Judy went off to cook breakfast, and Mannering lay and looked at Lorna, who was in a dark blue dressing-gown; beautiful, serene. He forced a twisted grin.

'Knock out drops for Hero Number One,' he said.

Lorna laughed. 'Darling, you needed them!'

'Now let's be serious,' said Mannering.

She sat on the side of the bed and took his hands. Her eyes were shadowed with fear she'd tried to fight away. Neither of them spoke. Suddenly she leaned forward and kissed him passionately. When she drew back, she said:

'Thank you, darling.'

'Thank *me*? Why, you—'

'Don't talk about it yet.' Lorna got up quickly, and went to the dressing-table. 'It's time I dressed. Everything's all right with Bristow. He's guessed the truth, of course, but there isn't much he can do about it, and not much that he wants to do, if I judged him aright.'

'That was last night. What did you tell him?'

Lorna explained.

Mannering nodded with satisfaction. 'It's nice and simple, and it answers everything,' he said. 'I can tell him how I went to Guildford ready to kill. His trouble will be the fat-faced stranger who rescued you!'

155

Judy brought in breakfast.

Lorna said: 'Forsythe told me about Flick.'

'Oh.'

'You know he died trying to help us, don't you?'

'Trying to help me, to be correct. Yes.' Suddenly, breakfast didn't appeal to either of them. 'There isn't much doubt that he was given the paste gems knowing he'd tell me, and that Lopez wanted to do a deal – the other stones in exchange for the Adalgo. When you turned up instead of me, they switched their plans.'

'Why kill Flick?'

'Because he recognized Lopey,' said Mannering.

'There isn't any proof that it *was* Lopey. It could have been someone else. I doubt it.'

The front door bell rang; it seemed always to be ringing.

'That'll be Larraby,' Lorna said, 'and it's nine o'clock, and I'm not ready. I don't think I can work this morning, anyhow.'

'You won't have the chance,' said Mannering. 'Larraby won't turn up.'

Lorna stared. 'Why not?'

'He was one of the men who surprised us at Guildford,' said Mannering quietly. 'I saw him. We know he's a pretty cool customer, but coming here will be too much for him.'

Lorna drew in her breath. 'Josh,' she said. 'Oh, Josh.'

'I know. But I saw him in the light of the torch, and I also saw him about to crack that policeman's skull. At least we know where we stand.'

'Does Bristow know?'

'I doubt it.'

'Will you tell him?'

'I can't, without giving too much away.'

They were silent, until Judy tapped at the door. When Lorna called out: 'Come in,' she opened it and poked her head inside and said:

'I'm sorry to worry you, ma'am, but it's the tra – I mean, it's your *model*. Mr. Larraby, I mean,' she added, and stared at Mannering's expression in astonishment. 'It's – it's all right to let him in, isn't it?'

'Tell him to wait,' Lorna said, and added as the door was closing: 'John, you were wrong.'

'I can't believe it,' Mannering said.

'I suppose he doesn't realize that you saw him. What are you going to do?'

'You dress, I'll think.'

She went to the wardrobe and took out her clothes. He looked at her as she stepped out of a silk nightdress, and didn't smile. Ten minutes later, she was ready.

'Well?'

'I'll see him,' said Mannering.

Lorna went out, leaving the door ajar. Larraby's voice was soothing, gentle. He was extremely sorry to hear that Mr. Mannering was hurt, and hoped that it was not serious. He was delighted that Mrs. Mannering—

Lorna said: 'Not really serious. He'd like to see you.'

'He's well enough for that? Good!'

Larraby came in, greying hair untidy about his ears and neck, but wearing a new suit; well, a different suit, which wasn't patched. It was too large for him, of sandy-coloured tweed, baggy at knees and elbows, dropping round his insteps; it made him look smaller, almost wizened.

'Good morning, Mr. Mannering. I'm sorry—'

Mannering said harshly: 'The joke's over, you don't have to be sorry.'

He missed nothing; the sudden change in Larraby's expression, the almost pathetic droop of his lips, the way his hands raised, then flopped to his side. After that, Larraby stood quite still.

'Where were you last night, Larraby?'

'I—'

'I asked you to stay here. You agreed. Where did you go?'

'The police made me leave,' said Larraby in a taut voice. 'They called soon after you'd left – it was the man Tring. I told him you'd asked me to stay but he didn't believe me, said he'd charge me with being on enclosed premises if I didn't leave – he may do that, yet. I persuaded him not to, until he had talked to you.'

That couldn't be a lie; Larraby wouldn't use Tring's name if it were.

'And then?'

Larraby said: 'Mr. Mannering, I don't believe you would

start this again unless you thought you had a good reason. Will you please tell me why you think it necessary?'

It was difficult to believe that this man had smashed a weapon against a policeman's head; or lied, tricked, cheated and fooled him time and time again.

'Last night, an acquaintance of mine was at a house in Guildford – a house called *Green Ways*, Bingham Street.'

There was no sign on Larraby's face that the name of the house or the mention of Guildford meant anything to him.

'There was a burglary there,' Mannering went on. 'You were seen.'

Larraby started. 'It's impossible!'

'He is prepared to say so in Court.'

'In – Court!' sighed Larraby. He advanced a step, with his hands outstretched. 'Mr. Mannering, it isn't true! I was in London all last night. I—' he drew in a sharp breath.

'You've just remembered that you weren't, have you?'

Larraby said in a low-pitched voice:

'What time was this, Mr. Mannering?'

'About eleven o'clock.'

'About – eleven.' Larraby began to speak in broken phrases. 'I was – travelling from my wife's house, at that time. I went over to see her. Fortified by your – your promise of help, I thought that it might be my lucky day. I went out to Harrow, where she lives. She wasn't at home. I waited until half past ten, and then a neighbour told me that she had gone away for a few days. My luck wasn't in, after all. No, my luck wasn't in.'

Mannering said slowly:

'So you've no alibi.'

'I spoke – to this neighbour. It was in the dark street – a woman who turned into the next door gate. She would not have seen me clearly, and I was anxious not to be seen.' Larraby licked his lips. 'You – you've scared me, Mr. Mannering.'

'You've reason to be scared. Do you know that Leverson was murdered?'

'I have – read about it. But I was *here*, then.'

'You left here when young Harding came,' said Mannering, 'and you hurried away from me. The next time I heard of you, you were outside Leverson's house. The police saw you there, too. You had time to kill Leverson, and—'

'Mannering!' Not even a 'Mister.'

Mannering said evenly: 'You served time, Larraby, and the police will want to know what you were doing at the house.'

'Yes – I know. Immediately I read of Leverson's murder, I knew that I would be questioned. But that didn't scare me. I didn't enter the house, I was waiting for you. I know nothing about what happened there, except what I read in the newspapers. That doesn't worry me, Mr. Mannering, but – this man who was seen—'

'Well?'

'Will – will your acquaintance tell the police?'

'If you weren't at Guildford, what harm can it do?'

Larraby said: 'A great deal of harm, Mr. Mannering. A man – with my record – my love of jewels – if it is even suspected that I was near there, the police will—' Larraby broke off, clenched his hands and shook them at the ceiling. 'I wasn't there! I swear to God that I was not in Guildford. Your friend was mistaken!' After a pause he lowered his hands and dropped his voice. 'Mr. Mannering, I wasn't there. I was not seen. Someone like me was seen, Mr. Mannering. And – this is what I have never told you. I have never told anyone, it seemed so useless. I did steal once and was justly sentenced, but I was supposed to have been seen at the scene of another robbery about the same time; I was arrested as a result of that, not as a result of the one which I committed. They charged me with the real crime, they couldn't prove the other. The man who was mistaken for me—'

'Turned up again last night?' Mannering laughed bitterly. 'Try another.'

Larraby said. 'Of course, it's unbelievable. Of course. Well – tell the police, Mr. Mannering. I would rather get it over with.'

Was this a *guilty* man? If he were, would he gaze so desperately into Mannering's eyes?

'Did you speak to this neighbour last night?'

'You – believe me?'

'If you spoke to someone at Harrow at half past ten, you couldn't have been at Guildford. If the Harrow witness will take the stand, you should be all right.'

'I did speak to this woman,' Larraby insisted. 'There was nothing criminal about it, I didn't want my wife to be told I'd been there, just wanted to see her. If it could have been said that I hung about the house when she was out, it might have had the wrong effect. I must go to see that woman! I think she was next door when I lived there.' He swung round.

As he did so, the door opened.

Bristow stepped in, with a nervous Judy behind him.

'The Superintendent wouldn't let me tell you he was here, sir!' Judy cried. 'Mrs. Mannering's in the studio, I was cleaning the letter-box, and he came in. He wouldn't—'

'All right, Judy, no harm done.'

Bristow pushed the door to and glanced at Mannering, but was more interested in Larraby. The beggar moved away, gulping, his hands trembling; the big suit seemed to shake.

'Well, Bill?' Mannering spoke sharply. 'Do you know you're breaking the law by forcing entry and intimidating a girl who—'

'Forget it, I haven't come for you. Tring!'

Tring came in, carrying his bowler.

'I'm going to charge him,' Bristow said, and touched Larraby's shoulder. Larraby stood like stone, staring at Mannering. 'Joshua Larraby, I charge you with wilful bodily harm to Police Constable Higson in the garden of Green Ways, Bingham Road, Guildford, Surrey, on the night of . . .'

'No!' cried Larraby in a strangled voice.

'. . . and warn you that anything you say may be used in evidence. Take him away, Inspector.'

Tring actually licked his lips.

Mannering said: 'Wait a minute. Tanker, did you come here last night and compel Larraby to leave the apartment?'

'Supposing—'

'*Did you?*'

'Yes, I did. He was on enclosed premises—'

'With the owner's permission. A nice piece of evidence of police malice and persecution,' said Mannering. 'Take it easy, Josh, this isn't the first mistake they've made.'

CHAPTER TWENTY

THE REPORTER AND A REVELATION

THE door closed on Tring and Larraby, and Bristow moved to the side of the bed, sat down and rested a hand slightly on the covered cage above Mannering's knee. He lit a cigarette.

'Are you mobile?'

'Not yet.'

'You don't know it, but that's your good luck. What makes you take Larraby's side?'

'I think he's more honest than you or Tring. He admits his mistakes.'

'He was there,' Bristow said confidently. 'You're slipping, you shouldn't have trusted him. Cigarette?'

'Thanks.'

Bristow flicked his lighter and held it out.

'That's if you did trust him,' he went on. 'I wouldn't put it past you to pretend to fall for him simply to fool us. We aren't so easily fooled. He's a stool-pigeon, here to snatch the Adalgo when you think everything's all right. Where is the Adalgo? It's not at Quinn's.'

'I removed it last night. It's here now.'

'Not before its time,' said Bristow. 'How did you find *Green Ways*?'

'That was easy. I had a telephone call asking me to meet a man at Guildford, under the clock. I went, but preferred to look for Lorna myself. I saw a man with a small high-bridged nose, and recognized him from Lorna's description. I followed him to Bingham Street, went to look round—'

'You went away to disguise yourself.'

'What an imagination! I wanted time to reconnoitre, my knee wasn't too good even then, and I couldn't do much. Believe it or not, I was going to call you when I had another look at the house – and Lorna came out. Enough being as good as a feast, we left. The local police were about by then, and I slipped off the kerb, busting my knee properly.'

'I suppose I'll have to accept that until I can disprove it,' said Bristow. 'Let's get back to your original story about the search for gems like the Adalgo. What's the truth about that?'

'I've told you the truth.' Mannering hitched himself up. 'Bill, listen to me. Larraby's story has to be checked. He says he was near his old home, and spoke to the neighbour.'

'He even makes you dumb! What would be easier than to arrange for a friend to visit his wife's house and speak to anyone who came along? A neat way to establish an alibi. He didn't reckon on being seen at Guildford.'

'He could have a double.'

'You're not so good this morning.'

'It was dark. He was seen in a poorish light, and the policeman who was attacked certainly couldn't have got a good view of him. I hold no special brief for Larraby,' Mannering said, 'But I don't want him blamed for a job he didn't do.'

'It's an open and shut case. The rest of it will be, before long, including your part. I've seen that window at the house. It was a perfect Baron job. I don't know that anyone could blame you for doing what you did, and you had the sense not to mask yourself and put up the usual Barn smokescreen. If you're worried because an admission would make it obvious that you can force entry with any known cracksman, you needn't—'

'I didn't force my way in.'

'That lock was beautifully forced,' Bristow said, and stifled a yawn.

Mannering grinned. 'Lock?'

'That's right, lock. Any objection?'

'No objection, I don't know whether he went in at the window, the door or down the chimney. Try again, Bill!'

Bristow laughed.

'I wish you'd put your mind out, for a change. I've brought you some news.'

'Murderer in your hands?'

'All but. We caught the man known as Lopey.'

Mannering said softly: 'Did you, then. That's a pity. I hoped he'd stay free just long enough for me to get my hands on him, If ever I do that, he'll remember it.'

Bristow said: 'I hand it to you. Last night you could have

smashed his face to putty!' He stood up. 'If you change your mind and decide to come across, give me a call. Larraby will squeal as soon as we've talked to him, he may have noticed more than you think.'

'Everywhere I go, a yawning pit,' said Mannering. 'Why don't you go and talk to some bad men?'

'I will,' said Bristow.

There was a lilt in his voice and a spring in his step – and it wasn't because of Larraby's arrest. When he'd announced the capture of 'Lopey', he'd been in high fettle. Why? Because 'Lopey' was known to be the murderer? Or was Bristow full of the joys for another reason?

Mannering's mind seethed.

Was he being a sentimental fool about Larraby? Why had Bristow admitted having 'Lopey' with such glee? Why were there so many diamonds like the real one, as well as so many fakes? Why had Leverson and Bray been killed – and why choose Gray's shop for the murder? Bray had certainly been lured there, to his death. Had that been connected with the Harding-Bray quarrel? Why had Bray been killed? Was 'Lopey' working for himself or for someone else? If for himself, who were the second lot of thieves at *Green Ways*? That led to another puzzle: why had 'Lopey' wanted Marjorie Addel a prisoner, taking the risk of kidnapping a girl who was watched by the police? Evading the police was one thing, carrying a girl from under their nose another. There was a different angle that couldn't be overlooked – the release of Marjorie Addel, Zara and the Hardings.

Lorna brought in some coffee and the early evening papers. All carried the story of Leverson's murder and an account of the affair at Guildford, but there was nothing new. Both Mannering and Lorna were mentioned in passing.

Mannering found himself thinking of Larraby, and Lorna said: 'Are we wrong about Josh?'

'We'll learn. Out of about ten thousand questions, one emerges as the most significant.'

'What?'

'Why all those Adalgo imitations, and who is really behind it? What should the name Lopey mean to us?'

'Lopey or dopey?' Lorna asked. 'Darling, I'll scream if I don't get some fresh air.'

'Don't scream,' Mannering said.

She laughed and went out; but he knew she was heavy-hearted, because of Larraby, not for herself or him.

She looked in, five minutes later, with her hat on.

'I won't be long.'

'Don't go far, and keep your eye on policemen.'

'Yes,' she said. 'John, do you think it possible that Bristow has always known or suspected the real mystery behind the Adalgo?'

Mannering frowned. 'It could be. He's acted like an oaf half the time, and he isn't one. Also—'

'He's seriously suspected you, and he gave up thinking you were still a-Baroning years ago,' Lorna said. 'So he doesn't really think you've been cracking cribs for the sake of the loot, darling. He may think – especially if he knows the real reason – that you consider this a just cause for risking a long visit to His Majesty's rest homes. I mean, how do you spell 'Lopey'? With a 'z'?'

Mannering said: 'Well, well, you picked that up fast.'

'I have a mind,' said Lorna. 'I know it's only a pale imitation of yours, but that idea's worth thinking about. What would be a sufficient cause?'

'If I were a secret supporter of the claims of the Adalgo family to the Spanish throne, as advanced by a certain Senor Pedro Lopez—'

'That's it,' said Lorna. 'You aren't, are you?'

'No. I'd weighed this up, and decided it wasn't a royalist campaign. At first I thought it might be, but when the killings came I ruled that out. This kind of skull-duggery wouldn't win the Adalgos any support anywhere, it would more likely make them lose some.'

'Well, think again,' said Lorna. 'Where is the Adalgo?'

'Here.'

'Where?'

'In my waistcoat pocket.'

'Oh, you fool!' She hurried to the waistcoat which hung beneath a coat, over a chairback. 'Are you sure—'

'I feel it every two minutes, for fear of ghosts. Incidentally, the Larraby at Guildford might have been a kind of ghost, Larraby looks four-dimensional. If you mean, don't I think it's time that diamond wasn't here—'

'I do!'

Mannering said: 'Take it to Bristow, will you? Ask him to have it put away safely, tell him I've a feeling that the bad men are worked up about it and they might try to break into Scotland Yard in order to get it. That'll make him laugh like anything.'

Lorna said: 'Are you serious?'

'About taking it, yes. Ask a policeman to go with you – one will be following you, anyhow, you may as well keep him alert with chatty conversation. You might ask Bristow if he's checked Larraby's Harrow story, too.'

Lorna took out a wadge of cotton-wool, felt the diamond inside it, laughed a little wildly, and said:

'Was it here all night?'

'Yes, I forgot the damned thing, that was almost the last thing I tried to say as I went under. I was ready to suspect even the good doctor.'

'I hope I never see it again,' said Lorna. 'John—'

'Yes, I love you!'

'Then help Larraby.' Lorna turned, and went out.

Mannering dozed; and that was not a thing he liked to boast about after lunch. The newspapers were spread out over the bed, when Lorna looked, and still Mannering 'dozed.' It was nearly three o'clock, and the flat was quiet, little sound came through the window.

A faint noise disturbed Mannering. When he roused himself it was more than faint, it was a voice just outside the door.

'Mr. Mannering will always see me, my pet, that's one of the cardinal rules of his life. He knows that I am one of his best friends – and what a friend!' There was excitement in the caller's voice, and that cheered Mannering.

Judy opened the door and said:

'Mr. Forsythe, sir.'

Forsythe strode in, eyes aglow. He stood at the foot of the bed, and then made a clownish face.

'You *have* done something for yourself!'

'The question is, what are you going to do for me?'

'My dear chap, I'm going to be your right-leg man, as it were,' declared Forsythe. 'You do the thinking, I'll do the acting. This business is going to break all records before it's over. Bless your heart, I always knew that if I stuck to you like a leech, the day would come when I would stop regretting it.'

Mannering nodded to a chair. Forsythe sat astride it, leaning on the back, took out cigarettes and tossed one to Mannering.

'Thanks,' said Mannering. 'And have you stopped regretting it?'

'Have I! But you're an old so-and-so for sitting on dynamite. Even a whisper would have done me a world of good. Background and off the record, you know.'

'There's nothing I could have whispered about.'

'Ha-ha! He hugs his secret to the last!'

'No secret. I'm prepared to believe I've been the world's blindest bat.'

'Great Scott and little Hamishes!' gasped Forsythe. 'I would never have believed it!' He got up and stepped towards Mannering. 'You *are* serious? You mean it? You didn't know the truth all along? And I thought you were being really cunning over this. John, I apologize.'

'You might even tell me what you're so excited about,' said Mannering.

'Oh, yes, I will. The big Adalgo, the little Adalgos and the fakes which would have impersonated the Adalgo. And you really don't know the story behind it? I've got it out of Tring, which reminds me. Beware Tanker, he's spiteful. He thinks you're backing Lopez – oh, you do know that Pedro Lopez has been arrested, don't you?'

'*Pedro* Lopey,' Mannering said softly.

'Lo*pay* – L-O-P-E-Z. With a Z, old chap. Once warrior-in-chief for the restoration of a Spanish throne. Remember?'

Mannering said: 'Well, well!'

'Go on, concentrate,' urged Forsythe. 'Of course, Lopez's English accent is fairly good, few people realize he's as Spanish as he looks. The accent isn't surprising, as he's been in England for ten years and more – and he came here after the first brush between the monarchists in Spain and the people. Remember? Pedro Lopez my dear chap? Firebrand Spanish Royalist. Down with Negrin, down with Giral, down with Franco, down with everyone except the Royal Family and his particular branch of the Spanish Royal Family, too. No truck with the exiled monarch, only the Adalgo branch interested our friend Lopez. He made a song and dance about it – the Adalgo family

166

was really *the* Royal Family. He once even tried to take the throne for the Duke of Adalgo, and his little game was neatly stopped by Franco. I see that the truth's dawning on you,' added Forsythe, gently.

So it was not just crime; it went deeper – and he'd rejected the obvious because it was too obvious.

'I see a gleam of understanding in the pain-wracked eyes,' said Forsythe. 'Can you bear more?'

'Much more,' said Mannering heavily.

'Stout heart ne're lost the last battle,' said Forsythe. 'It's really quite simple.'

'Mannering said: 'Yes. Let me have a stab now. It all fits in, but I didn't want to believe that this was a royalist racket. Oh, I knew the Adalgo belonged originally to the ducal family, who wanted money. I suppose Lopez saw this as the easiest way of getting some. He or someone else of warped brilliance of mind, thought up a winning idea, once they accepted murder and violence as proper means to the end. The Adalgo was stolen once before, long before the Royal Family recovered it and put it on the market openly. Everyone who owned it ran into trouble. That gave the diamond a legendary value, put a kind of spell on to it, and for some people, increased its cash value.'

'Why did you first buy it?' Forsythe asked.

'I had a notion to find out what would happen.'

'I won't tell your wife,' promised Forsythe. 'Go on.'

'While it was missing, other rose-tinted diamonds were cut to resemble it. Lopez, for the Adalgo family, sponsored this faking and imitating, wanting cash and getting plenty above face value for each supposed Adalgo. The copies were sold to various collectors at fantastic prices, and each collector thought he had the real one. As it was known to have been stolen, no one could admit possession of it.'

'Then the real one turned up,' Forsythe broke in. 'No one who had bought a pup dared say so. They unloaded the pups on the under-cover market, until *you* bought the real one. Lopez was after it – just why I don't know, but possibly old friend greed. He wasn't quite sure whether yours was the real one, so traced everyone who had a diamond that was blood-brother to the Adalgo, and finally reached you – at last learning that you were the legal owner of the one and only Adalgo. The owners of the other real diamonds boasted, as collectors do, of owning *the* Adalgo. That made him laugh, I presume. Shall I go on?'

'You deserve to.'

'Thanks. Lopez made a number of imitations in paste. These he planned to substitute for the real stones, by a series of burglaries about which no one could complain, as each possessed a stolen stone. He did that, until he had all the stones except the genuine antique. Everything was hunkey-dorey until he himself was robbed of them all, some six months ago.'

Mannering rubbed his nose.

'Too strong for you?' asked Forsythe, sympathetically.

'Rub it in,' said Mannering.

'There isn't much more. When Lopez was robbed he couldn't do much about it at first. Biter bit. He waited his chance. These stones and fakes were spread about and sold – all under cover. Several of them were lodged with fences or in the collections of people who, knowing they had no legal right to them, began to worry when so much interest was shown. Then the world was told that you had the real McCoy. You found yourself with an embarrassment of riches, so to speak – and small wonder, as they were under-cover stuff and the owners were anxious to unload.' Forsythe rounded his eyes. 'My, my!' he exclaimed. 'What will the police think of the owner of Quinn's buying doubtful jewels?'

'I wonder,' said Mannering heavily.

'Well, there's the story as far as Tring and I know it. Don Lopez is now comfortably in jail, the story is unfolded. Not much doubt of the truth. Why didn't you want to believe that the Adalgo family was behind it? That must have stuck out a mile.'

Mannering said slowly: 'I've read the family history, and they seem a good crowd. There's still something we don't know.'

'Face-saving,' murmured Forsythe. 'Can't say I blame you. Well, one of Lopez's boy-friends talked, so all is over – except one little thing, the second parcel of booty-hunters at the Guildford house last night. By the way, the police have pinched Josh Larraby, I'm told.'

'Yes.'

'You haven't any idea who this rival bunch is, I suppose? It's rather odd, isn't it, if Larraby's one of them and you should make a point of befriending Larraby? Odd to the police, I mean.'

Mannering contemplated him in silence.

'Sorry if you're sore,' Forsythe said. 'I feel as if I'm teaching granny to suck eggs, but—'

'You are and she needs teaching.' Mannering laughed. 'Do you still want to know who the second party was at Bingham Street?'

'Do I!'

Mannering said: 'As soon as I can get about on this leg, I'll tell you.'

'If you know—'

'I'm guessing. You wouldn't want to put guesswork in your newspaper, would you?' Mannering laughed again; the movement shook him and hurt his knee, but he went on laughing. When Lorna—'

'Why wait for her?'

'Sorry. If you can't see the rest of the story now, you're as wilful blind as I was. Remember two parties are interested, as was proved last night. Also, remember that we're told Lopez tried to put the fear of the Devil into young Harding and Marjorie, and that Marjorie was kidnapped by Lopez.'

Forsythe said slowly: 'Hum, yes. The Addels and the Hardings being the second party.'

'That's it.'

'Hardly sensational,' Forsythe said.

'It will be,' Mannering chuckled again.

'What *is* funny?' demanded Forsythe.

'I am. And you. And Bristow. Well, I can see why Bristow thought I'd been up to the old – er – why he thought I would sink to crime.' Mannering swallowed hard. 'Forsythe, take pity on an old crook. Go chasing about and looking for the answer to three questions. Why did Harding Senior offer a jewel for sale and then withdraw it? Why did Paul and Marjorie appear to be so scared of the police, and then why did Paul change his mind? Why, in fact, did they pretend to be the naïvest of the naïve – is there such a word as Naïvest?'

'After today, there is. Third question?'

'Why was Zara Addel so anxious to prevent the police from seeing a letter written by Bray and found at the shop? If the

Adalgo family is in it, the family name of Zara for the daughters is too obvious to miss.'

'Was she anxious about that letter?'

'Yes. Bristow doesn't know – forget to tell him, will you?'

Forsythe said: 'Don't you be too sure about Bristow, he stores a lot of stuff in that old noddle of his. Anything else?'

'Yes. Ask your Research people to try to find photographs of pictures of a male member of the Adalgo family. I've seen dozens of women, but no men.'

'Why?'

'You'll probably get the answer when you see the picture,' Mannering said.

CHAPTER TWENTY-ONE

THE SUPERINTENDENT AND THE INSPECTOR

BRISTOW had a heavy day.

He went to Guildford for conferences with the local police, interviewed Pedro Lopez and the other prisoners until he was dizzy. Only the man with the wrinkled forehead, named Barnes, had talked; whatever qualities the brute of *Green Ways* lacked, loyalty was not one of them; he wouldn't say a word. Yet so much could be pieced together, now that Lopez was identified, that it would only be a matter of days before the rest fell into place – except one thing: what action to take with Mannering.

Late in the afternoon, Bristow went into the Assistant-Commissioner's office.

You're finding the pace hot, aren't you?' greeted Anderson-Kerr.

'It's getting pretty fast, sir, some of it outstrips me.'

'You've plenty of time to catch up,' said the A.C. 'Finding that Pedro Lopez was at the back of it, is half the job.'

'In one way, yes. In another I'm not so sure,' said Bristow. 'We've got to accept one thing: we caught Lopez and the other two because Mannering or his wife sent for the Guildford police after visiting the house. I doubt whether we shall ever get proof, but there it is. I just can't be sure what Mannering's up to. I don't believe he's blind to the reason for Adalgos by the dozen, or that he's above lending a hand to the Adalgo family. He'd regard a royalist cause as his, and outside law and order.'

'Yet you think he shopped Lopez.'

'We know that Lopez was an Adalgo royalist years ago, we don't know that he is today,' said Bristow. 'We do know that someone else raided *Green Ways*, presumably to get the diamonds. We also know that Larraby was there. Mannering had shown remarkable friendliness towards Larraby, and so Mannering might be working with Larraby's crowd – the real instigators of the trouble. I can't see Mannering starting this affair in the way that he says he did – out of curiosity. If he lied, he knew that the real diamonds which are so much like the Adalgo, had been stolen.'

'Could he have known?'

'Mannering's like most of the big collectors – he learns what's for sale under cover. Deals running into hundreds of thousands of pounds go on regularly, and we know nothing about them. Let's get down to cases. We've established that Lopez first had the rose-tinted diamonds cut like the Adalgo to get an inflated price for each; that he stole them from their owners, who realized they'd been fooled once they knew Mannering had the real Adalgo, but sat tight. They couldn't complain, as they bought what they thought was the Adalgo at a time when it was listed as stolen goods. We've also established that Mannering went headfirst into the market for the duplicate stones. Surely it's reasonable to assume that he knew they were stolen – and therefore to say that he bought stolen goods.'

Anderson-Kerr looked owlish.

'What about the murder of Bray and the murder of Leverson? Have you any proof that Lopez—'

'Lopez killed Leverson,' said Bristow abruptly. 'Barnes has talked enough to establish that. Lopez really wanted the real Adalgo, Mannering had it in the window, where it was as safe as anywhere and attracted a lot of attention. After Lopez had stolen the other jewels from Mannering he sent a man to offer the stones to Leverson, sure that Leverson would get in touch with Mannering. Lopez wanted to meet Mannering and force him to give up the Adalgo, but Mrs. Mannering turned up. Afterwards, Leverson recognized Lopez – Barnes is quite sure about that.

'Lopez killed Leverson after tricking Mrs. Mannering into going away with him – and Mannering went after her, as Lopez hoped he would. Lopez came unstuck because Mannering's what he is.

'We also know that Lopez killed P.C. Harris at Mannering's flat,' Bristow went on. 'We don't know who killed Bray. It's Bray's death which brings the Addel women and the Hardings into it. Harding Senior, being a collector in a small way, had one of these pseudo-Adalgo diamonds. He had Spanish interests, too – how deep, I don't know. I've a feeling that Mannering, the Hardings and the Addels have been working together, and that Mannering put us on to *Addel & Co.* both to save himself – and to fox us. That's the kind of tortuous trick that would appeal to him.'

'Can we hold Mannering?'

'We couldn't make any charge stick.'

'Then don't chance it, yet. If it weren't for Larraby, you'd be less certain of Mannering's part. What about Larraby?'

'He sticks to his story.' Bristow hesitated. 'It's nonsense, of course, but I've heard some rumours about him having a brother who resembles him. If we get Larraby, we'll get Mannering – that's about the size of it.'

Anderson-Kerr said: 'Well, don't forget to let Tring make the charge, when it comes.'

Bristow laughed, but wasn't amused. 'I'm not so sure. Tring talked too freely to the Press, gave far too much away. Have you seen the papers?'

'Yes. Will it do much harm?'

'Forsythe knows pretty well as much as we do – and but for Tring, no one would know who 'Lopey' really is. Remember Forsythe is in Mannering's pocket, too.'

'Discipline Tring yourself,' said Anderson-Kerr.

Bristow nodded, and went out.

He heard voices as he paused outside his own office. Tring's voice was raised, giving vent to a spate of bitter vituperation, but occasionally he recognized the voice of Forsythe.

'Damn it, you gave me the stuff and didn't say it was off the record,' Forsythe said.

'I forgot. You ought to have known. You—'

Bristow thrust open the door. Tring glared, Forsythe turned from a desk to Bristow, with a broad smile.

'Hallo, Super! I've been waiting for you.'

'There's a waiting-room downstairs for you people,' said Bristow sharply. 'If you come upstairs again without my permission, I'll ask your paper to keep you away from here. Clear out.'

Forsythe's face dropped.

'Oh, come! Tring had already told me—'

Bristow pushed the door wide open.

'Out.'

Forsythe shrugged, and went out briskly; grinning.

Bristow closed the door, sat down, and lit a cigarette. Tring watched him as if hypnotized. After a pause, Bristow put his hands flat on the desk.

'Tring,' he said, 'if you give any statement to the Press without authority, I'll have you relegated to sergeant's rank. If ever I hear you talking about Mannering or anyone else to the Press as if you believed him guilty, if ever I hear you giving out hints for journalists to write up in their scandal sheets, I'll have you drummed out of the Force. I'd like to wring your neck!'

Tring licked his lips.

'Can't you open your mouth?' snapped Bristow.

Tring opened and closed it.

'All right – get out,' growled Bristow.

Tring started to speak again, changed his mind, and turned to the door. Then he spoke. He intended to speak under his breath but the depth of his feeling made the words audible.

'You're too fond of Mannering, that's what your trouble is.'

'Tring!' bellowed Bristow.

Tring jumped a foot, and spun round. Bristow got up, his face white.

'Repeat that,' said Bristow. 'Don't mumble, repeat it.'

Tring drew in his breath; and suddenly, words tumbled from his lips.

'All right, I'll repeat it! I think you're too fond of Mannering. If it was anyone else you'd have them here, you'd give them hell, that's what you'd do. But because it's Mannering, you let him get away with murder. I don't care what happens to me, it's all wrong. Right's right, that's what I say, I always have and I always shall. Right's *right*.'

'I – see,' said Bristow flatly. 'All right, Tring. You can go. Remember that if you make any statements to the Press without my permission you'll be disobeying orders.'

Tring tightened his lips, and went slowly towards the door and out into the passage.

Bristow didn't feel so sore as numbed. Was Tring right? Had he allowed himself to be influenced by personal liking for Mannering? Would he have been harsher with someone else, and taken more chances? Had Mannering been Leverson, or any other man suspected of crime, would he have left Mannering free? Would he have insisted on getting a warrant and leaving a man in Mannering's apartment, to take his statement before he could conspire with his wife? Or was it the simple truth that Mannering always beat him to it? Mannering knew the law inside out, had powerful friends in Fleet Street, and used a form of blackmail – make one mistake with him and the Press would scream it from the housetops.

But – Tring was half right.

Tring would have taken chances, because he was so bitter; Bristow wouldn't, because of that personal liking. It was there all the time, he couldn't define it and couldn't ignore it.

What was he? A recruit from the police college or a Yard chief with twenty-five years service behind him?

Prove the case against Larraby and he'd prove one against Mannering. All right, he'd prove one!

Larraby was at Cannon Row, the low roofed, grey forbidding police station so near Scotland Yard that it seemed part of the same headquarters. He called the sergeant-in-charge-of-cells to say he was on the way.

Nothing would shake Larraby's story; the Mannerings had befriended him, and he had not been to Guildford. Bristow was dry when he'd finished talking, Larraby almost exhausted but as stubborn as ever.

Tring was in the canteen when Bristow went for a glass of beer. Tring studiously avoided him.

Bristow telephoned Mannering's apartment, was told that Mannering would be laid up for the better part of a week, and detailed a man to watch Green Street day and night and to note all visitors. He was not justified now in doubling the guard; the greatest danger was over with the arrest of Lopez and the others. There was plenty of high-pressure routine work, and it was a relief not to have to watch Mannering.

The case against Lopez and the others for the murders of P.C. Harris and Leverson, built up remorselessly. Beneath a floor at Bingham Street, they found the gun with which the policeman had been shot and there were bloodstains on the butt; Lopez had beaten Leverson to death with the same gun.

But there was no evidence that he or any of his men had been to *Addel & Co.*'s Lander Street shop; the murder of Bray was still unsolved.

Lopez refused to talk.

There was no evidence that any of the Adalgo family were in England. Nor was there evidence against the Addel women or the Hardings.

The name of Marjorie's sister-in-law was a coincidence almost too obvious to be significant; the fifth and other Duchess of Adalgo had been named Zara. Zara Addel's story was simple, and couldn't be disproved. Bristow knew what Mannering knew about her. She had lived in France most of her life, lost her parents during the war, when she had married Marjorie's brother. He had been killed, and she had come to England to live with Marjorie. She had no interests that Bristow could trace, except at the gown shop. The Hardings and the Addels had met through Paul; love at a party and at first sight. There was no reason to doubt the truth of any of this.

He sent a routine request to *Sûreté Generale* in Paris for all possible information about Zara, expecting that it would be at least a week before he received any answer.

Marjorie Addel's story of her presence at Guildford was unshakable. She said she had no idea why she had been taken there. She had been going to see the Hardings, after her release from Scotland Yard, and as she was walking along a quiet street, a car had pulled up alongside her and she had been bundled inside. Investigation brought forth two witnesses who had seen the incident. Her story seemed genuine enough, and Barnes didn't know why she'd been kidnapped, except that it had been on Lopez's orders. Harding Senior maintained the story which Paul Harding had told Mannering; suspicion of his father handling smuggled jewels could have accounted for Paul Harding's first nervousness of the police; could also have explained Marjorie's fears.

No reason, thought Bristow bitterly, and every reason; someone was lying.

Larraby – or a man who might have been Larraby – had been seen in Harrow Street, near the house where his wife and daughter lived. Bristow couldn't trace a brother, but picked up rumours that Larraby had one, who was abroad.

The Bray murder and the whole story gradually faded out of the newspapers . . .

Nothing faded out of Tring's mind, and Bristow found himself muttering an almost daily incantation: fix Larraby, fix Mannering.

The telephone bell rang in the apartment, and Mannering heard Lorna answer it. She wasn't long before she came in.

He looked up from the bed.

'Who?'

'Paul Harding.'

'Oh-ho!'

'He says his father is still very anxious to see you.'

'Needing help?'

'He didn't say so.'

'Did you ask him here?'

'No,' said Lorna. 'I don't want him here.' She went to the door. 'Did you expect a call from them?'

'I did.'

'Why?'

'They want the Adalgo.'

Lorna said: 'I'd gladly give it to them,' and went out.

Three days later, Mannering stood at the side of his bed and said: 'Watch me pirouette, my sweet!'

'Sit down, you fool!'

'But I can stand, look. I can walk. *Look.*' Mannering took three short steps, then rested on his sound leg and bent the right knee gingerly. 'How long have I been in this dungeon with an ogress for company?'

'Three days, precisely. From beloved wife to ogress, in seventy-two hours.'

'Rather a nice ogress.' Mannering limped across the room to Lorna's side. 'Wearing a troubled frown, it's true. Why? Had Harding called again?'

'Marjorie did, they're changing the bait.'

Mannering laughed: 'No love for her now? What's really the trouble?'

'I suppose it's Josh.'

'Ah, yes. Bristow won't come and tell us all about everything, so we don't know whether Josh has a chance or not.'

'We know he's still under remand.'

'Yes. Any other reason for gloom?'

Lorna poked her fingers through her hair.

177

'Not really. It's over and yet it isn't over, I feel as if we're going to get a nasty shock one of these days. John, *could* Larraby have lied?'

'Yes.'

'If Bristow proves that he did, then you and I—'

'Come under deep suspicion for harbouring a crook, but we've been under suspicion before.'

'Not quite like this.'

'Worse.'

'Darling, why pretend you're all happy and gay?'

Mannering laughed.

'Would it help if I were glum and depressed? My mind won't depress, anyhow – I think you're right, there'll be another flare-up, and when it comes there'll be plenty of smoke but we won't get burned. I hope. The oddest part of an odd affair is the virtual disappearance of the Addel–Harding combination from the scene. Forsythe can't get a line on them beyond what we already know, and the police doubtless have it on their dossier. A nice, respectable if superior little crowd. If Bray hadn't died, they wouldn't even be on the suspect list. If Marjorie hadn't come to see me – well, she did and I'm wasting our breath. And now Harding *père* wants to see me. When do you think I can get up?'

'What day is it?'

'Friday.'

'Three weeks next Friday.'

Mannering chuckled, and kissed her.

There was always a policeman in Green Street; always a feeling of being watched. After the third day, Mannering expected visitors – Paul Harding or the girl – and was disappointed because neither came. But Paul Harding telephoned each day, anxious and inquiring – and inviting. This, Tring and Larraby were the three main topics of conversation, until, on the seventh day, Lorna came into the bedroom and saw Mannering fully dressed.

'Doctor said I could,' he protested before she said a word.

'He didn't say you could go to Guildford.'

'Coming?'

'How did you guess—'

'I heard you asking Forsythe for directions when he rang up last night.'

178

'What else did you hear?'

'That he hasn't found a picture of a male Adalgo, and doesn't understand why you want one.'

'That's easy. If it's the face I expect, we won't have to ask many more questions. What else did your eavesdropping tell you?'

'That Forsythe is spending a lot of time at Guildford, and concentrating on Marjorie. Can't you get her ripeness out of your mind?'

'No. Can you?'

'I wish we'd never heard of her. Don't go, John. Take me out to dinner.'

'There's our old Josh, too.'

Lorna said: 'Oh, you'd better go. Have one more day's rest, and—'

The telephone bell rang.

'That'll be Paul,' Lorna said. 'Why *do* they keep ringing?'

Mannering shrugged, and went to the telephone.

'Perhaps my voice fascinates him. Hallo – *hallo*, Forsythe. Any news?'

Forsythe said: 'Go to the Hardings' house, John, make it snappy and take a gun. I told you how to get there, last night. I can't stay.'

It was a warm morning with a cooling breeze. The *Talbot* had been polished during the few days of rest until it shone like a mirror. Mannering drove, glad to be at the wheel, to feel the easy freedom of his leg. It was his first real outing since his accident, and he enjoyed driving at speed along the Guildford Bypass. He was amused when he drove up the High Street, and glanced at the clock under which he had met Lopez's man. The urgency in Forsythe's call was dulled by the drive. The two mysteries still unanswered were the murder of Bray and the identity of the second party raiders at *Green Ways*. Were they connected?

'Top of the hill, straight on, third right and first left,' said Mannering, glancing at a list of directions which Forsythe had given him. 'Should I have telephoned Harding to say I was coming? Pity if he's out!'

'Getting conventional, darling?'

'Ogress,' said Mannering. 'I – hallo, look.'

He had turned off the main road and, at the next corner they had to take, which should lead them to *The Lees*, was Forsythe. He glanced round, recognized them on the instant, and swung towards them. Mannering slowed down.

Forsythe exclaimed:

'Give *The Lees* a miss for a jiffy – I've got something else.' He climbed into the back of the car, and dropped on to the seat. He was breathing heavily, and as Mannering passed the end of the road where *The Lees* stood, he glanced along it almost nervously.

Mannering took the next turning, and pulled up.

'Now what's all this about?'

Forsythe patted his chest heavily.

'I'll have to go into training – or stop smoking, or something! Sorry. I was coming to 'phone you again, and I didn't want to waste time. Also, I didn't want to be seen. You're going to thank me for this.'

'For a newspaperman you take a hell of a time to get to the point,' Mannering said.

Forsythe said: 'Believe it or not. Item one, I've seen Larraby's double.'

'You've *what*?'

'No!' cried Lorna.

'I saw him with my own eyes, and couldn't believe them at first. It's *not* Larraby. Even if our Josh weren't cooling his heels at Brixton, it still wouldn't be him. But the likeness knocked me over. He left the Hardings' house. in a fast car. On a dark night anyone could be muddled. Item two: there was a Guildford policeman watching the house until half an hour ago. He's vanished. This is the first time the house hasn't been watched. I've a lovely feeling the bobby's been biffed on the head. Say thanks.'

CHAPTER TWENTY-TWO

THE MAN WHO WAS NOT LARRABY

MANNERING said: 'Yes. Thanks.' He grinned crookedly at the excitement in Lorna's eyes. 'Meet my wife, who didn't want me to come.'

'Josh wasn't lying,' sighed Lorna.

'There isn't a shadow of doubt,' said Forsythe. 'This merchant came out of *The Lees*, as bold as brass. I hopped along to call you, aiming to get back in three jiffs. And I ought to be on my way,' he said. 'Drop me down where you picked me up, will you?'

Mannering let in the clutch, turned, and drove slowly to the end of the next road, talking all the time.

'Keep a careful watch, especially after I've gone into the house. I'm going to see Harding, and if Larraby's double comes back it won't do any harm.'

'What about Mrs. John?'

'I'm going with him,' said Lorna. 'I don't trust him with lusciousness which tempts him daily by telephone.'

Mannering patted the back of her hand.

'You were coming,' he said. 'Now you're not. You're going to wait for me in the car, because I might want to get off in a hurry and you drive quite nicely.'

Forsythe grinned.

'Drop me here and have your fight alone,' he said, and looked round. 'Hallo! I see a man wearing a black hat and brown shoes. Did you know Tring was on your tail?'

'Tring's always on my tail,' said Mannering.

'Well, it's you he's after.' Forsythe got out, waved to Tring and strolled towards *The Lees*. It was a big grey faced house which stood in its own grounds, not pretty, not ugly. A high grey wall surrounded it.

Mannering did not speak again until he pulled up outside.

'I suppose you're right,' conceded Lorna.

'This time, yes. Tanker will entertain you, my poppet. I won't turn into the drive, and you won't be seen from the house if you stay here.'

'John, do you know why they want to see you?'

'I've told you – for the Adalgo.'

Mannering left her at the wheel and walked along the drive of *The Lees*. It was a solidly built late Georgian period residence standing in well kept grounds. A youngish gardener was working among the flowers, which made a riot of colour in the bright sunlight. The gardener touched his cap and remarked that it was a nice day.

'Wonderful!' agreed Mannering.

It was wonderful. He hoped he could see Larraby's face when he was told of this. He felt on top of the world; anxiety wouldn't last much longer, now.

He reached the massive, green-painted front door, and pressed the bright brass bell.

There was a long pause before he heard footsteps inside. With Tring nearby, and Lorna and Forsythe within hail, the signals were at 'go'. But for a missing policeman . . .

A woman was hurrying towards the front door, quick taps on a wooden floor.

Zara Addel opened the door, sleek, lovely, remote – and suddenly frightened, at sight of him.

She backed away when she saw who it was, and her hands rose to silk clad breasts which shimmered with her agitated breathing.

'Good morning,' said Mannering brightly.

'Good morning.'

'Is Mr. Harding in? Not Paul, his father. He's asked me to call.'

'Yes, I – I think so.' She had expected someone, but certainly not Mannering, and she wasn't sure of herself. 'Will you please come in?'

She was more beautiful then he had realized; regal, too.

Mannering stepped into a spacious, well-furnished hall. Zara left him and ran upstairs. As she disappeared, Mannering looked round keenly. Some of the furniture was in the rococo Spanish-Moroccan style. A Spanish shawl, a lovely shimmering thing, hung on one wall.

Minutes ticked by; he thought a lot about a missing police-man, about Harding's daily message, the spider's invitation to the fly.

Then a door opened at the head of the stairs, and Paul Harding came running down.

'Hallo, Mannering! This is wonderful!'

'Nice of you.'

'We'd given up thinking you would come,' said Paul. He looked boyish, delighted and eager. 'My father won't keep you long.' He pushed open the door of the drawing-room wider, and stood aside for Mannering to pass.

'I see you've other guests,' said Mannering.

'Oh, hardly guests. Marjorie and Zara are staying here, they're almost members of the family.' Paul was brisk, proffered cigarettes and offered a drink.

'It's a bit early,' Mannering demurred.

'Oh, not for a small one,' insisted Paul. 'Whisky?'

He busied himself with the drinks, and looked twice towards the door, doing everything jerkily; a man on edge. There wasn't a sound outside. Mannering glanced about this lovely room, and saw a small portrait, by itself on one wall. A crest on the frame was like a crown for the head.

It was the portrait of a young man, a handsome, dashing rakehell of a man – not Larraby, but as Larraby might have been, twenty years ago.

There was a word worked into the crest: *Adalgo.*

Harding brought Mannering a whisky-and-soda.

'An end to crime! But you thrive on it, don't you?'

Mannering laughed. 'Is your father still buying?'

'Oh, odds and ends,' said Paul. 'He's not a big fish, you know, just likes a few sparklers about him.' The laugh which followed was forced, he looked at the door again. 'He doesn't go in for it as you do, but he's always wanted to meet you. That's why – I think he's coming!' Paul stepped quickly to the door, as someone came down the stairs. Mannering moved so that he could see into the hall as the door opened.

Marjorie Addel appeared.

'Oh, hallo!' exclaimed Paul. 'It's you. Where's the old boy?'

'He's coming,' said Marjorie. She was agitated; was she always like this? Her blue eyes were like deep pools. 'Mr. Mannering. I want to apologize.'

'Great Scott, why?'

'For – for the way I behaved to you. It was crazy, I was beside myself.'

Then Harding came in.

He walked slowly, to impress. He was shorter than Paul; as short as Zara and – beautiful? That wasn't an absurd thought. He was a lean, grey haired, perfectly built man, and gravity sat on him like a clock, with something more – confidence, poise, self-possession – he had them all. He was exquisitely dressed; he didn't really belong here, had no place in this day and age.

He bowed.

'This is Mr. Man—' Paul began.

'Yes, Paul.' Harding smiled. 'We will send for you and Marjorie.'

'But—' Paul began to protest.

'Come on, Paul.' Marjorie took his hand; as she passed Harding, Mannering had an absurd feeling that she would genuflect as before a presence.

The door closed.

Harding said: 'I feel sure we shall understand each other.'

'I hope so,' Mannering mumured.

'Have you brought the Adalgo?'

Mannering said: 'Did you think I would?'

'Of course. That is why I sent for you.'

'Well, we all make mistakes.'

'In the past and present and future,' Harding said. His voice was mellow and aloof; like Zara's. 'I make few mistakes.'

'I wonder.'

Harding laughed; it was an icy sound.

'You will find out. You are going to give me the Adalgo diamond.'

'Well, well! A free gift?'

'As barter. The Adalgo for your freedom.'

It was warm in the room, but Harding, like his voice, was cold. Mannering watched him, fascinated and almost afraid.

'You treasure freedom,' Harding said. 'You can have it for the diamond. You see, I know *all* about you.'

He believed that; he made Mannering believe it. The room wasn't hot, it was cold.

'That is why I invited you here,' said Harding. 'As I say, I make few mistakes. I knew you would come eventually, Mr.

Mannering. I have learned a great deal about you since our paths first crossed.'

Mannering said: 'Is there much to learn?'

Harding's eyes were grey, clear as polished steel. There was a smile on his lips but none in that steel.

He had expected the visit; he'd been sure it would come.

'I have also made a close study of criminal law,' he said. 'That is necessary when one goes a little too near the dividing line between the legal and the criminal, a habit common to most collectors of precious stones. I know what is evidence and what is hearsay. What you and I talk about is hearsay, not evidence – you can safely discuss the truth with me, as freely as I can with you. I have been wanting the Adalgo diamond for some time – before you bought it. I did not know for sure that it was in your possession until recently – when you made such an ostentatious display of it in your window. Why *did* you do that, Mr. Mannering?'

'Candles attract moths.'

'I have no wings to singe,' said Harding. 'I have been seeking the Adalgo diamond for a very close friend of mine.'

'How close?'

'Perhaps the phrase "a relation by marriage" will satisfy you?'

'It'll pass.'

'My wife, who died when Paul was born, was the second daughter of the Duke of Adalgo,' said Harding calmly. 'At the time of our marriage I had interests in Spain. The Adalgo family were and are my friends. But I do not think I need to go into great detail about them, Mr. Mannering. You know who they are, you know that they claim the Spanish throne, you know that they are never likely to ascend it unless they become so wealthy that they can press their claim. One of my tasks has been to make sure that they become so wealthy.'

'Pedro Lopez had a cut at that.'

'Lopez was never more than a mercenary – a good mercenary, yes, with the gift of oratory and the gift of organization. But he lost his faith, soon after the Civil War. Since then he has been interested not in the fortunes of the family but of himself. You know the story of the imitation Adalgos and their sale as the genuine diamond, I presume.'

'Yes.'

'And you think Lopez was responsible for planning that?'

'Wasn't he?'

'No. I gave him instructions. Afterwards, he betrayed me and worked on his own. Consequently he is in prison, awaiting trial for murder. I don't think any man would enjoy prison, do you?'

'Who killed Bray?' Mannering asked flatly. 'Remember we're being honest with each other.'

'It is beside the point. I want to impress on you the fact that I am loyal to the Adalgo family. Whatever you have paid for it, whatever your legal right to it, the Adalgo diamond belongs to the Adalgo family.'

'A case might be made out, but they sold—'

'They did not sell it, Mannering. It was stolen from them by another bunch of the royal family. It was always the property of the House of Adalgo.'

Mannering laughed, and lit a cigarette. The laugh jarred, even on himself. This calm, coolly agressive man had the same immature frankness as Marjorie; a form of naïveté, but it wasn't childish and it could be damning.

'Let's agree that it's morally theirs,' he said. 'It's legally mine. It's value—'

'It cannot be valued in terms of money. Listen to me. I knew what Lopez was doing. I wanted him to get the diamond, and planned to take it from him. That is why I arranged a visit to *Green Ways* on the evening you were there. Unfortunately the police came too soon. Did you give the diamond to him?'

'I didn't go to the house.'

Harding smiled; he was utterly sure of himself, as if he didn't consider the possibility of failure.

'You did, Mannering, and I can prove that you did.'

'So you can work miracles and prove what isn't true.'

Harding smiled gently.

'Yes, I could prove it, even if it weren't true. I have many friends, Mannering, who will swear black is white, if it will help the cause. I have others in high places and with influence internationally. There have been two campaigns running side by side. The one, you know about – Lopez, with his cunning and his treachery and his idiocy. He had no idea that I realized that he was going to – what is the word? – ah, yes, doublecross me. True, he forced me into making one of my few mistakes, by persuading me that the diamond in your window was not the Adalgo, and convincing me that Bray had the one I wanted. That is why I sent Marjorie and Paul to get Bray's gem from you. They were nervous, they did badly, but by the later talk of smuggling and Paul's most unfilial suspicions of me, there was an adequate explanation. You will also want to know why I told Paul to tell of my quarrel with Bray.'

Mannering said: 'I'm dying to know.'

'It's better that you should. When you know it all, you will realize the inevitability of giving me the Adalgo. I did quarrel with Bray. The police were bound to find out. So, I sent Paul to tell you of it, believing that it would excite your curiosity and bring you to see me. I did not know that Bray was dead until I saw the newspapers.'

'Lies,' said Mannering.

'Truth,' retorted Harding. 'I believe that Lopez had discovered that I was watching him very closely, and killed Bray to make difficulties for me. He chose the shop, because it would embarrass Marjorie and Zara, and he thought that would distress me. It distressed the girls, that is all. There was really no need for them to worry. Remember that I have friends in high places, Mannering. I do not suggest that those friends could persuade the police to connive at crime, but Scotland Yard dare not hold me or any of my friends without the strongest possible evidence – and their evidence was not strong enough.'

Mannering said lightly: 'You don't know the Yard – another of your mistakes. They let you go for one of two reasons: either they were satisfied that on the evidence they couldn't legally hold you, or else they gave you plenty of rope with which to hang yourself.'

'If that satisfies you, believe it.'

'It satisfies me. Why did you quarrel with Bray?'

'When I believed that he owned the Adalgo, I wanted him to get it back from you and to withdraw his request for you to sell. Being in financial difficulties, he refused. It was an unfortunate, unnecessary interlude—'

'Which will get you hanged.'

'There is far less risk of me being hanged than of you going to prison,' Harding said. 'Haven't we talked enough? I want the Adalgo or I shall give the police all the proof they need about your adventurous past. I should be sorry, because I like a man who flouts convention.'

Mannering went to the cabinet and poured himself a drink.

'Yes, you need that,' murmured Harding. 'Where is the Adalgo?'

Mannering sipped his drink.

'Where is Larraby's double?'

Harding's eyes turned towards the portrait. He hesitated, at a loss for words for the first time.

Mannering said gently: 'I might hand the diamond over if I know the truth about that. Where is he? *Who* is he?'

'Mannering—'

'No statement, no Adalgo.'

Harding said softly: 'Very well, Mannering. You are looking at a portrait of the Duke of Adalgo. The man you know as Larraby, a love child, is his half-brother. *And* he knows it.'

'And the Duke was out last night?'

'He—'

'Knocking policemen over the head, too.'

Harding said coldly: 'It was unfortunate but necessary. I doubt if identification can be assured, but His Highness is already flying out of England, for safety's sake. *Now* will you give me the Adalgo.'

'No,' said Mannering.

CHAPTER TWENTY-THREE

THE BARON AND THE PAST

HARDING said harshly: 'You blind, stubborn fool! Don't you realize what I can do to you? Do you think I'm bluffing? You'll give me that diamond or I will give the police all the evidence they need that you are the Baron. *Are*, do you understand, not were. I'll bring it up to date, I'll have your name dragged through the muck, you disgraced and your wife dishonoured. I mean it.'

'Yes, you mean it.' Mannering went across to the photograph and studied it, his back to Harding. The man strode towards him.

'Mannering—'

'Nice chap,' said Mannering. 'The Duke and you – both very nice chaps. You mean it, all right, there isn't a foul trick you wouldn't play. Nor the Duke. I do not like you, Duc d'Aldago, and I do not like your friends.'

Harding said in a quivering voice: 'You will not insult His Highness. You will—'

'I'll spend the rest of my life in jail rather than let either of you get away with this,' said Mannering. 'Poor old Josh! Tricked, cheated, harassed, frightened – he's as fine as they come. He wouldn't betray you or his fine feathered relative by a hint or whisper. He'd rather go to jail. He knows his so-called brother is fixing this latest job on him, but won't make the statement which puts him in the clear. Now there's a man worth knowing.'

Harding said: 'Be a reasonable man, not a sentimental fool. Larraby was lost from the family for years, and had no idea who he was. He was approached some time ago and asked to help in the cause, but refused. He was married to a silly little woman, he had what he thought was a safe job, and he wouldn't risk it. He did once try to steal some jewels from me, said they were his birthright. But he is a timid, slow-witted fool.'

'And worth about twenty of you.'

'He stole—'

'You make me sick,' said Mannering. 'You make me think of crawling things and corruption. You have the nerve to sneer at Josh for his one mistake while you plan murder and violence, and use blackmail – get away from me, I might break your neck.'

Harding backed away, then stopped himself abruptly.

'If you think I'm afraid of you, Mannering, you're—'

'Oh, you're not afraid. You've proved it. Bloodsucking spider in the centre of his web, using your own son, Marjorie, Zara, Lopez – anyone who'd fallen foul of your web, before you'd take a risk yourself. You hadn't even the guts to come and see me. Who is Zara?'

'Never mind.'

'*Who is Zara?*'

Harding said: 'The Duchess. Mannering—'

'Was the gown shop used as a royalist meeting place?'

'Yes.' Harding's face was chalk white and his lips quivered. 'I'll have that diamond or you will go for trial. I can produce that evidence.'

'You can produce it until the cows come home,' said Mannering. 'No diamond. Sit down.'

'Man—'

'Sit down!'

Harding backed to a chair and sat on the edge.

'And keep still, my fine royalist, or you'll get hurt. I can hardly keep my hands off you as it is. Be quiet and listen, for a change. You think I'm a man with a past and think you can say *hey presto* and bring the past to life. You can't, and no one can. The police are so tired of people saying that I'm the Baron that they've a special file for the anonymous letters and mimeographed replies. My past will stand anyone's scrutiny, in dock or out of it. Remember that.'

'It won't,' said Harding. His voice was reedy with anger. 'Even if it could have done, it can't now. When you were first associated with the Adalgo I found out all there is to know about you. The story of you being the Baron came from three sources – one as far away as the United States. I collected those statements, Mannering, and then I had others invented, giving eye-witness proof of you as the Baron. I searched the news-papers for Baron crimes to get all my dates and my data right. You haven't a chance.'

'To hell with you,' said Mannering. 'No diamond.'

Was it checkmate?

As Mannering's anger evaporated, the cold facts pressed themselves into his mind. Harding was not bluffing, and would do exactly what he threatened if he were once convinced that Mannering would retain the Adalgo. But there were other facts. Larraby, in jail, loyal to a family to which he owed only contempt and hatred; he would serve ten years if the attack on a policeman were proved against him.

There was no alternative to fighting.

He saw Harding struggling to regain his self-control, and thought: 'I could frighten the wits out of him, now.' Was that worth trying? He stepped towards the man, and as he did so, saw a movement out of the window; someone passed there, bending low, anxious not to be seen.

Could it be Forsythe? Or – Tring?

How Tring would revel in this 'evidence.'

Tanker Tring had never felt so vindictive or so angry, as he did now. For the first time since he had worked with Bristow, they were bad friends. That was Mannering's fault; Tring didn't blame Bristow, only Mannering. He was sure that Bristow would never carry out the threat to take away his new rank, but felt that he had lost his one real friend at the Yard.

If only he could prove his case, if only he could make Bristow realize that right was right, no matter what anyone said and no matter what Mannering was doing now, the breach might be healed. Years of training, years of hopeful planning, years of failure, keyed Tring up to make one final effort. So, he dogged Mannering's footsteps.

He saw Lorna at the wheel of the *Talbot* and Forsythe in the street: and knew that Mannering was in Harding's house. There had probably always been something between Mannering and Harding; now, he might find the proof of it.

He went through the garden of the house behind *The Lees*, climbed over the wall, hidden from the house by trees – and approached the house behind a thick beech hedge. He spied out the land, then made a dash for the house, convinced that he had not been seen.

He heard voices, and peered through a window, saw Mannering and Harding were together in the room. The window was open an inch at the top. Tring stood quite still, eager not to miss a word. He missed plenty, but what he heard was of absorbing interest. He kept motionless, sheltered by a small shrubbery from a gardener who was working not twenty yards away.

'Evidence – proof – trial – Baron—'

What could this mean, but one thing?

Proof – *proof* – that Mannering was the Baron, was in this house! Tring's heart began to beat so fast that he could hardly breathe. Should he handle this himself? Or creep away and call Bristow? As he fought an inward battle, he heard the gardener approaching, bent low and crept past the window, to hide behind a bush. He didn't realize that the sun cast his shadow on the side of the window.

Mannering could only see a shadow, but knew that it was the shadow of a man. Harding did not know that anyone was there, and was screwing himself up to another effort.

Mannering said: 'You'll clear Larraby, if it's the last thing you do. When you've told the police about the Duke, I'll talk to you again.'

If he were allowed to leave, it would mean they would even risk implicating the Duke, by helping Larraby, so as to get that diamond. Why did they want it so desperately? Not just as an omen, because of its history, because of the tradition that the rightful owner was – a Queen?

Harding did not move.

Mannering opened the door and stepped into the hall. Paul Harding stood at the foot of the stairs with an automatic in his hand.

There was a strained, half eager and boyish smile on Paul's face. The gun did not waver. He must have been sitting at the foot of the stairs, waiting for this moment.

Harding followed Mannering out of the room.

'Another mistake,' Mannering sneered.

Harding said: 'Paul was told to wait here, in case of emergency. I am less confident than I was that I can compel you to give up the stone on my present evidence, but I am going to have it. You are going to write instructions to your manager at Quinn's to give the stone to Mrs. Mannering. She is waiting outside, as you know. Paul will go with her and see that she gets the stone. She will not refuse, knowing that your future is in the balance, Mannering. She'll be told to get the diamond or a wreath.'

The Adalgo diamond was in the strong room at Scotland Yard.

CHAPTER TWENTY-FOUR

THE DUCHESS AND THE TRUTH

'ENJOYING yourself, Mannering?' Paul broke the silence; and he grinned. It was a silly, trite thing to say and had no importance, but it turned the iciness in Mannering to red-hot fury. He sprang at the youth, saw Paul flinch and raise the gun, saw the glitter of alarm in the eager eyes – and knew that Paul's forefinger was trembling on the trigger.

He pulled up.

'That was lucky for you,' Paul said in a harsh voice.

'Stand farther away, Paul,' said Harding. He went behind Mannering and felt his pockets, drew the automatic out and put it on to a chair. 'Mannering, you are being foolish, there isn't a chance for you. Everyone in this household will commit murder to obtain possession of the Adalgo diamond, and you will not leave here until we have it. Whether you leave for a free life or for prison depends on what you do now.'

Forsythe or Tring had been outside that window, might have heard enough to make them rush for the telephone; minutes might make the difference between life and death, between a future and oblivion.

Mannering said: 'I'm going to light a cigarette.' He watched Paul, whose finger tightened on the trigger and relaxed only when the cigarette was alight. 'All right, Harding, you've the trump cards.'

'You will—' Harding's voice cracked in relief.

'When I know why you're so anxious to get the Adalgo, I might think you're justified in all this.'

Paul laughed. 'That's what a look at death does to a man.'

'Be quiet, Paul.' Harding held his hands together; where they pressed against each other, the flesh was white. 'I will even tell you that. The Adalgo diamond *must* be in the possession of the Queen. There is, as you doubtless know, a great deal of royalist sentiment in Spain, and much dissatisfaction with the Franco regime. The royalist sentiment is frustrated, because Alphonso is not really popular. Almost any other claimant to the throne will win great support, and the Adalgo family is second to none in popularity. You understand all that?'

'Yes.'

'The Duke married his cousin, the Zara whom you know. The story of the dead husband was false, of course, but carefully documented to convince all who made inquiries. The two main branches of the Adalgo family are thus united in marriage. Preparations for a *coup d'état* are complete. The economic plight of Spain is worsening rapidly, the only likely solution to the economic problem is a share of American aid. Franco won't get it, but the Duke and his adherents have powerful friends in the United States. The first thing that the Duke will do on his accession is to declare a political amnesty, and after that he will hold free elections. Can you imagine Spain being kept out of the Atlantic Pact for long after that?'

'Not bad,' said Mannering.

Paul laughed again. His eyes were too bright and his hand unpleasantly shaky.

'Not bad! It's perfect. It'll be worth a political amnesty and one free election to get on the winning horse, won't it? After that—'

'Paul!' snapped his father.

'Why try to fool Mannering? He knows—'

'I know I wouldn't trust the Duke of Adalgo or his adherents for ten minutes, and wouldn't give them a pennyworth of anyone's aid,' Mannering said. He knew much more; they would not let him live, now that he had this information. They'd bribe him with the promise of safety when he had delivered the diamond, but when they knew he couldn't give it to them, they'd treat him as they had Bray. 'Spain will work out its problems without the help of another gang of thugs,' he went on. 'That's no reason why I should risk my neck any more.'

'The great hero with feet of clay,' sneered Paul. 'Where's that diamond?'

'I still don't know why it's so important.'

'You're bad at guessing,' Paul said.

'Be quiet.' His father stood deliberately in front of him, for a tantalizing moment was between Paul and the gun. 'When the

Duchess Zara reaches Madrid with the diamond, Mannering, that will be the signal for the rising. Elements in the army, navy and air force are ready for the signal.'

Paul said: 'Keep out of the way.' He slewed the gun round towards Mannering. 'Go back, Mannering.'

Mannering stood still.

'Call Marjorie,' Harding said.

Paul raised his head: 'Hal-*loooo*, there! Hal-*loooo!*' The call wasn't loud but would carry – outside as well as in.

Who was outside? Tring, Forsythe, Lorna – why wasn't there a move from one of them?

After a pause, they heard the girl hurrying, from somewhere downstairs. A door at the end of the hall passage opened, and she appeared; her blue eyes so bright that they looked like sparkling steel.

'Hallo, sweet,' Paul said. 'It's nearly over. Go and tell Mrs. Mannering that her husband—'

Marjorie said: 'Paul! There's been trouble outside. That newspaperman Forsythe and a detective—'

Mannering felt almost suffocated. Alarm leapt to Harding's eyes, the shock hit Paul so hard that he almost forgot the gun in his hand.

'Well?' rasped Harding.

'They were in the grounds, we've had to overpower them.'

'That's fine,' said Paul, with relief.

'Are they safe?' Harding demanded sharply.

'Yes, they're unconscious in—'

It was now or never; and Mannering leapt.

Paul, although looking at Marjorie, saw him coming and swivelled round. The shot roared out as Mannering swayed to one side, the bullet smacked into the wall. Mannering flung himself forward, touching the barrel of the gun with his outstretched hand, and Paul backed and kicked against a stool. He fell backwards, arms waving. Mannering heard him crash. Mannering beat Harding to the chair where his own gun lay.

'No!' screamed Marjorie. 'Zara, Zara!'

Harding said: 'Mannering, don't be a crazy fool. If you don't do what you are told, that evidence will damn you. It won't help you if we suffer too.'

'Forget it,' Mannering said.

'*Zara!*' screamed Marjorie.

Mannering went across and struck her beneath the chin with his free left hand; she collapsed. Paul scrambled up, and Mannering fired. His bullet caught Paul's automatic. The gun dropped, blood sprang crimson on to Paul's fingers and he backed against the staircase, muttering. Harding sprang towards the stairs.

'With me,' Mannering said. He grabbed the man by his right arm, forced it up behind his back in a hammerlock and pushed him towards the stairs. Footsteps rumbled near the door from which Marjorie had come. Mannering said: 'Hurry!' and thrust Harding forward. They reached the landing as a door opened and two men appeared, one with a gun.

Mannering fired, twice; that was enough. One man turned and ran, the other doubled up, gasping. Marjorie moaned. Mannering forced Harding across the landing, thrust open a door and looked round for a telephone. There was one in a corner. He went towards it, pushed Harding on to a bed and kept him covered, and dialled Whitehall 1212. The ringing sound began at once.

Harding tried to sit up.

'Quiet,' said Mannering. 'Hallo . . . Yes, you can help me. An urgent message for Bristow – strong men and armed men needed at Harding's house, at once. Got that?'

'Harding's house?' the operator said.

'Yes, he'll know.'

He saw two things at once. The door opened, and Harding rolled over on the bed; Harding had a gun at his hip pocket. Mannering dropped the receiver and swayed, felt a bullet snatch at his arm, fired again and shattered Harding's wrist. He swivelled the gun towards the door.

He didn't shoot again.

Zara came in.

She wasn't armed, was dressed in black as he had seen her at the show, yet there was a difference, a quality which was all its own. It was in her eyes, her poise, her movements. She closed the door behind her, showing neither fear nor haste. In her right hand was a large envelope.

'Stay where you are,' Mannering said.

Lorna would have heard that shooting; she would come tearing in, she was fool enough and in love. Paul wasn't badly hurt, and with Marjorie's help he could do a lot of damage.

The window was open; he heard running footsteps on the gravel.

He backed towards the window and shouted: 'Lorna, I'm all right, stay where you are.'

She didn't answer.

Harding sat up, clutching his wrist, his face as pale as the cream wall behind him.

'Zara, go away. Hurry.'

'Not yet,' said Mannering. The footsteps outside were nearer the house. If it were Lorna, she was no longer running; at least he'd made her cautious. 'Where are those lying documents, Harding?'

Harding said: 'Zara! Go away.'

'She knows the right end of a gun,' Mannering said. 'She won't have a chance to get away if I don't get those documents. Hurry.'

A door banged, downstairs.

'I have them here,' said Zara. She came across fearlessly, took the papers from the envelope and held them out to Mannering. There was a sheaf of typewritten sheets, and he saw a photograph clipped to them. He snatched them, and backed away.

'*Zara,*' sighed Harding.

'I have been troubled for some time,' she said, in the husky, fascinating voice, 'and now I know why. Mr. Mannering, there were many things I did not know. I live to serve Spain. I do not think Spain can be served in this way. I heard what was said between you downstairs, for some time I have been able to hear from my room, which is above that. I prised up a floor board—'

'*Go away!*' cried Harding. 'The police—'

'The police may do as they wish,' said Zara. 'I am not a tool for assassins, whether the assassin be my husband or my friend. I shall tell the police everything, where to find my husband – everything. Mr. Mannering, I did you a grave injustice. When I first heard of you I believed you were a friend of the man Lopez. I believed that you had killed Bray at the shop and gave you that letter – it seemed the right thing to do. Since then, I have learned a great deal. I know that Paul and Marjorie killed Bray. Oh, they meant well, but—'

Harding muttered something; Mannering couldn't hear the

words. The dark eyes of the Duchess of Adalgo hypnotized him.

'John!' That was Lorna, from downstairs. 'John! Where are you?'

Mannering shouted: 'Be careful!'

Lorna's footsteps sounded on the stairs – and a car door banged outside, men's voices were raised. The police? A patrol car could be here by now.

'There have been so many lies,' Zara said. 'They shielded me from the truth, but I was not satisfied and discovered so many things that were damnable. Even my husband conspired to hide the truth from me. They pretended that only Lopez was responsible for the violence, and I believed it was true. When Lopez kidnapped Marjorie, it seemed to prove it. But now I know differently. They were prepared to use the fruits of violence and crime, let Lopez do his foul work, encouraged and helped him – meaning, when he had done what they needed, to kill him. Has Lopez told the police of *me?*'

'No.'

'He is loyal,' she said, and her eyes were hard with contempt when she looked at Harding. 'You would save yourself and all of us and blame Lopez for it all. Mr. Mannering, I want you to believe this. My friends considered that they were doing the right thing. They were wrong, but they had the merit of sincerity and faith.'

Lorna was on the landing, and sounded desperate. '*John, where are you?*'

'Will you please leave us now?' Zara said.

Harding was sitting on the side of the bed, nursing his hand, looking at her dully. The gun was near him.

'No,' said Mannering. 'Don't worry, you'll be—'

'Please go. I wish to talk to Mr. Harding.'

'*John!*'

'In here,' Mannering called. 'I – don't come in!'

He saw Harding grab at the gun with his shattered hand, fired again, caught the man in the shoulder but didn't make him drop the gun. Harding fired again – at Zara. The bullet struck her in the forehead. She raised her hands; and before she fell, Harding turned the gun on himself.

Lorna screamed: 'John!' and flung open the door.

'It's all right, my sweet,' said Mannering, 'it's all right.' His left arm was about her and he could feel her trembling body. 'There's nothing to worry about. Slip these into your dress.' He pushed the papers into her hands. 'The police are here, it's all right.'

He looked at Zara's lifeless body.

'And it was the right way out,' he whispered, 'she'd have gone through hell, that would have been inevitable. This was the best way for her.' Men were running up the stairs. 'Take it easy, my sweet.'

Lorna was crying.

The man whom Mannering had shot, Paul Harding and Marjorie were still in the hall when the Mannerings went downstairs. Another police car had arrived and more men spilled into the hall. Mannering turned to the door of the domestic quarters, his arm still round Lorna's shoulders, and they went into the big, white tiled kitchen. Tring was unconscious, with a head wound. Forsythe sat against the wall, his hands tied behind his back, a bruise on his forehead.

'John, by all that's holy, you got away with it!'

'That's right.'

'Cut me loose,' begged Forsythe. 'Cut me loose, I must get to that telephone.'

He had finished at the telephone before Tring left in an ambulance for the local hospital.

Mannering read through Harding's evidence as Lorna sat on a pouf in front of him. She leaned her head against his knee, and he played with a strand of her hair absently. He finished and handed her the papers.

'Want to read them?'

'Are they worth reading?'

'Tring would think so. A very slick piece of forged documentary evidence, my sweet, and I wouldn't have stood a chance if they'd been sent to the Yard, even if I'd been covered with glory over this affair. Mr. Harding was not a nice man.'

'He must have been mad.'

'Was that madness? Well, perhaps – a form of obsession. He'd married a prominent member of the Adalgo family, who died years ago.'

Lorna said: 'I'm glad he's dead.' She jumped up. 'I'm going to make a bonfire of these.'

Mannering watched her as she stood at the domestic boiler in the kitchen, and flames roared up the chimney. She stirred the ashes with a poker, and let the front of the boiler fall with a crash.

'Goodbye to all that,' murmured Mannering. 'My sweet, I haven't told you lately that I think you're the most wonderful woman in the world. But when you hear a shot, you ought to run away from it, not towards it.'

'When you start running away, I'll join you. John, what will happen?'

'Next to nothing. A sensational story in the Press, some half-truths about the Adalgo family and a possible purge in Spain. Marjorie and Paul will probably be hanged, Lopez certainly will be. I shall offer the Adalgo to the exiled Spanish Government and have an idea they'll be glad to have it.'

'Or you could throw it away.'

Mannering laughed. 'It did cost a packet, you know. Penny for your thoughts.'

'About Josh. Will he be all right?'

'I expect Bristow to release him as soon as he gets back to the Yard. Forsythe heard quite a bit of the story, and Marjorie was beginning to crack before we left. She'll tell him everything before long – if only to save her neck from being stretched. She was quite the oddest piece in the puzzle, our not so naïve Marjorie. The Hardings gave her an alibi, of course, for the night of Bray's murder. Not bad. On the whole, they did a good job.'

'Good!' cried Lorna.

Mannering said: 'In its way. As for Josh, we know why the Adalgo fascinated him, now. We also know why he was just the model for you – the tragedy, in an ordinary man, of being caught up in great affairs.'

'You knew who he was, didn't you?' Lorna asked.

'I was late with it. But once I knew the Adalgo family was involved, and Larraby had come across them before, it hit me between the eyes. Hence the vain hunt for a picture of their Dukeships!'

It was midnight before they had a visitor; then it was Bristow. Mannering let him in, and he strode briskly across the drawing-room, smiled at Lorna, and said brightly:

'Well, John? How's the knee?'

'So we're all pals again?'

'Now that I'm satisfied you weren't playing the fool, why not? I thought you'd strong royalist tendencies over this job. I couldn't imagine anything else which would make you play the fool with that diamond. Why did you?'

Mannering shrugged: 'It had all the makings of a nice little puzzle.'

'I think you had an idea what kind of puzzle. Well, forget it. We've everything tidied up. Marjorie Addel has made a full confession. Paul Harding is stubborn, but he'll talk before it's over. The only thing he's opened his mouth about is a dossier on a certain Mr. Mannering, which was supposed to be in his father's bedroom. Remarkable thing, it wasn't there when we searched.'

'Probably it never existed. Harding talked a lot of hot air.'

Bristow laughed. 'You'll do!'

'How's Tring?'

'Not too bad,' said Bristow. 'Conscious and muttering dark threats against the Harding family. He's changed his target for venom. Tring's all right, his chief trouble is that he's an obsession against you in certain moods. He seems to think that you saved him from becoming a corpse this time, so he'll spend the rest of his days in the force looking for another obsession. We found a lot of stuff at the house about a royalist plot in Spain – and that's why I'm here.'

'Oh?'

'It's off the record,' Bristow said. 'Forsythe got some background stuff for a story, but that's about the end of it. I'm here to make it clear that you're requested not to make any statement affecting the Adalgo family, to the Press.'

'If that's the only reason for coming, it was a waste of time. It's not in my mind to talk.'

'Oh, a pleasant half hour with the Mannerings is always good for me,' said Bristow genially. 'There's one other trifling thing. Marjorie has told us about Josh Larraby's early past and his half-brother. I've seen Josh.'

Lorna said sharply: 'Have you released him?'

'Oh, yes, he's loose somewhere. I think you backed the right horse, although if it hadn't been for Josh Larraby, I would have had less doubt about your motives. It was so obviously a phoney set-up that I couldn't believe you'd just taken pity on the chap.'

'That's the difference between a human being and a police-man,' said Lorna tartly.

'All right, all right, I asked for that. What did you know about him, John?'

'Not much – not anything like enough. I know a great deal, now. He'd rejected what Harding had the nerve to call his birthright but he couldn't keep away from the Adalgo. I often wondered why, I don't wonder now. He had his pride – I believe he would have served ten years rather than betray the family. What about the Duke who ran away? Any idea where he is?'

'No, and I don't want to know. It's being handled at a higher level than Scotland Yard, now, and it can stay there. Hallo, visitors at this time of night?' Bristow looked round as the front door bell rang. 'I must be off!'

Mannering let him out; and let Larraby in.

Lorna saw who it was from the drawing-room door, hurried across and took his hands – and then quite spontaneously, kissed him on the cheek.

The private view of the Royal Academy was crowded. Josh Larraby, neatly dressed and with his hair shorter and carefully brushed, wandered about the big rooms of the gallery, grad-ually drawing nearer to the large group which stood in front of his own portrait. He looked at it, over the heads of the crowd. He was still sad; and the Mannerings, watching him from the other side of the room, saw him peering at every woman who came in.

They saw his eyes light up.

A neaty dressed, middle-aged woman, with a girl in her teens whose likeness to Larraby couldn't be mistaken, saw the portrait as they came in. The girl said:

'Mum, it *is* Dad's picture!'

The woman said gruffly: 'I can see for myself, can't I?' She looked round, and saw Larraby.

Lorna held Mannering's hand so tightly that it hurt.

'Will she – John, it's all right, *look*!'

Mrs. Larraby went straight up to Josh, who held out his hands. They gripped, and looked at each other for a long time,

203

while tears glistened in the girl's eyes. Then Josh said in a clear, carrying voice:

'I still feel the same about you, Lil.'

The Mannerings didn't hear the woman's reply, but they saw the radiant smile which stole the sadness from Larraby's face.

CALL FOR THE BARON BY JOHN CREASEY

writing as Anthony Morton, creator of The Baron

A series of minor thefts at Vere House prompts Martin and Diana Vere to call in their old friend John Mannering to investigate. But while Mannering is doing so, the jewels and the famous Deverall necklace belonging to Lady Usk, a guest of the Vere's are stolen. Reluctantly, the police are brought in and much to Mannering's disquiet, Scotland Yard send their top man, Chief Inspector Bristow, one of the few who suspect Mannering to be the Baron – the cleverest jewel thief in the country.

And Mannering realizes it is even more imperative that he prove his innocence when he discovers someone has planted the stolen Deverall necklace in his room . . .

552 09297 5   30p

DEATH IN HIGH PLACES

BY JOHN CREASEY, writing as Gordon Ashe.

Capt. Patrick Dawlish is on manoeuvres in the wilds of Salisbury downs when he receives a cryptic message from Colonel Cranton to meet him next day in Salisbury. Once there, he finds his old friends Tim Jeremy, Ted Beresford and his fiancée Felicity, have also been summoned – but no-one knows why.

Then, just as Colonel Cranton arrives, his car is involved in a strange accident that Dawlish realizes was deliberate and in which the Colonel has been seriously injured. Leaping into another car he sets off on a dangerous chase that is to lead him through a maze of murder, espionage and blackmail before he is able to crack the riddle of Colonel Cranton's message – and the organization behind it all . . .

552 09384 X   30p

THE DESTROYER: DEATH THERAPY

BY RICHARD SAPIR AND WARREN MURPHY

The security systems of America had failed. Every government agent was being systematically wiped-out by an organization whose aim it was to control the most powerful nation in the world – and then sell it to the highest bidder! There was only one man who could save Congress from becoming the sole item in the biggest auction of all-time – one man who could not be tortured physically or mentally – REMO WILLIAMS, the man who called himself THE DESTROYER . . .

552 09595 8   35p

THE PATRIOT BY CHARLES DURBIN

The exiled king of the international Mafia – killer, sadist, heroin millionaire. But first of all, an American . . .

THE PATRIOT

A raw, revealing 'insider's' novel about the methods, murders, and men of the mob . . . 'Spares nothing in the way of violent brutality and sexual depravity . . . Destined to be a highly popular success!'

552 09486 2   50p

THE EXECUTIONER: CARIBBEAN KILL

BY DON PENDLETON

The police in thirty states are on the lookout for him. The FBI is on his trail. He's on the VIP list at Interpol. There's virtually no law enforcement agency that isn't familiar with his name, and his game.

But the people most anxious to put him out of business are on the other side of the law – that organized cartel of crime and corruption called the Mafia. And Bolan's sole purpose in life is to extinguish every trace of the Mafia – alone if need be.

Impossible ? Yes. But Bolan's doing it. In this chapter of his domesday book, the Executioner invades the Mafia strongholds in the Caribbean, and although the odds aren't in his favour, all the scores are.

552 09326 2   30p

THE EXECUTIONER: CALIFORNIA HIT

BY DON PENDLETON

San Francisco, City of the Golden Gate and stronghold of the most organized crime syndicate in the world, becomes Mack Bolan's next target in *California Hit*. With the toughest cops in the USA gunning for him the Executioner continues his deadly vendetta against the corrupted empire of the Mafia . . .

But this time there's an extra name on Bolan's list, someone bigger even than the Mafia, someone who controls every criminal operation in the west, someone known only as Mr. King . . .

552 09443 9   30p

A SELECTED LIST OF CRIME STORIES FOR YOUR READING PLEASURE

All these books are available at your bookshop or newsagent; or can be ordered direct from the publisher. Just tick the titles you want and fill in the form below.

CORGI BOOKS, Cash Sales Department, P.O. Box 11, Falmouth, Cornwall.
Please send cheque or postal order. No currency, and allow 10p to cover the cost of postage and packing (plus 5p each for additional copies).

NAME (Block letters) ....

ADDRESS...

....

(MAY 74) ....

While every effort is made to keep prices low, it is sometimes necessary to increase prices at short notice. Corgi Books reserve the right to show new retail prices on covers which may differ from those previously advertised in the text or elsewhere.